Praise for *John Bell: Th*

'It is a celebration of a remarkabl
than a confession, by the actor anu director who has played
a unique role in shaping our theatre.'
—Joyce Morgan, *Sydney Morning Herald*

'Bell recounts some wonderful stories . . . This is the actor
and director and manager still thrilled by the legerdemain
of those tent shows he loved as a boy . . . the recollections
of an engaged, committed eyewitness to the opening and
closing of countless stage doors, back doors and trapdoors.'
—Graeme Blundell, *Weekend Australian*

'Australia was lucky to keep him [Bell].'
—Barry Oakley, *Bulletin*

'As much of the book is devoted to his obsession with
Shakespeare as it is to finding ways to forge a distinctively
Australian style in which to play him.'
—Geoffrey Milne, *Sydney Morning Herald*

'Bell's love of life and sense of fortune come through
strongly . . .'
—Elizabeth Delaney, *Mercury*

'John Bell's narration is imbued with his passion for Shakespeare and the development of Australian theatre: his
enthusiasm drives the text.'
—*Australian Bookseller & Publisher*

The Book Den
144A Vincent St
Cessnock NSW 2325
Ph & Fax 02 4991 3577

# John Bell

## The time of my life

ALLEN&UNWIN

First published in 2002
This paperback edition published in 2003

This project has been assisted by the Commonwealth Government through the
Australia Council, its arts funding and advisory body.

Allen & Unwin
83 Alexander Street
Crows Nest NSW 2065
Australia
Phone:  (61 2) 8425 0100
Fax:      (61 2) 9906 2218
Email:  info@allenandunwin.com
Web:    www.allenandunwin.com

National Library of Australia
Cataloguing-in-Publication entry:

Bell, John, 1940- .
    John Bell : the time of my life.

    Includes index.
    ISBN 1 74114 134 6.

    1. Bell, John, 1940- . 2. Actors - Australia - Biography.
    3. Theatrical producers and directors - Australia -
    Biography. I. Title.

792.028092

Set in Sabon (Old Style Figures) by Bookhouse, Sydney
Printed in Australia by McPherson's Printing Group

10 9 8 7 6 5 4 3 2 1

# Contents

# Prologue

I remember the moment clearly. It was the first day of rehearsals for the Bell Shakespeare Company, a sunny morning in November 1990. I was leading a group of my young actors across the campus of the University of New South Wales where we were rehearsing. We passed an old tin shed with the name Fig Tree Theatre on it. I stopped and pointed: 'Well, would you believe? That's where it all began—the original Old Tote!' My companions looked at the shed blankly and then looked at me.

'What was the Old Tote?'

I was fairly taken aback. This batch of bright young actors had recently graduated from NIDA and other state drama schools where they had studied History of Theatre. They could tell me all sorts of interesting stuff about the Berliner Ensemble, the Moscow Arts and the New York Actors' Studio—but none of them had ever heard of the Old Tote, Sydney's first full-time professional theatre company. The Tote had flourished for fifteen years from 1963 till 1978. From the tin shed it had moved to the Parade Theatre, Kensington (now demolished) and from there to the Sydney Opera House. It had been a major force in Australian theatre and had only been defunct for twelve years—but none of these kids had heard of it.

As I write this, in 2002, I am aware that most young actors today have never heard of Nimrod or the Pram Factory either—other major forces in Australian theatre.

It seems to me that our actors should know something of their own theatre history and maybe the theatre-going public should too. They should understand where our theatre has come from, the efforts and achievements of those who paved the way for us. I am constantly inspired as I delve into Australia's rich theatrical heritage and realise what an enormous amount of talent this small country has produced, and I am moved by the battle it had to survive.

But I realise too that we theatre workers have to add our own bits of the story. Hence this volume of impressions and recollections, which I hope may add a little more information and personal detail to what is on record.

It's a tangled tale, part personal, part professional—how do you separate the strands? Most of all it's an attempt to articulate what drives me, and others like me, to follow the road we have chosen . . .

*Part I*

# GETTING
# EDUCATED

# Feeneys, Bells and Ryans

I always thought my grandfather's name was Joe. He was christened Patrick Joseph Feeney but was called Joe all his life. My father was christened Albert John Bell and was known all his life as Jack. Is that an Australian thing?

My mother's side was 100 per cent Irish—Ryans, Feeneys and Maloneys. With a name like Bell I presumed my father's side was English or Scots, but found out recently that his mother's name was Hannah O'Connor and even the Bell was from County Cavan. So I couldn't be more Irish than that.

My father never talked much about his family. His own father was gassed on the Somme and didn't live long after he came back. I don't know much about the rest of the family except that they moved to Queensland in the mid 1900s. Dad was devoted to his sister Ida, a sweet and gentle creature who I knew only a little. I get the impression that life otherwise was pretty miserable for him—I guess the Somme would have had nothing on going to a Christian Brothers school in Queensland in the 1920s.

My mother's family, on the other hand, was a treasure-house of folklore and tradition; it was close-knit and overflowing with generosity, love, laughter and mutual support—all the best elements, and none of the worst, of the working-class Irish.

Joe Feeney had five brothers and three sisters scattered around Millers Forest in the Hunter Valley, where they were farmers, blacksmiths and market gardeners. The Forest was where Joe met Aggie Ryan, my grandmother. She had been orphaned at eight years old and put into domestic service. Aggie and Joe, Nan and Da, were the light of my childhood. I was devoted to my parents, but Nan and Da indulged me shamefully (grandparents' privilege) and their house was a place of wonder, so different to ours. My father was determined to have everything new and modern. On his small-town bank manager's salary he struggled to put five kids through Catholic schools, but he despised the cheap and the shoddy. He looked down his nose at my grandparents' humble dwelling where everything was a bit threadbare and old-fashioned.

Their house, which was called San José, was in Railway Street, Wickham—a lively, shabby Newcastle suburb, now demolished and turned into a concrete wasteland. San José was impeccably clean and tidy. A small bungalow with a long dark hallway down one side, a sunny breakfast room where most activity took place, a parlour barely used except for sitting around the big open fire on winter nights, a lounge room where all the best china was kept and photographs on the piano. This room had a sofa and armchairs and came alive for Saturday night sing-alongs. But mostly it was preserved for important visitors, such as when the parish priest visited for afternoon tea. The kitchen had a fuel stove; the ice man trudged down the hall with blocks of ice held by pincers to load the ice-box, and the laundry was a dark, clammy place with a wood-fired copper and a mangle. That's where the chooks got their heads chopped off at Christmas, so I had rather an aversion to the place. The sunroom looked out onto the fernery canopied with grapevines. My Da was devoted to his goldfish, his vegetable garden and his chooks (even the ones we had to eat). His pet bantam hen sat on his shoulder as he pottered around, and a series of cats and dogs held sway on the settees and armchairs.

Of all the dogs who came and went over the years my favourite was Sprat, a wily fox terrier who could read minds and would be sitting in the driver's seat of the soft-top '27 Chevy before the rest of us knew we were going anywhere. The Chevy proved to be Sprat's undoing because at the ripe old age of fifteen he was leaning out too far (he loved the wind in his hair) when Da drove over a pothole and Sprat fell out on his head. But for most of his eventful life Sprat held the house to ransom, especially on Saturday nights. Sprat hated the sing-alongs and as soon as the singing began he would scuttle under the house, sit directly under the piano and set up the most dismal howling. We kids would jig from foot to foot with delight: 'Sprat's singing! Sprat's singing.' Nan was mortified in front of her guests and, bustling about with mountains of scones and buckets of tea, would say, 'For God's sake, Joe, get rid of that jolly dog.' Da would set to with the broom handle and the hose, but nothing would dislodge Sprat and nothing could silence him until the singing stopped.

My grandparents had done it tough, what with the Depression and two world wars, but they scraped and saved and insisted that all three daughters have elocution, piano and violin lessons. The neighbours mocked them for such extravagance but Nan and Da insisted that their daughters should have every chance in life and want for none of the social graces.

Australia was just beginning to emerge from an era of intense religious bigotry. My father darkly hinted that his career at the bank had been stymied by the Masons. I never met a Protestant until I went to university. We lived in a cosy, hermetically sealed Irish Catholic ghetto. Every weekend saw a picnic in the bush, up Medowie way or Raymond Terrace. This always involved a group effort to gather cow manure in chaff bags or blackberries in billycans. 'You kids are eating more berries than you pick—I think I'll just put pastry round the lot of you . . .' The flies gave us hell and we wrestled with them over the ritual feast of cold corned beef, sliced beetroot, tomato and iceberg lettuce, washed down with billy tea.

Politics were rarely discussed at home. My grandparents, with their Irish working-class memories of the depression, were loyal to the memory of Ben Chifley and the Light on the Hill. My parents, victims of the Menzies era, bowed to the advice that thundered from the pulpit every Sunday: a vote for the ALP meant a vote for atheistic communism. As soon as Labor got in, you could expect to see Russian tanks rumbling down George Street, the Hammer and Sickle raised over Sydney Town Hall and Cardinal Gilroy bustled off to a concentration camp. So I suspect my parents voted for the Liberals, or worse still, the breakaway bunch of right-wing scabs who called themselves the Democratic Labor Party. So the family never talked politics—it was considered too divisive.

Born in 1940, by the time I was ten I had three sisters—
Carmel, Keri and Maureen—all of us roughly three years
apart. My brother Michael didn't arrive on the scene until
I was eighteen and about to leave home. My mother spent
hours on her knees praying for 'another John'—and she
got him. Even today I am unnerved by our clone-like resemblance. (Needless to say, my mother felt her faith in the
power of prayer to be fully vindicated.) My sisters were my
public, my first audience. I performed shows and devised
games for them. East Maitland was still something of a
suburban sprawl, bordering the bush. There weren't many
other kids around, so we had to make our own fun much
of the time. I'm afraid I betrayed early signs of being a
tyrant and an impresario. I manufactured my own currency
out of silver paper and doled it out to my sisters in return
for errands. But at weekends I demanded it all back again
for the puppet shows and handmade comic strips I forced
on them.

School holidays were spent in a fibro shack at Nelson
Bay—no electricity and a tin can out the back for a dunny.
The days were spent rocking up and down in a rowboat
fishing for leatherjacket or rock cod until the mozzies drove
us home at sunset. Fish for dinner every night, and then
yarns and stories around the hurricane lamp.

During holidays at home I spent the evenings crouched
in front of the wireless cabinet, drawing and sketching, listening to the Lux Radio Theatre; but if I had holidays at
Nan's I could listen to all the morning soap-operas as well—
*Portia Faces Life*, *When a Girl Marries*, *Doctor Paul*—and
no matter what was happening in the house, everyone
downed tools at lunchtime to gather around the daily
episode of *Blue Hills*.

My Nan took me to the pictures too, and suffered many a western and pirate epic for my sake, just as I suffered the musicals and soppy love stories for hers. There was nothing in my life you could strictly call 'theatre' but from my earliest years, circus tents were a key part of my life.

Among my earliest memories are these: sawdust, tinsel, the bright lights and brassy band of a circus tent; the excitement, the racket, the precarious bleacher seating, the thrill and horror of it all. I hated the lion tamer and shuddered whenever they started to erect the lion cage inside the ring. I hated the crack of his whip and the heavy thud as the giant cats jumped up on tubs, snarling and swiping their paws and kicking up dust. I trembled again as those manic trapeze artists shimmied up the poles to the highwire. ('Why do they have to do it? . . . That's enough—please don't do any more . . .') I even trembled for the jugglers, praying they wouldn't drop anything. But most of all I feared and hated the clowns—terrifying anarchists with crazy hair and faces, who might at any moment dart out of the ring, haul you into the mayhem and have everyone laugh at you! I always hoped for a seat up the back. Still, the word 'circus' thrilled me like no other and I couldn't wait for my next fix of jubilant terror.

The circus (the big ones were Wirths and Bullen Brothers) came to Newcastle once a year but with Christmas came another tent show I loved even more. Pitched in Civic Park, opposite the Newcastle Town Hall, was Sorlies' tent and for a couple of magical weeks they'd run a panto in the afternoons and a variety show at night for the grown-ups. I guess I was four or five when my mum and Nan first took me to Sorlies' panto, but it became the most anticipated event of the year until I was about ten. The title of the show changed every year. It could be *Aladdin* or *Cinderella* or

*Jack and the Beanstalk*—it didn't matter; the jokes and costumes were always the same.

Some things about it got my goat. I usually had an aversion to the busty brunette in her tight jerkin, fishnet stockings, high heels and garish makeup posing as Jack, Aladdin, Sinbad or whoever. But I was smitten by the princess. How could anything be that gorgeous? The company manager usually played the villain—Baron Hardup, Demon King etc.—and he was hopeless. I could spot a lousy actor. This one had a dour expression, moved awkwardly and had a restless, roving eye—he was probably counting the house. The sword fights were lousy too, just the old one-two-three, one-two-three, the foils tricked up with electric leads so sparks would fly. Phooey.

The company always worked in the latest pop songs from the charts. The band would pound them out as a chorus line of silver-knickered nymphs from the local ballet school tried to look like the Rockettes. That was a yawn, as was all the love stuff, but it was worth sitting through just to build up to the moment when HE would come on— Bobby le Brun as the Dame, with his wig of red sausage curls, cherry nose, obviously fake bosom and capacious apron. He was the cheeriest Dame you could ever have seen and I never tired of his stock routines; indeed I longed for them, even though I knew them by heart: the pastry-making scene, the wallpapering scene, the white-washing—in short, anything that created a glorious mess.

This was like the circus—the canvas tent, bleacher seats, sawdust floor, bright lights and noisy band—but it was all fun, warm and fuzzy, with none of the cruelty or anxiety of the circus. For years Bobby le Brun would hold sway as my first theatre icon and role model.

# If you're a Catholic you can believe anything

My school career got off to a rocky start. I walked out of kindergarten. I said that playing with cotton reels all day was a waste of time—I had other things to do . . . So I pretty well skipped 'kinder' altogether, and at five years old I trotted through the gate of St Peter's School, Stockton, my hand trustingly clasped inside that of my mother. She knocked on the schoolhouse door, and imagine my horror when it was opened by a man in drag. Well, I'd never seen a man in drag—but a man in drag this had to be, with a big hairless face squeezed into a stiff white coif, a towering figure all in black with a long black veil, a sturdy leather belt and heavy rosary beads. Sister Pius turned out to be a honey, but a child's first sight of a nun can be pretty unnerving.

Anyway, I was ushered into a classroom full of tiny total strangers with staring eyes and hostile giggles—abandoned by my mother for the first time ever. I got to like the nuns and soon sussed out their feminine soft spots. Sister James was a round, red-faced little aunty who let me paint and draw to my heart's content; and Sister Gerard was a gaunt, shy sixteen-year-old with huge brown eyes—my first serious crush. Sister Benedict, on the other hand, was a yellow-faced, shrivelled little old witch who wielded a long thin cane with venomous relish.

Still, being at the nuns' was a doddle—I didn't know what terror was until I fell into the hands of The Brothers. When I was in my fourth year, Dad got shifted by the Commonwealth Bank to Kurri Kurri in the Hunter Valley. We bought a house in East Maitland and I started attending Marist Brothers College, Maitland, a school regarded by some of the fraternity as the end of the line—the place they sent the nervous wrecks or those who had got into deep shit elsewhere. But looking back I think I got off lightly—there were a couple of crackpots, sure, but most of the teachers I suffered under were decent, hard-working monks, and a couple of them were brilliant teachers who had a profound effect on my life.

My first teacher at the new school was Brother Francis, a pimply, red-haired eighteen-year-old. He had a lively sense of fun but was heavy with the strap.

I had been apprehensive about going to a new school in Maitland. It was twenty whole miles away from Newcastle. 'Will they speak English there?' I asked. My father snorted, 'Of course they will!' But after only ten minutes on my first day analysing a sentence about wild beasts, Brother Francis asked: 'What is the opposite of "wild"?'

I shot my hand up: 'Tame, Brother.'

He looked puzzled. 'No, there's no such word.'

I was quietly furious. 'There, they *don't* speak English!'

To this day I am perplexed by this failure of communication.

I soon had a reputation for clowning around and doing comic turns. Brother Francis became highly excited about coaching me to recite Banjo Paterson's *The Man from Ironbark* for the school concert. He would hug himself with glee and the kids would shriek when I came to the line 'Murder! Bloody Murder! yelled the Man from Ironbark'.

I got all kitted up in swaggy clothes and a beard made of black wool and waited in the wings. I could see Brother Francis hopping about with excitement as he watched the audience file in. Suddenly he turned ashen and dashed backstage to me: 'Hey, Belly, the Bishop's in—I think you'd better cut the bloody.' So when I came to the poem's classic line and declaimed 'Murder! . . . Murder, yelled the Man from Ironbark', there was an audible groan of disappointment from all the kids out front.

About a dozen Brothers lived in a house adjacent to the school. Their lifestyle was basic, not to say meagre. They devoted all their working hours to their vocation—no wives or families to distract them—and took endless pains to 'bring out the best' in their charges. All day long the school echoed to the whack of the strap or cane, the chanting of hymns, the hum of the rosary, the roaring and bawling-out of numbskull students; and after hours, the whistles and shouts of football coaches, the thwack of the handball and the rat-a-tat-tat of the drum corps practising for the St Patrick's Day march.

The playground was a bitumen wasteland with a couple of wire cage cricket pitches and crumbling Moreton Bay figs, drooping with flying foxes. During lunchbreaks Brothers on playground duty sauntered about the prison yard, menacingly swinging the tasselled cords of their black soutanes and breaking up groups of boys who were loitering and talking. The talk was bound to be smutty, so, 'Break it up—go and play handball or boot the footy.'

Given how much time we spent praying and hymn-singing, it's surprising we learned anything at all. But the inculcation of knowledge was relentless and the school actually had quite a decent academic record. What was *more* bizarre, looking back on it, was how a teacher could leap from teaching us medieval superstition (Creationism, the bodily Assumption of Mary into heaven, or her house flying miraculously through the sky) to the latest in contemporary physics without the slightest indication of incongruity. Anything that seemed just too wacky for words had to be accepted and believed as 'a Mystery of Faith'.

We didn't spend much time on the Old Testament (too sexy) but studied Six Proofs for the Existence of God and Why the Catholic Church is the One True Church. These latter studies were to equip us to refute the Protestants and even atheists we might encounter once we left school. We were told we wouldn't have much trouble if we joined the public service because that was nearly 100 per cent Irish Catholic.

The hymns we droned out daily were slow, lugubrious and Mary-centric:

Oh Mother, I could weep for mirth [we intoned dolefully]
Joy fills my heart so fast
My soul today is heaven on earth
O, could the transport last . . .
Mother of Christ, Star of the Sea,
Pray for the Wanderer,
Pray for Me.

The hymns were conducted by a Brother wielding a cane, and woe betide anyone who smirked, gazed out the window, yielded to the temptation to inject a bit of 'swing' into the rhythm or, worst of all, snuck in alternative smutty lyrics.

The Irish sense of persecution was encapsulated in one of the regular favourites, *Faith of Our Fathers*. One verse ran:

> Our fathers, chain'd in prison dark,
> were still in heart and conscience free.
> How sweet would be their children's fate
> if they, like them, could die for thee.
> Faith of our fathers, holy faith!
> We will be true to thee till death.

Despite the messy syntax, the message is clear. Needless to say another hot favourite was 'Hail Glorious Saint Patrick, Dear Saint of Our Isle'. I assumed that we were referring to Australia. It never occurred to me that the Isle in question was the Emerald one. Yet another popular hymn was addressed to the 'dear little Shamrock, the sweet little Shamrock, the dear little, sweet little Shamrock of Ire-laaand'. I'm not sure if it's sound theology to address a hymn to a common or garden weed, but we did anyhow.

Our headmaster was Brother Justinian. He had cold blue eyes that struck terror into us. He taught us Religious Doctrine and Ancient History, and he was only ever two pages ahead of us in the textbooks. He had us praying on the hour and was always urging us to offer up an ejaculation — a brief prayer such as 'Jesus, Mary and Joseph', or 'Lord help me!' 'Boys,' he would say to us, 'you mightn't always have time for an Our Father or a Hail Mary or even a Glory Be, but you've always time for a quick ejaculation!'

I run into him sometimes in Centennial Park, walking his dog Jack. He jumped over the wall years ago and got married. I marvel that anyone as shy and gentle as he could ever have passed himself off as Captain Bligh and gotten away with it.

Brother Gonzaga was a bit of a cot-case, a bit of a worry. One day he made us close all the classroom windows as he had a deadly secret to impart. 'Boys,' he whispered in hushed tones, his wild eyes roving over a room of trembling twelve-year-olds, 'I want you to know that last night I saw the devil! Yes, boys, I was awakened by the suffocating smell of sulphur. I sat up in bed and the room was full of smoke and fumes . . . But I could make him out, sitting on the end of my bed with huge glowing red eyes, just sitting and staring at me . . .'

Years later I told Ron Blair and he worked it into *The Christian Brothers*, but even Ron thought the devil story was a bit rich for audiences to accept, so he watered it down to a vision of the Virgin Mary.

At the age of fifteen I encountered my first truly inspirational teacher, Brother Elgar, published in poetry anthologies as RD Murphy. He was a big man with a head like the Roman emperor Galba. He had a deep resonant voice, a quick temper and an exhilarating love of poetry and literature. It's very largely due to him that my life and career took the course they did. I'd never heard of Shakespeare but Elgar hauled out copies of *A Midsummer Night's Dream* and proceeded to take us through it by acting out all the parts himself, striding up and down and throwing himself right into it, especially the role of Bottom. What's more, he'd seen it on stage, so he delighted in describing the sets, costumes and gags as well as playing the text. As a result I got hooked on Shakespeare pretty quickly. Luckily, it was at this time that Olivier's Shakespeare movies started to hit the screen and we were marched off to the local cinema to see *Henry V*. When it was over we trooped out into the sunlight and the other kids wandered off home. But I stood there, stunned and blinking. I couldn't believe what I'd just experienced—so I went back in and watched it all over again.

Olivier's Globe was just like the circus or Bobby le Brun—the actors playing to the excited crowd, the comedy and buffoonery, the sawdust and tattiness. But added to this were pageantry and spectacle, and most of all, this thrilling language. I hadn't dreamt people could *talk* like that! I seemed to understand most of it, but the odd phrase puzzled me, like when the Duke of Burgundy said, 'The coulter rusts that should deracinate such savagery.' I didn't know what a coulter was or what deracinate meant, but I couldn't wait to get home and look them up. In the meantime I walked along rolling the phrase around in my mouth like a boiled lolly and repeating it aloud: 'The coulter rusts that should deracinate such savagery.'

Shortly after this I was crouched in front of the wireless, scribbling away as usual, when the ABC broadcast *Julius Caesar*. I'm pretty sure it was Ron Haddrick playing Brutus. Anyway, I was following the story along until it came to Brutus's first soliloquy when he contemplates killing Caesar and says, 'It is the bright day that brings forth the adder, and that craves wary walking.' I felt the hairs on my neck stand on end and suddenly I knew what poetry meant. It was something that bypassed the purely rational part of your brain and touched your senses. The compactness of that image of Caesar's ambition being like a deadly snake lurking in the dark until aroused by the brilliance of power was balanced by the tentative rhythm and assonance of 'that craves wary walking . . .'. As in so much good poetry, it's the menace of understatement, of what's left unsaid, that is most affecting.

In the years following, Olivier's *Hamlet* and *Richard III* appeared and my fate was sealed. All I wanted was to walk in Olivier's footsteps and have the thrill of playing Henry V, Hamlet and Richard III . . . Elgar—or Murph, as I later came to know him—encouraged my enthusiasm and offered to me, besides, whole realms of poetry and fiction. He formed our class into a verse-speaking choir for school concerts and by generous application of the stick he drilled into us an appreciation of rhythm, metre, alliteration and onomatopoeia. This was my first acting lesson. When he was moved on, as teachers were every few years so they wouldn't get 'attached', I was in despair, but struck it lucky again with his replacement, Brother Geoffrey.

Younger and a bit more of a daredevil than Murph, Geoffrey brought a touch of the big bad city to sleepy Maitland. He was pretty shameless in cultivating favourites, usually the sporty types, as he was a superb swimming coach. But I made it to the inner circle by virtue of my academic prowess. He had my career mapped out for me. I would take three Honours courses (English, Ancient History and Modern History) for the Leaving Certificate and he would personally coach me in all three. I would go to Sydney University, take an arts degree and then become an actor. This appealed to me greatly, but put the wind up my poor parents. They saw nothing wrong with the theatre per se, but it was even more notoriously insecure then than it is now. Still, 'Brother knows best' was their motto, and so I was fairly set.

Geoffrey also believed in 'his boys' having a bit more experience of the world than Maitland could offer, so one night (I was sixteen at the time) he hired a car and drove four or five of us to Sydney to see the Borovansky Ballet Company. After the show he took us to Kings Cross, where we sauntered along at midnight feeling very grown-up, wearing sunglasses and puffing the cigars he handed around. When we sat down in a coffee bar and he ordered cappuccinos I thought, this is the Big Time!

I was boning up all I could on the life and career of Laurence Olivier and knew all about his famous roles such as Oedipus and Hotspur—how he played them, the makeup he used, etc. Along with my studies I was bursting for a chance to strut my stuff as an actor and prevailed upon Geoff to put on a school play night. Maitland Marist had never heard of such a thing, but Geoff was much taken with the idea. I suggested a program of three pieces— I would design the whole thing and play all the leading roles, and he could direct it. I proposed *Oedipus Rex*, a scene from *Henry IV* featuring Hotspur, and a pantomime in which I would play the Bobby le Brun role—all my favourites in one evening.

Geoff went to enormous trouble and hired the costumes from Sydney, I daresay at huge expense. He devised a series of acts in the pantomime which displayed the prowess of the gymnastic team and set them to Tchaikovsky. The whole thing was a glorious dog's breakfast but packed the Maitland Town Hall and was the talk of the town.

Another thing that drove me to act was a determination to conquer a frightful stutter. I had begun stammering round about the age of twelve; by the time I was fifteen I couldn't get a word out without turning crimson, choking and stuttering. I read that Demosthenes, the greatest orator of all time, had the same problem and overcame it by filling his mouth with pebbles and speaking in spite of them. So I knew it could be beaten; I would have to beat it by acting in public. It was tough going at first and I often had to change words or adlib to get through. It took me twenty years to finally master the problem, and even today, when I am tired or overwrought, I get an attack of the stammers—but thankfully not on stage.

I did well with my Leaving Certificate and Honours subjects and was accepted into Sydney University with a Commonwealth Scholarship, which covered my fees and provided a meagre living allowance. I also auditioned for a new drama school that was to be called the National Institute of Dramatic Art (NIDA), and was accepted into the first intake. I would dearly have loved to take up the offer, but deferred to my parents' wishes that I go to university first and leave the acting until later. As my mother assured me, 'Once you've got a BA, you'll never be out of work.'

I sometimes fume about the negatives of my education, the brutalisation, the narrow-mindedness, the constant fear of failure; but I also have a lot to be grateful for. For one thing it was a very useful background for an actor: if you're a Catholic you can believe anything. My whole childhood and adolescence was rife with religious mythology, visions of heaven and hell, angels and devils, stories of miracles and martyrs, a sense of eternity and a spiritual world coexisting with this material one. All powerful stuff for feeding the imagination and providing a direct hotline to ancient, medieval and even Elizabethan mind-sets.

But as well as that, my teachers set me living examples of people dedicated to a vocation, a 'calling'. They sacrificed professional careers, families and material comforts, and devoted their lives to the next generation. Whatever their individual cranks and failings, they possessed a generosity of spirit that commanded respect and gratitude. The rage and turmoil I underwent in separating myself from the Church has quietened down now, and I look back on family and teachers with affection for the good, well-meaning people that they were.

# Green corduroys
and suede
'brothel creepers'

Arriving in Sydney and at the university in 1959 subjected me to a series of shocks and awakenings. Here I was, on my own in the Big Smoke, a hundred miles from home, after eight years of rigorous Catholic education in a single-sex school. All of a sudden I was surrounded by a throng of young, bright, excited men and women from a wide variety of educational and social backgrounds. They were competitive, rebellious, wildly egocentric, scornful of much that I held dear, and desperate to experiment with 'Life'. I couldn't wait to fit in and squandered much of my meagre resources on olive green corduroys and a pair of suede 'brothel creepers'. Within a week I was puffing on cheap packets of Ardath cigarettes. I didn't enjoy the experience but persisted for conformity's sake. I soon decided it would be even more prestigious to purchase a pipe and a tin of Three Nuns tobacco. That affectation didn't last either. In a similar vein, early attempts at relationships with girls were fumbling and shamefully inept. So most of us stuck to being boysy and proclaimed our masculinity by downing schooners at the Forest Lodge. I should add that most of the girls were similarly gauche.

Many of these kids came from comfortable backgrounds and went home to the North Shore or Vaucluse and three square meals a day. I was a scholarship boy living in dreary lodging houses under the watchful eyes of tight-lipped land-ladies in Bondi Junction and Randwick. I used to catch a tram to Central then walk up Broadway to uni, scanning the pavement for dropped coins as I went. Most days I found at least sixpence, which meant I could buy a coffee. But I felt no envy or resentment. I was having too much fun. This was the way students were meant to live. I had to juggle my resources and my parents helped out when they could—but my father's salary was pretty stretched with my three sisters still in Catholic schools.

When I hit the campus for Orientation Week I was over-whelmed by the array of student societies with their booths and placards soliciting membership. There were two com-peting drama societies—the old established Sydney University Dramatic Society and the new breakaway Players. By chance I came across the Players booth first and joined up. That move was to be of some consequence in my later life, since the driving force behind the Players at that time was law student Ken Horler, with whom I would, a little over ten years later, set up the Nimrod Theatre Company.

I drank red wine out of casks at post-show parties, got outrageously drunk and sang 'Michael Row the Boat Ashore' as loud as the best of them. I told 'sick' jokes, talked like the Goons, roared at Stan Freberg and eyed with cautious wonder the shenanigans of those sophisticates who were Libertarians or belonged to the Push. I discovered that all the best movies were black-and-white with subtitles— Eisenstein, Kurosawa, Buñuel, Bergman. I was fashionably late with essays and assignments, baffled by tutors conversing in Old Norse, and idled away my time between the Refectory and Manning House, drinking cups of muddy coffee and listening to the big kids being witty.

I don't know if it was a fluke of timing or intense peer pressure that brought so much talent to the fore, but I seemed to be surrounded by geniuses. There was much mutual back-slapping and keen competition for acting roles, having poems or cartoons published in the student newspaper, *Honi Soit*, and commanding the largest coterie of hangers-on. Robert Hughes had just graduated but his spirit loomed large and set the pace for our generation, which included Clive James, Germaine Greer, Leo Schofield, John Gaden, Richard Wherrett, Bruce Beresford, Richard Walsh, Mungo McCallum, Arthur Dignam, Les Murray, Bob Ellis, Laurie Oakes and Ken Horler.

We were all trying to be somebody. The easiest way was to be somebody else, to have a role model. I worked hard at being Laurence Olivier. I bought his records so I could copy the inflections and I imitated his makeup whenever I went on stage. Ken Horler, busy being Bert Brecht, sported a black leather cap and a cigar. I think John Gaden was being Wilfred Hyde-White, but it wasn't nice to ask. Bob Ellis cultivated a deep, rumbling oracular voice; unsure whether he was being Richard Burton or Winston Churchill, he ended up sounding like a weird synthesis of both. Clive James was nailing down Humphrey Bogart, or anything mildly American. He held court in the Refectory in the morning, Manning in the afternoon, and cast his spell with monologues about Scott Fitzgerald, e e cummings, and a lot of other Americans who weren't on our syllabus. He wore big chunky sweaters and tortured eyebrows, and sat hunched with his cigarette over his coffee, grinding out more or less spontaneous one-liners in a carefully calculated mid-Atlantic nasal twang. The freshettes, in their beatnik outfits, tossed their hair and hung on his every word. Clive wrote a lot of the revues which we performed in the smoky firetrap that was the old Union Theatre. On the day Adolf Eichmann was hanged in Israel, Clive wrote a sketch and performed it that night dressed in a hangman's shroud. It was incomprehensible, but obviously terribly topical and intellectual, so the crowd was hushed and impressed.

I developed a couple of severe crushes on girls in my own year, and found it awfully hard trying to stay a good Catholic. It was okay to get wildly drunk at parties and roll around the floor, pashing intensely, so long as it stopped there.

It was a big mistake to offer your parents' house for a student party because we were pretty good at trashing the place, spilling wine on the carpet or burning it with cigarettes. I remember Ken Horler getting into an apron and rubber gloves with a doily on his head, pushing a traymobile among the writhing bodies on the floor. He was serving up Johnny Ray 78s, cooked between slabs of bread.

A party wasn't a party unless the police were called at least twice, and we'd sit against the wall, sniggering at the young cops picking their way through the room with their shoulders squared, demanding to speak to the 'person in charge'.

Oh, and then there was John Clifton-Bligh; I don't know who he was trying to be, but he may have felt impelled by his double-barrelled name to sport a monocle and sola topee. His eyes would mist with tears as he read extracts of letters from his brother Rupert, who had made it into the Guards in London: 'As we clip-clop down Whitehall behind the Royal carriage, our spurs jingling and our plumes dancing in the breeze, it all somehow feels . . . satisfactory.' And the tears would brim over. Perhaps he was being the Raj . . .

I guess all our mutual admiration did us no harm. It built up a pretty solid self-confidence and sense of destiny, which the world would soon do its best to knock out of us.

# SUDS and the Players

One reason that university drama seemed important was that it was taken seriously by the press and attracted quite a large 'downtown' audience to the campus. There wasn't much else on offer. Sydney had no full-time professional theatre company. The Australian Elizabethan Theatre Trust gave us occasional productions and for a couple of exciting years in the early sixties presented a group called the Trust Players in short repertory seasons at the Elizabethan Theatre in Newtown (now demolished). The Trust Players consisted of good, solid actors in good, solid productions. I remember vividly Frank Thring's Ahab in *Moby Dick Rehearsed* by Orson Welles; Hugh Hunt's *Julius Caesar* with Ron Haddrick, Neva Carr-Glynn and Neil Fitzpatrick; and an imposing *Long Day's Journey* with Haddrick, Fitzpatrick, Frank Waters, Dinah Shearing and Lewis Fiander.

The Trust Players gave Sydney theatre a shot in the arm but didn't last the distance. Otherwise we had JC Williamson

doing reproductions of Broadway musicals (usually starring the American understudy); Doris Fitton's Independent,
where professional actors worked for nothing in between
their radio jobs—but she did keep the doors open for forty
years; Hayes Gordon's Ensemble, mainly staging recent
American works in the Round and showcasing students
from his school, including the startling talents of Reg
Livermore and Jon Ewing; and finally, Sydney's most successful professional theatre presenting revue at the Phillip
Street Theatre under the direction of Bill Orr. This was the
nursery of Ruth Cracknell, Maggie Dence, Barbara Wyndon
and one of Australia's greatest comic talents, Gordon
Chater.

That sounds like quite a healthy menu, but it was spor-
adic, and if you were a serious theatre-goer and wanted
Shakespeare, Aristophenes, Beckett, Sartre, Brecht, or anything 'experimental', you had to take in SUDS or the
Players. We performed mainly in the Wallace Lecture
Theatre or the old Union Hall, which was demolished to
make way for the Union Theatre in 1962. I got the chance
to play Malvolio, Coriolanus, and heaps of revue roles as
well as Giovanni in 'Tis Pity She's A Whore. This last was
significant in that it attracted my first fan letter. It came
from a gentleman named Tony Gilbert, who worked in his
family's automobile company. I thought I should treat a fan
with deference, so I replied to his letter and suggested we
meet for coffee. That was the beginning of a friendship that
has lasted forty years and planted the seed of the Bell Shakespeare Company.

Having run through a succession of grim landladies and
constricted quarters, in 1962 I decided to chum up with a
couple of other students and take a flat. We were extremely

lucky to find one advertised in a beautiful old sandstone house in Randwick. It belonged to a dignified, elderly actor named Charles Tasman. As Charles Tasman-Parkinson he had been headmaster of King's, but since retirement had taken to the boards. He was letting out the top half of his house while he and his sweet-tempered little old wife occupied downstairs and tended the extensive garden. So I moved in with two fellow students who, like me, were heavily involved in university theatre. One was Andrew McLennan, who went on to work at the ABC and created the innovative *Listening Room*; the other was Arthur Dignam, unbelievably vague and chaotic, but with a mellow voice that, like Orpheus, drew trees and stones, and particularly females, in his wake.

As well as sharing the excitement of treading the boards and the anxiety of exams and overdue assignments, we shared our genteel poverty in scenes reminiscent of *La Bohème*. I remember one night when we were all three stony broke and the only edible thing in the cupboard was half a bag of flour. I suggested we make a damper, but as none of us had ever cooked damper, we had to do it by guesswork. I assured the other two it was only a matter of adding water, moulding it into a loaf and whacking it in the oven. For four hours we sat hungrily staring at the glass door of the stove waiting for something to happen. When it had turned black I assumed it was time to take it out. Well, the black crust was firm enough, but under that it was just grey glue. We nibbled a bit of the charcoal crust and regretfully chucked the rest in the bin.

Some months before I moved to Charles Tasman's flat, I was hard up for accommodation and was put up by buddy Bruce Beresford at his parents' home in Wentworthville.

Bruce, a movie fanatic, had quite a collection of 16 millimetre prints which he used to screen for me, with a running commentary, on a sheet hung up in his room. This was my introduction to *Citizen Kane* and a score of other classics.

Bruce was also scraping together enough film stock and favours to make a twenty-minute feature called *The Devil to Pay*, and he asked me to play the lead role of a Faustian figure who cheats his way to the top (shades of *Citizen Kane*) but is finally gunned down in a stormwater channel (shades of *The Third Man*). The outstanding features of the production were Bruce's recklessness and sheer effrontery in scrounging resources. For half a day he risked life and limb lying on the bonnet of his parents' Rover, pointing a camera at me as we sped back and forth across the Sydney Harbour Bridge.

When he needed twenty voices singing 'For he's a jolly good fellow' he simply slipped a requisition form into the recording studios of the ABC and came back next day to pick up the tape. No-one asked what it was for.

His production manager was Richard Brennan, whose father was a judge. His Honour was persuaded not only to appear as an extra but to prevail on four burly detectives to show up at the stormwater channel, gun me down and carry me off into the sunset like Hamlet. It was a marvel to watch Bruce conning and charming people into letting him use various locations, from private homes to the renowned Adams Marble Bar in the Hotel Australia. His cameraman, Richard Keyes, now runs the National Film and Sound Archives. Whenever I visit Canberra he threatens to screen the only existing copy of *The Devil to Pay*.

I used to take weekend and holiday jobs to keep me in funds, spending most Sundays pulling up weeds with Bruce or pulling milkshakes at Coogee Beach. That was okay because I could consume all the milkshakes I wanted, as long as the boss wasn't looking. My long holiday jobs were less satisfactory. In one factory I was a storeman and packer, trundling crates around on a forklift. The only way to keep myself interested was to try to set new records for the number of boxes I could carry on one load. One day I managed to get a column of one hundred and forty boxes of flyspray onto the forklift, but as I started to move I saw the column tip towards me, as if in slow motion. I stepped aside and watched aghast as the whole lot crashed to the floor. I very quietly collected my lunchbox, left by the rear door and never went back.

Another time Bruce and I had a job proofreading the telephone book, triple-checking every name, address and number. We had a terrible time staying awake and felt a pang of gratification when it was later announced that the telephone directory had a record number of mistakes that year.

While maintaining a sturdy disrespect for authority and government in general, as a student body we were politically ignorant and inactive in the late fifties. This was pre-Vietnam and most of the country still wallowed in the lazy complacency of the Menzies era. There were small groups of libertarians and socialists on campus but we tended to write them off as the ratbag fringe. Because we'd had no education in Australian history we were sublimely unaware of the forces gathering around us. I had to leave Australia to become politically motivated, but when I returned in 1970, the anti-Vietnam movement was in full swing and Gough Whitlam was breathing the winds of change. Meanwhile we carried on with desultory study and amateur dramatics.

The new Union Theatre opened in 1962 with a production of John Arden's *Sergeant Musgrave's Dance*, directed by May Hollingworth, coaxed out of retirement by Ken Horler. I played the role of Sergeant Musgrave in Arden's bitter anti-war, anti-Establishment surreal fantasy. Our distinguished first-night audience was affronted and baffled—not only by the script, but by our attempts at Geordie accents. After the performance the cast had to line up to shake the hands of the New South Wales Governor, his lady-wife and other notables, who gave us an icy reception.

But at last we had a (for then) state-of-the-art student playhouse. I had a go at Coriolanus there and watched Germaine Greer haul her wagon round the stage as Mother Courage. It's rather depressing to see the Union Theatre forty years later, abandoned and neglected most of the time. Given its potential and its location at the very entrance to the university, one would hope to see it a hive of creative student activity.

Sydney still had lots of attractive and atmospheric theatres in the fifties, instead of the bland collection of brick and concrete boxes we're stuck with now. They were all Victorian or Edwardian—the Elizabethan, Her Majesty's, the Royal, the Regent, the exquisite little Palace Theatre— all demolished in the greedy building frenzy of the sixties. But there wasn't enough local product to keep them going. I remember pretty shonky productions by John Alden's Shakespeare Company in his last years when he must have been desperate financially.

The art scene was just beginning to take off, with little galleries opening in Paddington. Barry Stern opened a new gallery with lots of fanfare and I went along because Spike Milligan was going to do the honours. After being jammed tight in the crowd for half an hour with my plastic cup of cask white wine in my fist, I fought my way outside for some air. I found Spike sitting in the gutter. 'Aren't you supposed to be opening the show?' I asked. 'I was going to,' he said with a woeful expression, 'but I forgot my opener.'

I ended up taking a second-class English Honours degree, which is probably more than I deserved because most of my knowledge was the result of desperate, last-minute cramming. It was the fashion to flaunt your complete ignorance just prior to exams, then stay up four nights in a row popping pills and drinking black coffee, and turn up for the exam looking wild-eyed and exhilarated, shrieking, 'I don't know *anything*! It's going to be a *disaster*!' This was to cover yourself in case it was.

Over the four years and some dozen university shows, my family made the trip down from Maitland to see practically all of them. It was a four-hour drive in those days but they'd turn up in convoy—the old soft-top Chevy with my Nan and Da, and the Morris with Mum, Dad, my three sisters and baby brother. After the show there'd be a brief reunion on the footpath outside: the thermos and sandwiches (and occasional birthday cake) would appear, and after we'd said our farewells they'd all drive off into the night, getting home around 4 am. This support and devotion continued until I left Australia for the big wide world.

But probably their proudest day was the one when I graduated and they sat in the Great Hall of Sydney University to watch me process, in hired gown and mortarboard, up the aisle to the strains of 'Gaudeamus' and receive my degree from the hand of wise-old-owl Chancellor Sir

Charles Bickerton Blackburn. Among the hugs, tears, laughter and photographs on the lawn afterwards, I couldn't help wondering, as I stood clutching my certificate, What now? Where do I go from here?

As luck would have it, at that very moment plans were being laid at another campus, the University of New South Wales, to create Sydney's first full-time professional theatre company. In a corner of the campus adjacent to the Randwick Racecourse some buildings had been hived off for a theatre and rehearsal space. Since the main one was the old totalisator building, it was decided to call the theatre the Old Tote.

*Part 2*

# THE OLD TOTE AND ROYAL SHAKESPEARE COMPANY

# Trofimov,
# Hamlet and love

I needed to hang out my shingle and tell the world I'd arrived, so before the university year ended I committed an act of staggering cheek. I hired the 100-seat Genesian Theatre in Kent Street and put on a one-man show, or rather showcase. (Well, I didn't actually 'hire' the theatre. I'd done a few shows with the Genesians and they kindly gave me the space for free.) I took some twenty extracts from Shakespeare's history plays (all ten of them, from *King John* to *Henry VIII*) and strung together a history of England, giving myself the opportunity to perform all the great roles and speeches—not just the kings, but characters like the Bastard (*King John*), Jack Cade (*Henry VI*) and even a double-act as Shallow and Silence (*Henry IV*). I used a few props—crown, sword, cloak and a few funny hats—and linked the story with my own running commentary. I played over four nights and one critic turned up, which is actually one more than you'd expect for a one-man student show.

But he happened to be the most influential critic in town—
Roger Covell of the *Sydney Morning Herald*, whose word
was law. He gave me a good rap so although no professional directors saw the show, they all heard how good it
was, which was probably the better option. When I went
to audition for this new company, the Old Tote, my reputation preceded me.

Meanwhile things were moving along at the Tasman-
Parkinson house in Randwick. Andrew and Arthur, studies
completed, were moving out and Charles advertised the flat
for rental. He told me I could stay on in the little one-room
shack in the garden and use his bathroom and kitchen,
which I was happy to do.

One morning as I was showering and shaving in the flat
upstairs, Charles knocked on the door, announcing that
two ladies had come to inspect the flat. Would I mind if he
showed them around? I opened the door in my mousey old
dressing gown with a towel around my neck, my face pink
and shiny, my hair standing on end, and there beheld the
two most glamorous women I'd ever seen. They both
looked exotically European and were dressed to the nines—
hats, handbags and all. They stared at me and the younger
one burst out laughing. They were introduced as Mrs Spindler
and her daughter, a recent NIDA graduate who had decided
to abbreviate her father's name, Dobrovolska, and call her-
self Anna Volska. Anna was to be part of the new Old Tote
company, and so was Charles, who was to play the aged
retainer Feers in the first play of the season, *The Cherry
Orchard*.

So Anna took the flat, along with two other recent
female NIDA grads, and I moved into the garden hut. I set
my heart on joining the Old Tote. The timing seemed for-

tuitous and the Tote was being heralded as a great new
chapter in Australian theatre . . . besides, it was the only
professional theatre company in town. Luck was on my
side because a vacancy had just come up. The company
was to be headed by experienced stalwarts like Ron Haddrick, Owen Weingott and Gordon Chater, but made a
point of taking on a couple of recent NIDA graduates. This
was because NIDA and the Tote were interdependent. The
Tote would never have gotten off the ground without
NIDA's input. The actual Old Tote Theatre was a tin shed
lined with fibro; it had a hundred seats and a small stage
with no wings, flies or front curtain. It was part of the
NIDA complex of fibro huts and was run by NIDA staff.
Its directors, Robert Quentin, Tom Brown, John Clark and
Joe McCallum were all NIDA personnel and students were
used for bit parts and understudies. For its time it was a
healthy expansion of NIDA's activities and a valuable cross-
fertilisation of pros and students.

The two recent NIDA graduates chosen for the first Old
Tote season were Anna Volska and Dennis Olsen, who was
to play Trofimov in *The Cherry Orchard*. But then Dennis
had an offer to tour with an Elizabethan Theatre Trust
company called the Young Elizabethan Players and he asked
to be released. This left Robert Quentin short of a Trofimov.
Anna tipped me off that the part was up for grabs so I
pestered Quentin for an audition. After I'd read for him he
looked dubious and shook his head. 'You're not right for
the part—Trofimov is gaunt and hungry. He's scruffy and
flea-bitten. You look too healthy.'

I begged for a chance to come back again next morning
and stayed up most of the night to make myself as gaunt
as I could. I didn't shave, rubbed grease through my hair,

borrowed from Charles a pair of rimless specs, dressed in a baggy old overcoat and walked to the Tote making myself dirty and dusty along the way. This time I got the part and rushed home, overjoyed, to tell Charles and Anna.

Naturally Anna and I walked together to and from rehearsal each day, and of an evening she would often come to the garden hut to talk about the day's work and we'd listen to records on my battered turntable or read favourite poems to each other. Anna had been accepted into NIDA when she was sixteen. Now she was eighteen, I was twenty-two and fast becoming captivated, though she always claims it was she who made the first move. I've no doubt that it was entirely mutual. Before long we had taken to sitting on the big rock in the garden through the pitch black frangipani-perfumed night or taking moonlit walks along Coogee Beach.

Within a few weeks of her moving into the flat we were carrying on a full-scale romance, much to the consternation of those around us. As Juliet says, it all seemed 'too rash, too sudden'. One of Anna's flatmates, playing Big Sister, warned her off me, Charles gave me a stern ticking-off for cradle-snatching, Robert and June Quentin gave me a sombre lecture about putting my career first, and my mother, when she found out I had a 'girlfriend', became hostile and embattled. I'm afraid she remained wildly possessive of her first-born for many years. Only Anna's mother, Christine, bore it all with good grace, although she must have been full of trepidation.

Meanwhile Anna and I were blissfully happy and working hard at the Tote. We were both in the opening show, *The Cherry Orchard*, in which she played Dunyasha, and the following double-bill of Max Frisch's *The Fire Raisers* and Ionesco's *Bald Prima Donna*. We were somewhat over-awed by the rich vocal timbre of Ron Haddrick, the comic finesse of Chater, and the 'overseas' reputations of husband-and-wife team Sophie Stewart and Ellis Irving, whom Quentin had imported to launch the season. Each show would play an average of four weeks and the season ran for seven months. One day during the run of *The Cherry Orchard* I was taken aside by Tom Brown, who was slated to direct *Hamlet*. 'Can you fence?' he asked, and I thought, oh my God, he's going to offer me Laertes! Fantastic! So I assured him that I was a pretty dazzling swordsman—a gross exaggeration rather than a downright lie. 'How would you like to play Hamlet?' he asked, and I nearly fell over. This was too much too soon, but of course I leapt at it.

All through the rest of *The Cherry Orchard* season I was consumed by *Hamlet*, and Anna and I both hoped she would be cast as Ophelia. This was not to be, and maybe it was just as well. As in playing the Macbeths, playing Hamlet and Ophelia is not necessarily healthy for the offstage relationship—too much angst and spite. The production was very conventional—velvet cloaks and cardboard crowns—and I went for the jugular, giving in a tiny theatre a performance better suited to the Colosseum. Tom was an ex-stage manager and a part-time academic. He had few qualifications as a director, and I'd never had an acting lesson in my life, so I was doing it all by guesswork. Fortunately, the arrogance and ignorance of youth allowed me to take it all for granted.

The *Hamlet* season finished and I was out of work. I had not scored rave reviews, nor had I been a total failure—you can't really fail as Hamlet. I scrabbled around for a bit of television and radio, but was not particularly anxious.

Something would turn up, and it did. Robert Quentin summoned me to the Elizabethen Theatre Trust offices and asked whether I'd like to set up a new theatre company. He had the Trust's support for the venture. It would be very small—just a lunchtime affair presenting one-act plays in the beautiful little Palace Theatre (now demolished) in Pitt Street. We decided to charge the audience three shillings (about thirty cents) which would include coffee and a sandwich. The Three Bob Theatre opened in September 1963 with Edward Albee's *The American Dream* starring Neva Carr-Glynn and Gwen Plum. I faced, and failed, my first test as impresario when both leading ladies demanded the number one dressing room. I had no idea, at twenty-two, how to handle such an explosive negotiation and had to send for help.

Three Bob Theatre folded after four productions. We should have charged more or persisted longer until the idea caught on. The affair damaged neither my career nor self-esteem, but it cured me (for a while) of wanting to run a theatre company.

# Wasn't I ghastly tonight?

Now a truly exciting proposition came along. Tom Brown was to direct a Trust production of *Henry V* for the 1964 Adelaide Festival. He cast me as Henry and Anna as Princess Katherine. We were in heaven. Tom had spent some time as Assistant Director to Tyrone Guthrie setting up the Shakespeare Festival Theatre in Ontario. He had the prompt copy of Guthrie's *Henry V* and his own production was pretty much a straight replication. This was hailed as a huge plus—almost as good as the real thing! Guthrie had started in a circus tent, so the Trust had one made to similar specifications. We even had recordings of the trumpet fanfares Guthrie used to summon people into the tent. The set and costumes were pretty much identical to Guthrie's, as were the staging and choreography.

As with *Hamlet,* Tom was fine at getting on a show but not much help with the finer points of acting, handling the verse or vocal technique. Luckily, I had in Olivier a superb role model and referred to him continually rather than attempting anything radical or original. I was still very much in his shadow and happy to be there. But this didn't help solve my immediate problem—playing Henry V in a circus tent (eight hundred seats and terrible acoustics) eight times a week was a huge vocal strain. I had no idea of breath control, how to pitch, produce or resonate my voice. To make things worse, the park where our tent was situated in Adelaide had a highway on one side, a railway line on the other and a flight path overhead. And when it rained, the sound was deafening. So, in a word, I was struggling, and feeling vocally inadequate and untrained. But that's been something of a lifelong problem: six months at Bristol Old Vic didn't teach me anything useful, nor did the vocal coaching at the Royal Shakespeare Company (RSC). The first useful voice coaching I had was a couple of classes with Australian actor Jonathan Hardy—and that wasn't until I was in my mid fifties. Since then I have put in time with some excellent teachers—Rowena Balos and Lindy Davies among them. In my sixtieth year I began to feel confident that I had some idea of vocal technique and could play a heavy role for a long season without losing my voice.

Playing Henry V I felt most inadequate when listening to the voices of the older actors, especially Alex Hay, most impressive as a supercilious Constable of France. With his Lorenzo de Medici profile, flashing black eyes and resonant chest-notes, Alex had scored a triumph the previous year in the Tote's production of *Who's Afraid of Virginia Woolf?* opposite Jackie Kott. Alex presented an aloof exterior, but when I got to know him years later I found him to be the gentlest, kindest and most shy of people.

With its novel circus-tent setting, glamorous costumes, swirling banners and operatic staging, *Henry V* proved enormously popular, and nearly forty years later I still get buttonholed by people who remember it. It felt pretty heady being part of a major show in the Adelaide Festival. I was startled to receive applause on my first entrance. (It's never happened since!) But it was only because it was opening night and I was the 'star'. That's what an audience was supposed to do.

After the opening we were invited to a swell bash at the Town Hall where we were greeted by the soon-to-be premier of South Australia, Don Dunstan. Anna, Andrew McLennan (my former flatmate who was also in the show) and I felt pretty out of place among all the fancy hats and braid, and spotted a similarly discomfited group cowering behind a pillar. They were dressed in jeans and skivvies and sipped champagne as they eyed the whinnying and braying social set. 'They must be actors,' we said, and made our way over to them.

Actors they were—Harold Lang and his team from England, presenting a witty and informative Shakespeare show called *Macbeth in Camera*. We struck up an instant rapport and afterwards met regularly for post-show drinks or supper. Harold was the first truly camp, flamboyant and brilliant English theatre personality we'd met, full of hilarious anecdotes, gossip and impersonations. We pumped him incessantly for news of theatre 'over there'. Breathlessly I enquired, 'Have you seen Olivier's Othello?' Harold rolled his eyes, 'Oh my dear, dreary beyond words—just a Pearl Bailey black mammy. I saw it at a special matinee for actors and was so *bored*! I looked along the row and they were all heads down, fast asleep!! Then I looked again and they weren't asleep, they were all weeping!! All of them . . . so who knows?'

From Adelaide *Henry V* moved its circus tent to Sydney for a season in Rushcutters Bay Park. The Trust was entertaining the rather extravagant notion of building identical large concrete bowls in each capital city over which a travelling tent could be pitched, thus maintaining a long-term touring circuit. I think the novelty would have worn off pretty quickly and I'm relieved it didn't happen.

Despite my vocal anxieties I was having a whale of a time playing Henry. It was a role I had idolised and coveted ever since first seeing the Olivier movie—and here I was *doing* it, declaiming all the great speeches, making love to Anna Volska—and in a *circus tent*!

My love of sawdust and canvas was as ardent as it had been in the days of Sorlies' and Bobby le Brun. In fact circus tents have cropped up throughout my career. The Bell Shakespeare Company began its life in one; and if I couldn't have a real one, I sometimes reconstructed one inside a theatre as I did for a couple of my most successful shows, Nimrod's *Much Ado About Nothing* and *The Venetian Twins* in the Opera House Drama Theatre.

When *Henry V* finished I was once more high and dry, looking for a job and thinking hard about taking some acting lessons. To fill in time, and make some money, I put together a scratch company to stage a recital program in St James's Hall, Phillip Street. I wanted to do John Barton's *The Hollow Crown*, which had some great speeches, Shakespeare and others, and was a pushover for five actors and a piano. I applied for the rights but they were refused as the RSC was contemplating bringing the show to Australia. So I swapped a couple of speeches around, substituted others and retitled it *By Royal Command*. All the material was public property anyway.

The show was somewhat less than a sell-out and we didn't make any money, but it kept us out of mischief for a few weeks. The others in the cast were John Llewellyn, Doreen Warburton, Arthur Dignam and Anna. On the opening night we all rolled up in our hired dinner jackets and evening dress—except Arthur, who was in his old sweater and cords. He looked deliciously vague and drawled, 'Oh, I didn't realise . . .', so he made a phone call or two and soon a procession of young women materialised bearing a wide variety of white ties, tails, shiny pumps and cartons of makeup. Needless to say, he outshone us all. Except when he sat down to play the piano. Part of his job was to play the Beethoven Variations on God Save the King, which Art assured us were 'coming along', although we never heard them in rehearsal. On the first night he quietly muttered, 'I think I'd better drop the Beethoven—I'll just play the straight version.' When he commenced, the audience didn't know whether to stand or sit, laugh or scowl as Art picked his way through the national anthem with two clumsy fingers and a lot of mistakes.

Now came my first taste of commercial theatre with a whiff of the West End. I was offered a role in a Peter Shaffer double bill at the Phillip Theatre. It was a restaging of the West End production to be directed by the English stage manager, Frank Stevens, and was to star the English understudy, Judith Stott, who had covered Maggie Smith.

I was in the first play, *The Private Ear*, with Judith and Don Pascoe. The second play, *The Public Eye*, featured Judith, Gordon Chater and Max Osbitson. So far all my experience had been in the classics. This was my first taste of contemporary English comedy and, besides being highly instructive watching Judith and Gordon rehearsing with such expertise, it bore an unexpected bonus. Sir John Gielgud had come to town with his one-man Shakespeare recital *Ages of Man* and was performing at the old Theatre Royal. He and Judith were great chums from a season together at Stratford. She told me how she'd recently gone down to Stratford with Albert Finney, with whom she was having a pretty hot affair. Gielgud was playing Othello in Zefferelli's over-decorated production with Ian Bannen as his Iago. They were all four walking to the theatre for a matinee, Gielgud and Bannen in front, Judith and Finney behind, when Gielgud dropped one of his notorious clangers: 'How's *Othello* going, Sir John?' Judith had asked. 'Oh ghastly!' groaned the knight. 'Cumbersome sets, heavy costumes and the most dreadful Iago! You should have played it, Albert . . . oh, sorry, Ian.'

There was huge excitement all round when it was announced Sir John was coming to see our show. Second to Olivier, he was my acting idol. There was a party in Judith's dressing room afterwards and he was, as ever, charmingly complimentary to one and all.

Gordon suggested Sir John might like to go on a picnic on Sunday and we arrived at his Rose Bay hotel to pick him up. Sir John strolled down the steps in immaculate whites and Panama. 'Where are we going?' he asked. Gordon replied, 'Camp Cove, Sir John.' Slight pause, then Gielgud murmured, 'Ah, how appropriate.'

Since I was in the first half of the Shaffer double bill I was able to slip out at interval and hotfoot it down to the Royal. I knew the stage manager and he let me stand in the wings every night to watch the second half of Gielgud's recital. He was an extremely emotional performer and one night wept as he dedicated his *Julius Caesar* speech to John F Kennedy, who had been assassinated that day. Gielgud had performed for him the previous month at the White House.

As I got bolder each night, I'd creep a little closer in the wings to get a better look. One night I had my face close to the curtain to watch his Macbeth. He began, 'Is this a dagger that I see before me?', spun around, saw me standing there and uttered a startled shriek before going on with the speech. As soon as the curtain came down I beetled for the exit, but the stage manager caught me. 'Sir John wants to see you in his dressing room,' he said grimly. Oh cripes, now I'm for it, I thought as I knocked tentatively on the door.

'Come in . . .' fluted the familiar tones. 'Ah, dear boy, sit down, have a drink. Wasn't I ghastly tonight? The Hamlet was garbled, the Cassius too limp. What did you think?' And I found myself in the unusual position of having to reassure this icon of the British theatre that he'd actually put in a good night's work. Recounting the story some forty years later, it suddenly occurs to me that it may have been a pick-up. That's how dumb I am about some things.

# 'The right way—
# the English way'

It was 1992. I had just done a presentation of my upcoming Bell Shakespeare Company production of *Romeo & Juliet* for a group of supporters and interested parties. I had explained at length the reasoning behind the production's concept, design decisions, contemporary costumes and music. While everyone got stuck into the free wine and sandwiches, I found myself bailed up by a middle-aged lady with a tight smile and a glint in her eye.

'Thank you, but I won't be coming to see your production,' she announced sweetly.

'Oh . . .' I reeled a little, having anticipated a positive response. 'Why's that?'

'Well you see, I'm a *purist*,' she explained, 'and I just think if people have been doing Shakespeare the *right* way, I mean the *English* way for the last two thousand years, then who are we? Who are WE?' She pinned me to the wall with her glare and then confided: 'You know, when I was a gel'—she actually said 'gel'—'my mother had a book, and in that book were all the plays of Shakespeare—all in one book! And all written in the old language—you know, thee and thou; and I often think' (she cocked her eye wistfully) '...if only that book could be found again, what a wonderful world this would be.' By this time I was glued into the corner, my eyes darting about, looking for the men in white coats.

Still, that phrase of hers, 'the right way, the English way', stuck in my mind because it has bedevilled not only Australian art for so long, but also Australian life at many levels, socially and politically.

I was brought up a happy little Anglophile. Odd, because the family was Irish on both sides and had little to thank the English for. But of all the family, my grandfather, Joe Feeney, was the only one who protested the day Queen Elizabeth II visited Newcastle. While the rest of us got gussied up and lined the streets to wave little flags and cheer the royal couple, Da went fishing, his pipe clenched firmly between his teeth, muttering disparaging remarks about the Poms. We were brainwashed by the Anglophilia of Bob Menzies and his cohorts, by the gushing worship of the royals in the *Australian Women's Weekly*. We saw ourselves living in a no-man's-land, a cultural desert, Down Under. In 1950 it had been nearly a hundred years since the last heady push for republicanism and it would be more than forty years until the next.

England represented not only 'home and beauty', it epitomised all that was excellent in art and literature. Just as our landscape and our natural flora were considered drab and ugly alongside English hedgerows and cottage gardens, so our poets and dramatists were yokels ranged against the

greats of English letters. Literature meant English literature, apart from the occasional Australian poem like Henry
Kendall's *Bellbirds*, which had an English kind of poetic
elegance.

In high school we barely touched on Australian history.
We were tutored in the minutiae of the French Revolution
and the Treaty of Versailles as well as the Corn Laws of
the Roman Republic and the Punic Wars. But nothing about
the Holocaust, Hiroshima, the Great Depression or Gallipoli—things that had recently shaped our lives. Perhaps
as topics of conversation they were still too politically sensitive. Racism, anti-Semitism and political conservatism
were taken for granted. One of my Marist teachers used to
refer to Jews as 'DJs' (dirty Jews), and 'Abo' and 'coon'
jokes were popular.

So when I started acting I was told quite firmly by a
senior actor, 'Listen, son, you have two voices, one for the
stage and one for the pub, and don't ever mix them up or
you'll get clobbered for it.' This meant that whenever you
stepped on stage (or acted on radio) you deliberately
affected rounded vowels and a 'posh' phoney English
accent. That's what acting was. And as soon as you stepped
off stage, you switched to broad Australian in case anyone
thought you were 'up yourself' or a 'poofter'.

England was obviously the theatre Mecca and from the
age of fifteen I devoured every book in the slim collection
of the Maitland library that had to do with English theatre
and its luminaries. I sketched photographs of Olivier in
makeup and costume and when I started acting, did my
best to look and sound like him. Being stuck out in the
bush, I never got to see the English theatre companies when

they toured Australia, but I filled scrapbooks with photographs and reviews of them.

I had been acting professionally for just over a year when I had a phone call from a charming lady at the British Council asking me to meet her for a coffee. She explained that the end of the financial year was approaching and they had to get rid of some money in the kitty. How would I like a scholarship to study acting in England? I suppose having played both Hamlet and Henry V, I seemed to be a reasonable investment. I asked around and it seemed that Bristol Old Vic Theatre School was held in high esteem. The scholarship offered me a year's tuition with a modest living allowance. So plans were laid.

I took off in October 1964 at the age of twenty-three to fulfil my wildest dream. Anna and I weren't actually living together but were kind of unofficially engaged and she promised she would be joining me in a few months' time. We saw our destinies as intertwined: we were in love with each other and with the theatre. Like me, Anna was a devotee of Olivier and Shakespeare (the movie of *Henry V* had had the same effect on her as it had on me). She too was bent on making a pilgrimage to the West End of London.

Parting from my family was a wrench, but more for them, I'm afraid, as I was shaking with excitement. I had no idea how long I'd be away, so my poor mother was a sobbing heap. The deepest pang I felt was in saying goodbye to my dearest Nan and Da. Something in their still sadness told me they knew they'd never see me again. As it happened, they both died within a short time of each other about a year before I returned to Australia.

# Bristol Old Vic

Never having been in an aeroplane before, and never having set foot outside Australia, every minute of the thirty-two-hour flight was seared into my memory. Whenever we stopped for refuelling I thrilled to the exotic sights and sounds, the unfamiliar languages, the milling mobs of different coloured people in turbans and kaftans, the hot spicy air of Bangkok, the swaggering boy policemen with enormous guns on their hips, and to actually have one's feet on the ground in Rome!! (Even if it was only the airport lounge.)

And the excitement as we flew into London — I felt like Peter Pan gliding over Neverland. A weak golden sun was beginning to rise and everything looked just as it should — the neat hedgerows, the impossibly green trees and fields, the rows of little red rooftops and, above all, the thought: Laurence Olivier lives here! I half expected to see him looking up at the plane and waving: 'Hello, Johnno, welcome to England!'

Actually I was met at the airport by Ken Horler, who helped me hump my luggage to a flat in High Street, Kensington, where I'd be staying for a few days before going to Bristol. Shivering with excitement, my eyes drank in all the anticipated sights as we made our way through London— the bobbies in their helmets, the red buses, Trafalgar Square —I felt I shouldn't be able to sleep until I had charged down Whitehall from the National Gallery to the Abbey. Ken had been in London for a while now and pooh-poohed my wild colonial eagerness.

Ken's flat in High Street was in one of those big shabby Georgian terraces. A couple of other Aussie university mates were shacked up there—Clive James and Mike Newman; and Brett Whiteley lived and worked next door. I wasn't familiar with his paintings then, but was fascinated to sit and watch him at work on his Christie, Rillington Place series. The end of my first perfect day in London came with Ken's announcement, 'I've got us some tickets for the theatre tonight—we're going to see Ralph Richardson at the Haymarket.'

England was turning out to be everything I wanted it to be and on arriving in Bristol I was taken to a boarding house in an old terrace right next to the wildly picturesque Clifton Gorge. My landlady was a pious soul with a tight grey bun. To see a woman without makeup was unusual in those days. I was supposed to take meals with the other lodgers (all foreign students) while madam sat at the head of the table ladling out thin soup and maintaining genteel conversation. I knew I'd suffocate if I stayed there long and resolved to start searching for a flat quick smart. I found one not far from the school—the basement of a terrace owned by an old lady who seemed bemused by my occupation: 'So all you do is sing and dance all day?' (Sigh.) 'What a wonderful life!' Life was certainly wonderful but hardly comfortable. I was on very short rations and making ends meet was not easy.

Anna arrived in London three months after I did. We were eagerly looking forward to the reunion. I took a day off school to meet her at Heathrow but, unfortunately, she landed at Gatwick; I didn't know there were two airports. A flurry of messages resulted in our finally meeting at Victoria Station. I couldn't believe her suntan. Or maybe she was just smouldering over my stuff-up.

There was no hot water in my basement flat in Bristol and Anna's eyes popped when I welcomed her to my new abode by procuring for her a bath from a steaming kettle and an old iron tub. I think she was rather glad to escape from this freezing Dickensian establishment by going to find work in London. She had letters of introduction, a string of auditions and a living to earn. We planned on meeting up at weekends. Things might have got tough had I stayed long in Bristol, but that was not to be . . .

The Bristol Old Vic Theatre School was, and I presume still is, situated in a large white Georgian house opposite the Clifton Downs, a pleasant rambling wilderness. Nat Brenner was the principal, a dignified Viennese Jew whose closest ally on the staff was his compatriot Rudy Shelley, who was a bit more of the larrikin showman. Rudy was wildly emotional and demonstrative, with a touch of the Chico Marx about him. His classes were by far the most popular with students, being full of anecdotes, demonstrations and proverbial wisdom. We had singing classes with a cheerful baritone named John Oxley, and a voice teacher who insisted we copy her Somerset burr; there was a bit of ballet and fencing, and lessons in how to carry a fan, a cane and a pair of gloves, and how to curtsey. It was all quite entertaining and utterly useless.

I enjoyed my time in Bristol because I liked the staff, my fellow students and the city itself—an ideal small city with its university, beautiful cathedral and churches like St Mary Redcliffe, the busy port studded with ancient piratical pubs (Stevenson actually wrote *Treasure Island* in one of them), the Downs, the Gorge, the charming little zoo— everything within walking distance. And of course the Bristol Old Vic Theatre riding high on a solid reputation and some landmark productions such as Peter O'Toole's *Hamlet* and the icky-sticky *Salad Days*, which originated there and kept the company solvent through the ongoing royalties it provided. The theatre itself was an exquisite Georgian jewelbox, had a good company of actors, plus a lively alternative venue across the road to stage the newer, risky plays.

The other great thing about Bristol was its proximity to London, where Anna had a job at Boots the Chemist. We met up at weekends and stayed in her flat in Swiss Cottage and we got to a good deal of London theatre. I was fortunate to see several of Olivier's late great stage performances— his *Master Builder*, *Dance of Death*, Captain Brazen in *The Recruiting Officer*, Mr Tattle in *Love for Love*, but chiefly his Othello, which I saw four times, twice by sleeping on the footpath all night outside the Old Vic. It's still the most remarkable stage performance I have ever seen and bears little resemblance to the travesty that is the film version of the same production. Live, he effortlessly filled the theatre with an electrifying energy. He owned the place. I was sick with excitement watching him and at the end of the performance had to sit still while the audience filed out. I couldn't move—my legs had turned to jelly.

I must have made a favourable impression on Nat Brenner because after I'd been at the school about five months he summoned me to his office and said, 'I've had a letter from the RSC at Stratford. They're starting a new experimental studio there, attached to the company, for six months. They only want ten people and they're auditioning students from drama schools all over the country. Shall I put your name forward?'

I found myself confronting the legendary Michel Saint-Denis in a dusty church hall somewhere in the middle of London. Saint-Denis was one of the outstanding directors in English theatre for the first half of the twentieth century. He was also one of the founders of the Old Vic Centre and School and had the reputation of being a rigid disciplinarian. I did my piece for him and he seemed duly unimpressed, but did ask me to come back for the second round. This time I seemed to go down better and I was offered one of the ten places. Among my fellow students at Bristol three or four close friends were both tearful and buoyant about my good fortune. They packed my few belongings into an old car and drove me to Stratford one Saturday morning.

# The Holy Grail—
# Stratford-on-Avon

If London was the holy city, then Stratford-on-Avon was the Holy Grail itself. I couldn't believe that I was actually going to be living and working there, not only with this famous company, but walking in the very footprints of the immortal Will himself.

I spent all that weekend prior to starting work on Monday evening exploring every nook and cranny of the town—the birthplace, Anne Hathaway's cottage, the Wilmcote Farm belonging to Mary Arden, Shakespeare's mother, his grave at Holy Trinity Church, his garden at New Place—all the Shakespeare shrines. I was given accommodation in a rambling fifteenth-century house belonging to Denne Gilkes, the company's singing coach. She was a grand and statuesque old lady with a big nose on her big face, a deep resonant tone and a vigorous demeanour as she stumped about with her hearty stick and her flowing cape and shawl.

My room had creaking floorboards, a solid oak bed, half-timbered walls and little lead-glass casement windows that overlooked the main street. The room hadn't been altered in any major way for five hundred years, and on cold nights as the snow whirled around my casement I would burrow under the heavy counterpane and scare myself to sleep reading ghost stories by flickering candle-light. (I could have turned on the light switch, but I could blow out a candle without having to get out of bed and tiptoe across the icy floorboards. Besides, a rush candle was more atmospheric.)

Come Monday evening, the studio group of ten young actors assembled for the first time in the old library attached to the theatre on the banks of the Avon. The walls were lined with paintings of famous actors and we sat around a long oak table on upright chairs. Around me at one end were the nine other hopefuls whose faces I scanned with intense curiosity. All in their early twenties, they bore that glint of killer instinct in their eyes, hellbent on making a good first impression.

At the other end of the table sat the Heavy Brigade, Monsieur Saint-Denis in the middle. He was in his sixties, I guess, which seemed ancient then, and was quite small but solid, with a crisp, cursory way of addressing us. He was flanked by Peter Hall, the company's artistic director, looking dark and watchful in an avuncular sort of way; John Barton, a staff director, nervy, eccentric, chain-smoking and untidy; the sturdy Denne Gilkes, and half a dozen other administrative personnel. We all sized each other up and after a perfunctory greeting, Saint-Denis announced, 'We will now read *The Winter's Tale*. You will begin.' And he shoved a copy of the script along the table to where I was sitting.

I took a deep breath, cleared my throat and read the first line of the play. Saint-Denis stopped me. 'Please, my friend, don't try to perform it. Just read the words.' I didn't think I *had* been performing it; nevertheless it seemed appropriate to mumble an apology and begin again. I read the first line unexpressively and again he stopped me. 'I'm sorry, my friend, I think you misunderstood me. Don't *perform* it; don't *act*, don't *declaim* . . . just read the words.' Now my ears started to burn as I felt the critical eye of the Heavies at the end of the table boring into me and the other nine beginners shifting in their seats thanking Christ it wasn't them. I flattened my voice into a monotone and read the line as prosaically as I could. And again Saint-Denis stopped me. 'There is something wrong, my friend. Listen. Don't try to act, don't sing, don't mouth the words—just read the line.' Now the penny dropped. This was a set-up. I was the guinea pig demonstrating what we were in for over the next six months.

I made one last valiant effort to read the line sans expression, sans inflection, sans everything, and stumbled to a halt. Saint-Denis sighed deeply, shrugged his shoulders and looked around at the rest of the Heavies, who shook their heads sadly, dropped their eyes and stared morosely at the table. 'Well,' grunted our mentor, 'over the next six months we are going to discover new approaches to Shakespeare. Forget all you've learned. It's time to reassess our whole approach to performing these plays. You will work hard together for the next six months on language, on acting, on mime, on mask, and at the end of that time some of you will be absorbed into the main company. That's enough for tonight.'

So for the next six months I was locked in a room with nine other competitive egomaniacs. Most of Michel's own work was pretty old-hat—basic mime and mask stuff that felt a bit creaky. A suspicion grew in my mind that the RSC had found a little windfall of money and decided to put Michel out to grass instead of giving him main stage productions.

Denne's singing classes were a hoot—we all gathered in her musty Elizabethan sitting room crammed with ancient furniture, rugs, cats, books and papers spilling everywhere while Denne banged away on the piano. We did music hall songs like 'Daisy' and 'My Old Man', probably because the tunes were simple enough for our tin ears. But even here the competition was intense and Karl Rigg, his face flushed with fury, put his foot through the floor stamping out a frenzied 'Any Old Iron', determined to be the best! We all regarded the studio as an extended audition for the RSC.

We used the theatre cafeteria with the company actors, who looked at us with mingled scorn and suspicion. Who the hell did we think we were? Were we part of some plot to supplant them?

Eventually the six-month period of claustrophobic hell came to an end, and we were all taken into the company for a trial period. Now the real education began: playing small roles, we were able to sit in the rehearsal room day after day watching top directors and actors at work: Ian Richardson, Ian Holm, Glenda Jackson, Timothy West and—the biggest thrill of all—Paul Scofield, who was to play Timon of Athens in the first production of the season. I soon twigged that we were glorified dogsbodies—well, not even glorified. Walking on, carrying spears and under-studying for eight quid a week. Still, the experience was priceless and I spent most of the time tingling with excitement. Every night I'd stand in the wings watching Scofield as Timon when I wasn't in the scene, marvelling at his vocal cadences and peculiar intonations. The most exciting production that year (1965) was Peter Hall's *Hamlet* with newcomer David Warner.

Hall was at the peak of his achievement and was the first director I had heard clearly articulate the rationale for connecting Shakespeare's plays with contemporary events. The RSC was not overtly political but had that lefty anti-Establishment attitude that came with a fifties Oxbridge education. The RSC was certainly more obviously political than the National, and productions like Peter Brook's anti-Vietnam *U.S.* came out fighting. By maintaining the Aldwych Theatre in London (dedicated to new writing) as well as the company at Stratford, Hall instituted a deliberate policy of cross-fertilisation whereby the new plays would be served by directors and actors skilled in presenting well-structured classics with demanding language, while the artists involved in staging the classics wouldn't be immune to the influence of new writing and political activism. This kept the Jan Kott tag, 'Shakespeare, Our Contemporary', to the forefront of our minds.

In casting David Warner as Hamlet, Hall struck a chord with the rebellious, disenchanted youth of the mid sixties. Coming from the ranks, Warner had shot to prominence the previous season playing a melancholy, gauche and pious Henry VI in *The Wars of the Roses*. *Hamlet* was the next giant leap forward, but for all his natural attributes, Warner was arguably still too raw and inexperienced in technique to carry off such a huge role over a long season. He tended to shout his way through, and then shout louder to make a point. Vocally he lacked colour, variety and sense of shape. But in terms of temperament, appearance and attitude he captured brilliantly the mood of the moment. Lanky, emaciated and awkward, he had a mop of straw-blond hair, dishevelled dress and a long red scarf that trailed on the ground. It was that long red scarf that completed the contemporary image and allied him to a generation of students. His rage, petulance and nihilism had no particular focus, but seemed to embody those sentiments (anti-Vietnam, anti-US imperialism, anti-British Establishment) that were soon to find their expression in student demonstrations in Paris and elsewhere in Europe.

Hamlet is always an enigma, despite the clues to his motivation provided in the text. A successful Hamlet always dissolves the enigma by articulating the discontent and apprehensions of his generation. Warner's Hamlet, dismissed by many older patrons and critics as a snotty, whining adolescent, was recognised and embraced by a youthful audience and our season in Stratford witnessed one of those rare occasions when scores of young people camped outside the theatre night after night in the hope of procuring tickets the next day.

Setting off Warner's performance was a strong company of actors in an intelligent, consistent production. Costumes were Tudor in silhouette but made of pin-stripe fabric to add a dash of current Whitehall politics. Hall's view of the play was fashionably agnostic. 'The rest is silence' was uttered with a grim chuckle as the ultimate nihilistic statement. Despite critical controversy regarding Warner's expertise, the play was an enormous success and ran for two seasons at Stratford as well as one at the Aldwych.

It also provided me with my first break in the company. I began the season as a walk-on, understudying Michael Williams as Rosencrantz. When his services were required elsewhere I took over the part, and at the end of the season Hall offered me a three-year contract with the company, to the end of 1969.

In subsequent seasons I played Paris in *Romeo & Juliet*, directed by Athens' Karolos Koun (out of favour at the time with Greece's right-wing military regime), Lennox in Peter Hall's *Macbeth*, and understudied Paul Scofield in Hall's production of *The Government Inspector*, as well as lots of small roles in revivals of *Henry IV* (both parts), *Henry V*, John Barton's *Coriolanus* with Ian Richardson, and a patchy *Twelfth Night* with Diana Rigg as Viola and Warner as Andrew Aguecheek, somewhat redeemed by Ian Holm's pint-sized manic Malvolio.

Two of the company's leading men of that era, Ian Richardson and Ian Holm, presented a striking contrast in style. Richardson was the epitome of the well-polished classical actor—brilliant articulation and ringing vocal effects supported by a keen sense of timing, comic effect and 'presence'. His technique was as formidable as it was obvious.

Holm on the other hand was something of a puzzle. Small, unassuming and introverted, he became the exemplar of what the rest of the company called 'non acting'. Unlike the other actors, he exhibited no startling 'technique', but managed to sound remarkably colloquial and understated. When one keen young actor, anxious to crack his mystery, asked him 'What voice exercises do you do?', Holm replied simply, 'I play Henry V fives time a week.'

(Since we gave eight performances a week, in repertory, he played something else three times a week.)

Holm was a reversal of the standard classical actor the RSC seemed to breed and it was surprising to most people to see him cast as Henry V and Romeo. But in both roles his dogged integrity was moving and convincing. He was breaking the mould of the English classical actor and, by defying tradition, was opening the way for a new generation to take on the great roles. He was also redressing the balance by demonstrating that dazzling technique was hollow unless matched by originality, compassion and acute perception of human behaviour.

Hall's *Macbeth* starring Paul Scofield and Vivien Merchant was planned as the centrepiece of the 1966 season, to be followed by a tour of the USSR in 1967 as part of the celebrations of the fiftieth anniversary of the Russian Revolution. No sooner had rehearsals begun than the infamous *Macbeth* curse struck its first blow and Peter Hall went down with shingles. He was exhausted and stressed out; the production was put on ice for a couple of months until he recovered. The company scrambled around to find a replacement production, in a hurry and with minimal budget. The young staff director, Trevor Nunn, suggested he could quickly throw together a cheap production of Tourneur's *Revenger's Tragedy* using the *Hamlet* set and a few of the as yet untried company hopefuls—Helen Mirren, Alan Howard, Ben Kingsley and Patrick Stewart. It turned out to be the hit of the season, while the rest of us languished in limbo waiting for P Hall to recover.

Anna had joined me in Stratford a few months after I arrived there and we took the top floor of a guest house run by a young couple named Mike and Hilary Smith. They had three kids and worked flat-out doing bed and break-fast for other guests. They became our closest friends and forty years later we still maintain correspondence and the occasional visit.

Anna got a temporary job at the great Shakespeare quatre centenary exhibition across the river from the theatre. While there, she auditioned and was invited to join the company.

In August 1965 we decided to get married. Unfortu-nately the Sydney press got wind of it before I'd had a chance to tell my parents—so that didn't go down well.

The following July our first daughter, Hilary, was born. Rather recklessly we decided on a home-birth and thanks to midwife Pilkington it went off smoothly. I was simul-taneously exhilarated and emotionally drained by being at the birth, but then had to dash back to the theatre for an evening performance of *Hamlet*. As we took our bows David Warner whispered to the person next to him: 'John Bell has a daughter. Pass it along.'

Thanks to the help and care of the Smiths we managed pretty well with bringing up the baby and before long Anna was back on stage. Luckily we were both in the cast of *Macbeth* because it meant we could go to Russia together.

*Macbeth* got back on the rails but the curse was not lifted. The concept was design-heavy and what I would call anti-human. The characters were not dressed in anything like real clothes—they were part of a design statement. At the first rehearsal we were shown the model of John Bury's set—a great red cave made of fake fur, like the inside of a huge carcass, or the pit of hell itself.

'There are actually only two characters in the play, Mac-beth and his wife,' Hall announced. 'The rest of you are not people at all, but choric figures in the background, so we are dressing you all like chess pieces, or sculpted figures.' The costume designs backed his statement. We were all to wear long grey plastic tunics (lined with felt) and built-up boots, have identical pale wigs and beards and white faces splattered with paint to make us look like weather-beaten stone statues. We would not act like 'characters' but be choreographed in patterns and intone our lines ritualistically. It was a very primitive and Christian view of the play—operatic and formal.

It was fascinating to watch Scofield picking his way through the part like a minefield, testing every possible cadence and intonation. But it was difficult to spy any core of evil in the man. Scofield was great at emanating saintliness or melancholy or dry despair—or, as in *The Government Inspector*, a sublime silliness—but evil, no. It just didn't seem to be his part. Vivien Merchant had the glittering serpent intensity necessary for a Lady M but seemed dwarfed by the cavernous set and the three-foot-high cardboard crown on her head.

The plastic costumes were hot and sweaty, and it was awkward tottering around the fur carpet in our built-up boots. Worse still, the army of soldiers had to lie under the fake-fur carpet for half an hour while the audience filed into the theatre and then spring magically out of the ground. We were given handfuls of salt tablets to revive us. The whole thing was too choreographed, too formalised, lacking human drama and interaction.

By the end of the dress rehearsal Peter Hall seemed to feel likewise. Having showered and scraped the paint off ourselves, we stumbled into the stalls and waited for notes. A subdued Hall seated himself on the edge of the stage, drew thoughtfully on his pipe and then addressed us in the brave, cheerful tone familiar from old British war movies: 'Well, chaps, I think I've made a big mistake . . . You are *not* choric figures; you are people! Real living people! We open tomorrow night and I want you each to come on with a character . . . I don't care what it is, what accent you use—just come on as somebody! If we're heading for a disaster it may as well be a major one!'

We staggered home in a daze and when we hit the stage the following night we were confronted by a barrage of characters we'd never met before—sauntering or charging around with a range of accents stretching from Glasgow to Bangladesh. Yes, it was something of a disaster. The English reviews were at best 'mixed'. But it had its moments and the Russians loved it. While the costumes and performances had been modified, the set and concept remained abstract and symbolic. We played at the Kirov in St Petersburg, or Leningrad as it was then, and (big thrill) in Moscow at the Moscow Arts itself with Chekov's seagull still bravely winging its way across the house curtain. The companion piece to *Macbeth* was John Barton's production of *All's Well That Ends Well*. Anna was in it, but I wasn't, which made babysitting a bit easier.

# Russia and its aftermath

The train between Moscow and Leningrad was the Red Arrow, with a samovar in the corridor. The cold was intense and passers-by in Moscow were greatly concerned that baby Hilary's ears stayed covered. Hotels were amazingly helpful about rustling her up some tidbit or a piece of fruit while the rest of us endured awful food. The really hard part was leaving her alone in the hotel each night when we went off to perform. There was no provision for babysitters, so all we could do was signal to the aged babushka in the corridor to keep an ear out for her and hope she'd be all right till we got home. Russia had been jazzed up for the anniversary and Leningrad had been given a lick of paint. But behind the façades, wretched courtyards were visible. In the Hermitage Gallery (the old Winter Palace), Matisse's huge masterpiece of red dancing figures was illuminated by a naked lightbulb hanging on a string.

We were given tickets to the Kirov opera performance of *Quiet Flows the Don*. The audience members looked like workers straight from the factory—all cloth caps and mufflers. The conductor arrived a minute late to stony silence. People looked at their watches and frowned. He shouldn't keep his fellow workers waiting. But at the end of an emotional first act he got an ovation. As if to test this response, he arrived for the second act *two* minutes late—and got another ovation. Art overcame ideology.

The opera itself was a curiosity and well suited to the temperament of the audience. In St Petersburg in winter the Neva freezes over so solidly that it bears traffic, fairs and festivities. The arrival of spring is announced by the awesome sound of the ice cracking in the middle of the night, whereupon lights go on, bells are rung and canons fired in a frenzy of celebration. When the curtain rose on the first act of the opera, the audience loudly applauded the set with its wooded landscape and the river Don actually flowing (rear projection) down the backcloth. A sweet little wooden cottage stood downstage right and from it emerged the soldier's wife to bid a tearful farewell to her husband who was marching off to war. He looked very authentic in khaki, with kitbag and rifle in hand; the only detail that jarred was his blue eye shadow and bright red lipstick. There followed scenes of battle and carnage, all employing masses of Soviet soldiers covered in blood, bandages, blue eye shadow and bright red lipstick.

The final scene lasted all of two minutes: the curtain rose to gasps and groans of horror as the audience beheld the Act 1 set—but now, after battle, the trees were blasted, the earth scorched and the sweet little wooden cottage was a smoking ruin. On the backcloth the river Don was a mass of frozen ice. Our hero, battered and bloody (but, thank God, the eye shadow and lipstick intact) staggered on from the wings, dragging his heavy rifle. He stood with his back to the audience and surveyed the scene of devastation. Then, with a defiant gesture, he broke open his rifle, poured out the bullets and flung them at the frozen river. Immediately the ice cracked, the Don flowed again and the audience rose to its feet, cheering, weeping and clapping itself to a standstill.

In both cities curtain calls for our two productions went on for at least twenty minutes and people seemed pleased to make at least this very limited contact with visitors—the icy breath of the Cold War was still in the air. So the tour of *Macbeth*, along with *All's Well*, was at least a diplomatic success, whatever the artistic reservations may have been. This was also my first experience of a non-English-speaking country, my first encounter with real 'otherness'. Standing in an elevator in Moscow one time, I found myself surrounded by men in uniform—Tartars, Mongols, every variety of Slav. I was struck by the vastness of the USSR, its amalgam of races and cultures. It was a curious feeling, arriving back in London and seeing people in bowler hats strutting along the Strand, oblivious to the actuality of the Soviet Union, a few hours flight away.

Life in Stratford was crammed with incidental pleasures. We worked hard at the theatre and Anna had a difficult time juggling her workload with the care of a baby (sometimes she had to rehearse the *Romeo & Juliet* ball scene with Hilary on her hip), but we were still heady about being in the company most of the time. Stratford was still rusticated enough to be surrounded by fields and little patches of woods that were a delight in summertime, and at weekends we'd row along the Avon or take bus trips to Oxford and other nearby sacred sites.

Having to move back and forth to London to play in the Aldwych seasons was tricky, especially once we had acquired a dog and a cat as well as a baby, but London too was an inexhaustible source of activity. We had a flat not far from Kensington Gardens, a great place for baby and dog alike, and spare time was devoured at the National Gallery, the Tate, the V&A, British Museum as well as dozens of other places I knew by heart from reading about them—the Abbey, the Tower, St Paul's, the Wren churches, the Inns of Court and so on. I was a right little Anglophile, and still am to a large extent. I find no contradiction in simultaneously loving England's cultural heritage and being a rabid Australian republican.

But in England I was also becoming acutely aware of a class system and level of snobbery that, while present in Australia, have not permeated our society to the same degree—and I hope they never do. In Britain they are so entrenched I can see no end in sight for them. For all its lefty, liberal posturing, the RSC was a kind of microcosm of the system. This was reflected not only in salaries but which floor of the building you occupied, the number of people who shared your dressing room, where you stood in the curtain call. Most people thought it was perfectly in order at the National and RSC that the Sirs and Dames played royal personages and occupied number one dressing room, while the lesser mortals played lesser mortals and were crammed into the dressing rooms furthest from the stage, no matter how many quick changes they had. All these status symbols were jealously watched and guarded. It was all the more curious because theatre is, of its nature, a more egalitarian profession than most and thrives on a spirit of ensemble and camaraderie.

Reinforcing my perception of theatre as a microcosm of British society, I noted with amusement during one Aldwych season that our show came out around the same time as one starring Michael Denison and Dulcie Grey at the theatre on the next corner. Their play involved little more than walking onto the stage in evening dress, sipping cocktails, making witty remarks, taking a curtain call and walking out the stage door, still in evening dress, into a chauffeur-driven limo to be whisked off to the Savoy for a few more cocktails. As we scruffy RSC dogsbodies left our stage door and schlepped our way home in our mufflers and dufflecoats, we'd run into Michael and Dulcie coming out of their stage door looking impeccable in white tie and fur wrap, stepping into the limo while a throng of little old ladies in beanies made a waving, smiling guard of honour as if they were cheering royalty.

I accepted this as part of the legend of 'the West End' and quite enjoyed the quaint old-fashioned glitz of it all. I also enjoyed making my way to the Aldwych Theatre each day through Covent Garden with its piles of vegetables, shouting porters and bustling market—all gone and sanitised now, just another anonymous mall.

The iniquities of the class system hit me forcibly one Saturday afternoon when I was strolling up the city towards St Paul's and a wedding party emerged from one of the Wren churches. The bridal party, in morning dress, looked like a pack of thoroughbreds—all tall, immaculately groomed with impossibly white teeth! Watching from the sidelines was a gaggle of locals—little wizened men and women with yellow skin, yellow teeth and beady eyes, gazing with awe at their 'betters'. My immediate thought was, look at these two sets of bodies—one so well-fed, pampered and privileged over generations, the other deprived and shrunken.

I was becoming politicised. I was shocked that it had taken this long, but in Australia we were complacent and the social differences were not so glaringly obvious — at least not where I came from.

It was around this time that I decided to quit the Church. I had been brought up, to the age of eighteen, a devout and committed Catholic, but once I moved out of that comfortable womb into the real world, I became increasingly uneasy with the Church's simplistic certainties. Now, the discrepancies between the Church's priorities and the realities of everyday life began to tear me apart. The crunch came when I went to Mass one Sunday at a church in Kensington. Outside the church doors were newspaper banners proclaiming 'Thousands die in Rwanda famine'. Inside, old ladies wrapped in furs with poodles under their arms filed up to Communion and a pink, pudgy priest in a white frock preached some meaningless sermon about the beatitudes of the Virgin Mary. I wanted to scream, 'Look outside! Don't you know what's going on in the world?'

Nevertheless, I wrestled with Faith and Doubt over the next five years, not wanting to let go of something I had always been assured was more precious than life itself. Over the intervening thirty years I have explored other spiritual pathways and maintain some interest in Zen. Of the established religions only Buddhism has any appeal for me in the way it eschews dogma and honours all of existence, animals and nature equally with humanity. The other religions I find, in varying degrees, barbaric and repugnant. For me, art is the greatest form of spirituality, both as a form of sustenance and a platform for enquiry.

In England I also became aware of political and social
activism around me and applauded the efforts of organisations like OXFAM to raise consciousness and actively
involve people in tackling the world's problems rather than
shrugging them off onto government. This awareness was
no doubt heightened by Britain's relative proximity to the
rest of the world. Terrible things were happening not far
away, whereas the Australia I grew up in seemed to have
that kind of lotus land dreamy attitude: 'It's so far away—
it's nothing to do with us.' Unknown to me, things were
actually starting to hot up back home, due to our involvement in the Vietnam War.

Once all the plays were up and running at Stratford and
the excitement of rehearsals and opening nights over, the
seasons settled into a routine of repertory performance. As
each year drew towards an end, a lot of the feisty young
bloods who were doing bit parts and spear-carrying used
to go a little stir-crazy. Fuelled by boredom, petty rivalries
and too many pints at the Dirty Duck opposite the theatre,
brawls would break out. Karl Rigg (who had put his foot
through Denne Gilkes' floor) went crazy one night in our
dressing room and broke a few chairs over people's heads.
He didn't stay long after that.

To defuse the situation the RSC management instituted
an annual 'Flare-up', a three- or four-week workshop program designed to give the small part players a chance to
channel their excess energy and demonstrate some hidden
talents. For the 1966 Flare-up, Hall and Barton announced
a special project.

'English theatre has never had much success with the
Greeks,' Hall announced. 'We've never really cracked how
to do them—yet the Greeks are a most significant part of

our theatre heritage, indeed one could say the most significant part after Shakespeare ... So this Flare-up we are
going to involve the whole company, every actor and director, in exploring the Greeks. We are going to explore about
thirty plays, some extracts, some in their entirety, from the
earliest, primitive mimic pieces through Aristophanes and
the great tragedies. We are going to crack the mystery of
the Greeks, and then over the next season or two present
entire Greek cycles both here and in London.'

Of course there was great excitement right through the
company. The rehearsal room (now the Swan Theatre) was
converted into a Greek amphitheatre and special directors
were imported and recruited to share the load. Hall directed
some of the plays, as did Barton, Saint-Denis, Clifford
Williams, Robin Phillips and a couple of Americans whose
names escape me. In the whole team there was only one
Greek—a shy little man named Rovertos Saragas. He was
a movement teacher and he wandered rather glumly from
rehearsal to rehearsal observing all the frenetic activity and
occasionally obliging with a bit of choreography.

At the end of three weeks came the grand showing and
we all sat in the 'amphitheatre' for three days while the
whole panoply of Greek drama unfolded before us. We had
bawdy farces, musical-comedy takes, the inevitable stylised
moves and masks from Michel Saint-Denis, and cool posturing with cigarettes and black skivvies from Robin Phillips.
The entire staff and management of the RSC watched from
the bleachers. And when it was all over we waited expectantly while Peter Hall got slowly to his feet, thoughtfully
tapping his pipe. 'Well, chaps,' he began quietly, 'I think
we've done it. I think we have cracked the Greeks. We've
seen a huge range of experiments and ideas, but I feel we

have actually torn aside the veil of mystery and understood what makes the Greeks tick. And I confidently predict we'll be presenting Greek plays next season in our main venues . . . it's a tremendous achievement.'

We all murmured our humble agreement and gave ourselves a tiny hug. Barton and the rest glowed with pride and satisfaction. Hall looked around the room: 'Any further comments? Anyone . . . ? Oh, Rovertos, what did you think?' The shy little Greek got to his feet and said haltingly, 'Yes, it was all very nice . . . very interesting . . . There is just one difference. You see, for us the sun *is* a god, the sea *is* a god, the wine *is* a god—that's the difference.' He sat down again and there was total silence. It dawned on all of us that we hadn't even scratched the surface; we had no idea how to do the Greeks. We filed out of the amphitheatre and the Greeks weren't mentioned again for the next ten years.

# Itchy feet

Peter Hall's regime at the RSC was drawing to an end. He had his eye set on the National and Trevor Nunn was being groomed for the succession. I was not part of Trevor's 'team', and the new broom meant something of a clean sweep. I found myself siphoned off for a few months to Theatre-go-round, an education team performing in schools and regional areas. It was hard slog, but rewarding, and took me to parts of the country, including Glasgow, that I might not have seen otherwise. It also gave me an ongoing interest in school performances which I later re-invented as Actors at Work, one of Bell Shakespeare's most successful and important activities.

By the end of 1968 I was getting itchy feet—roles like Lennox and Paris weren't going to satisfy me for long. I had another year of my RSC contract to go if I wanted it, but I'd done a couple of shows with directors of whom I thought, I could do better than that! I had never contemplated directing, but now the idea excited me. So did the idea of returning to Australia. I was becoming increasingly aware of British theatre as a giant machine that could get along very nicely without one more little cog like me, whereas Australia I envisaged as a place with raw energy, crying out for development and offering a place to stretch one's wings. I could be useful back home. Besides, we now had two children (Lucy was born in December 1968) and I wanted them to grow up with sun, surf and bush picnics—not the nine months of drizzle and the damp, cold flats we were living in then. Anna had certainly had enough and was ready to come home. Her career was on hold, of course, with two babies to occupy her, and all her thoughts were of how best to provide for them. Australia seemed the place to do it.

But first I had a call from Phillip Hedley who was running the Theatre Royal in Lincoln. Phillip had done some great work with Joan Littlewood at Stratford East and had become reacquainted with Richard Wherrett who was teaching at the East 15 School. They were putting a season together at Lincoln and invited me to join them. So we packed our children and a few chattels, reluctantly gave away our cat and dog, and moved into a shonky old flat opposite the Lincoln railway station.

The theatre was a crumbling Edwardian edifice with gas-lighting backstage, the company of actors was fiercely committed (Rhys McConnochie was part of the team) and I was to play Romeo, Mirabell and a couple of smaller roles. Phillip was the first director I worked with who had a precise methodology, based on close analysis of the script and breaking it down, line by line, into 'actions'. Even today many directors head straight for result, effect or image and leave the actor to make his own way to the finishing post as best he can. I used Phillip's method conscientiously for the next few years until it became absorbed into my bloodstream and I found myself becoming too pedantic in employing it. I guess the more experienced a director becomes, the more he or she draws on a bank of knowledge and methods gleaned from various sources, and becomes adept in applying the appropriate one for the particular circumstances.

One area where England still leads the field is eccentricity. Lincoln played fortnightly repertory and we used to open a new show every second Wednesday night. On the Wednesday morning we did a preview for the local pensioners, and one old couple, in their coats and mufflers, always made a beeline for the Royal Box. There they'd sit patiently with a paper bag on their knees. If the show looked promising, they'd open the bag, take out their tortoise and sit him on the railing to watch the show. But if the play was boring or had 'language', he'd stay in his paper bag. So we always kept a hopeful eye on the Royal Box and gave each other a cheery thumbs up if the tortoise was watching . . . we had a hit on our hands.

By the end of my six months in Lincoln, I was keen to try my hand at directing and contacted my old mentor, Nat Brenner at Bristol Old Vic, who offered me a job as acting tutor. So once more children and bags were packed and we set up home in Bath, just a short train ride from Bristol. I also managed to squeeze in a season of three plays at the Bath Theatre Royal for the Lyric Hammersmith Company. The work was conventional old-fashioned repertory, which took me by surprise after the innovative approach of Phillip Hedley in Lincoln. On my first day's rehearsal for Shaw's

*Misalliance*, the director, Michael Meacham, said, 'Don't you know your lines yet?' I was taken aback, having come to the conclusion that you should only learn lines after you know what they mean and why you are saying them. But Mr Meacham wasn't having any of that: 'Well, go home and learn them,' he snapped, 'then come back and I'll tell you where to move.'

That was the kind of archaic director he was—'block' the play in two days and then spend three weeks 'polishing'. The use of the word 'block' was appropriate as it choked any invention or spontaneity, and 'polishing' meant just doing it over and over, getting slicker and emptier as you went. This was tired old English rep at its worst and I was glad to see the end of it.

Being back at Bristol, this time as a teacher, felt exciting but a touch fraudulent. I began to realise how much I didn't know; but I did develop my hankering to be a director. Meantime Anna was getting well and truly fed up coping with two babies in the temporary digs—the urge to go back to Australia was growing daily. So I wrote to John Clark, head of NIDA, in Sydney, to test the possibilities. To our delight he responded immediately with the offer of a job as head of acting, starting in a few months' time. I had only worked for one term as a teacher at Bristol Old Vic, but I decided to make a serious go of it as a teacher and took piles of notes from every book on acting theory I could devour. I also savoured the opportunity to direct student productions.

Our five-year sojourn in England had come to an end. What had I gained? A love of the countryside and a deeper appreciation of England's culture and history; I had satisfied a little my insatiable curiosity for ancient things—

artworks, archaeological digs, ruins, museums, cathedrals and country churches; we had made friendships and professional relationships that would endure a lifetime; we had seen great theatre and learned an enormous amount by working with and observing some of the best English talent of its day; and we'd had two children, one of whom would go on to become a writer and the other an actor, and both of whom could put on their passports 'born in Stratford-on-Avon'. And to recap on lessons I had learned from my most significant mentors:

From John Barton I had learned about the rules and structure of Shakespeare's language and how to employ them.

From Peter Hall I had learned the importance of bringing Shakespeare into line with contemporary issues and apprehensions.

From Peter Brook I inherited a belief that art has to be more than a comfortable pastime . . . the significance of theatre is as profound as our imaginations will let it be.

From Ian Richardson I learned the importance of flawless diction and technique.

From Ian Holm I learned the importance of concealing it.

From Paul Scofield I learned that one's own moral and spiritual being must inform one's work to lift it out of the conventional rut.

And from observing the grand old men of theatre—Olivier, Gielgud, Richardson and many others—practising their craft nightly, I understood the importance of a living tradition, mutual respect between older and younger actors, mentorship, and passing on the torch in a spirit of affection and passionate dedication to a priceless heritage.

We have many happy memories of that other time and place, but one of my favourites is the birth of our second daughter Lucy. Hilary had been born at home with the assistance of a midwife, but the succeeding days and nights were tiring for Anna. We decided this time we'd do it more realistically and booked into the little hospital in Tiddington, just outside Stratford.

I was there throughout the birth, as I had been with Hilary, and remember the wonderful moment of peace and calm when it was all over and Anna cradled our new chubby, black-haired, violet-eyed stranger. It was coming up to Christmas Eve and, looking out the window into the black night sky, I watched the snow softly falling onto the white fields and listened to the bells ringing from the candlelit church in the distance.

It could have been a lonely Christmas day for the half dozen mothers, but the nurses had knitted woollen toys and the head surgeon wheeled in a traymobile and carved the turkey with an expert eye.

So, all in all, there's a lot to be said for 'the English way'—especially in England. But that doesn't mean the same rules and values can easily be transported or applied elsewhere. When it comes to Australian art, literature, theatre, we have been struggling with the cultural cringe for two hundred years and are only now beginning, tentatively, to realise the struggle was unnecessary. But even as we confidently designate our work as 'world class' we are still betraying the vestiges of anxiety. Let's focus on Shakespeare, as an example.

Does Australia need Shakespeare?

Can his work be part of our own national culture?

Is there, and should there be, an 'Australian way' of performing him?

Insofar as any society 'needs' great art, Australia needs Shakespeare. Sure, if he didn't exist, or if we totally ignored him, the sky wouldn't fall. People would still go to work, have kids and enjoy going to the beach and the movies. And yes, the number of Australians who watch Shakespeare in performance each year wouldn't fill the MCG. Nor would those who go to symphony concerts, art galleries or the opera. But start subtracting those things one by one as being 'unnecessary' and you're heading towards an anaemic society—one that has no voice, nothing to show, nothing to say for itself, no mystique, no identity.

Unless we continually expand and replenish our spiritual selves through art, philosophy, intellectual debate, how are we going to make the big moral decisions, experience compassion, dare to think big?

Shakespeare is one of those wellsprings of spiritual replenishment at our disposal. But unlike Beethoven or Jackson Pollock (inspiring as they may be), Shakespeare is not fixed in time and place, but capable of infinite malleability, constantly demanding reinterpretation and re-presentation. Through him we address ourselves and our immediate concerns. Some of these are universals—the love, ambition, revenge motifs that apply across the board to all humanity. But then there are the particulars to do with nationalism, racism, sexism that will be of more immediate concern one year than the next. A successful and 'relevant' production is one that expresses the universals while homing in on some theme of immediate local concern and articulating it in a way that is fresh and revelatory.

If this is the approach taken by Australian directors and actors, then the plays will readily become part of our own national identity, speaking in our own voices about things that concern us. If, on the other hand, we eschew the local and the topical and aim for some vaguely 'classical/ traditional' production, the work will indeed seem remote and pointless.

As for an 'Australian way', it is certainly emerging and needs to be nourished. At its best Australian Shakespeare is informed by an energy, a freshness of approach, generous ensemble playing and lack of pretentiousness. We avoid most of the worst manifestations of the English system of hierarchy and star-vehicle selfishness, and we don't tolerate too much in the way of pomposity and self-importance (I'm only talking about theatre here!).

On the other hand, because we've always had a resentment of 'blowhards', 'skites', 'chatterboxes' and 'show-offs' we tend to back away from a glorious tradition of Australian rhetoric, tall stories, campfire yarns, and a linguistic flamboyance still exercised on a good day in Parliament. This taciturnity, this laconic attitude, has been further exacerbated by movie and TV role models who insist that it's 'cool' to be monosyllabic and understated. That is no way to approach Shakespeare, not in a large theatre anyway.

So as well as focusing on local, contemporary themes and issues in the play and stretching our spirits to encompass the universals, we have to reclaim the joy and exhilaration of giving great language full throttle, to make it as transporting as music. That takes expert training and some years of experience. Peter O'Toole once said it takes ten years of playing Shakespeare to become good at it. It certainly took me at least that long to begin to feel competent, especially in my search for a good voice teacher. Raw energy and youthful enthusiasm will get you part of the way, but the technique required to sustain a major role is hard won.

When we arrived back in Australia, early in 1970, the place had changed enormously. Coming from cold England to the intense heat of the Australian summer underlined the impression. Australia was in the grip of a rush of materialistic greed—a minerals boom was in full swing and people seemed unduly hedonistic, short-sighted and uncaring about the rest of the world. OXFAM was unheard of and there didn't seem much concern as to why it was necessary.

Arriving at NIDA, looking at the Australian theatre scene, my immediate thought was: the whole repertoire, the whole approach here, is stuffy and irrelevant. We have to throw it all out and start again. We need a theatre that is rough, rude, popular and shocking. So forget England, forget Stratford, forget classical theatre and all those things you learned—it's been a total waste of time. Scrub the slate clean. But over the years I have discovered that nothing of what I learned was useless. It has been valuable, sustaining and I continue to draw from that experience day after day.

After the initial shock it was great to be home. The white light was dazzling and the air full of promise. The grandparents were overjoyed to see the babies and my strongest image of their homecoming was a trip to the beach: Hilary ran and splashed the water in ecstasy . . . Lucy, just a year old, stared goggle-eyed at the sparkling ocean and delicately dipped her toe in the water.

Bruce Beresford (centre, with papers in hand) making his first movie, *The Devil to Pay*, with myself on the far right. Richard Keyes is the cameraman, Ron Blair is extreme left and John Clifton-Bligh, with the beard, lurks in the background; Sydney University, 1961.

The Sydney University Players in *Twelfth Night*, 1961. In the back row, on the left, is Bruce Beresford and John Gaden. In the centre of the middle row is Mungo MacCallum and myself. Ken Horler sits centre of front row.

*Overleaf*: Playing Coriolanus (Sydney University Players) with Arthur Dignam, Union Theatre, Sydney University, 1962.

In rehearsal for Hamlet, Old Tote Theatre, 1963. *(Photo Robert Walker)*

*Previous page*: My one-man Shakespeare show at the Genesian Theatre, 1962, as Chorus from *Henry V. (Photo Robert Walker)*

My first Hamlet, Old Tote, 1963. *(Photo Robert Walker)*

*Overleaf*: Anna as the Princess of France in *Henry V*, with her ladies-in-waiting. Tent Theatre, Adelaide Festival, 1964.

With Anna, Hilary and Lucy in our home in Surry Hills, soon after our return to Australia, 1970.

*Previous page*: Playing Rosencrantz to David Warner's Hamlet, with Jimmy Laurenson as Guildenstern, Royal Shakespeare Company, Stratford, 1965. *(Photo Reg Wilson)*

*Part 3*

# THE NIMROD
# YEARS

# NIDA and
# King O'Malley

We took a flat in a new redbrick block in Market Street, Randwick, not far from the University of New South Wales campus where NIDA was situated. The flat was squeaky clean and characterless, except for one of the neighbours. She was a freckled Australian with a small baby. The husband was a large German with a lantern jaw, swept-back blond hair and a mad glint in his steely blue eyes. We used to shudder with horror when his weekly supply of flagon riesling arrived because we knew that by midnight he'd be blind drunk, *Siegfried* would be playing at full belt, and soon he'd be weeping, then roaring, then throwing his wife around the room. Once or twice she came screaming to us for refuge, but always went back to him the next day and abused us if we mentioned it. It was a relief when we moved.

I still felt rather ill-equipped to set myself up as a teacher of acting, but by now I had assembled quite a few books of acting exercises and was looking for opportunities to direct the students in plays rather than just teaching theory. I don't suppose I did my students more harm than many another acting teacher but I wish I knew then what I know now—that you can't teach acting anyway. The best you can do is delicately remove psychological and emotional blocks to free expression, encourage whatever embryonic talent you can spot and help develop physical and vocal flexibility. The rest the audience will teach you.

I had a good range of students, many of whom I would work with after they graduated: John Hargreaves, Pamela Stephenson, Ivar Kants, Wendy Hughes and Tony Llewellyn-Jones were among them. I had an office in the elegant old two-storey house formerly used by the jockeys at the Randwick Racecourse over the road. The original Old Tote tin shed was still there but was now used only by NIDA students. The company had moved down the road a bit to the new and sterile Parade Theatre on Anzac Parade, seating three hundred.

One of my colleagues was the large, shambling and quietly anarchic Englishman, Michael Boddy. The name couldn't have been more appropriate, because besides being over six feet tall, he was of considerable girth, a state enhanced by a healthy appetite. It was a treat to go to Boddy's favourite Chinese restaurant and watch him run a pudgy finger down the menu, intoning 'I'll have a go at that . . . and that . . . and that . . .'

The big pink-flushed face, ginger beard and sweaty brow concealed an astute and critical Cambridge-trained mind. I asked him his first impression of Australia. 'Well, I landed in Hobart,' he told me, 'and walked across the quay to the pub. There were only two blokes there, sitting in the corner, and they looked me up and down. After a while one of them strolled over to me at the bar and said, "Hey, sport, how much do you weigh?" "Twenty-two stone," I answered. He went back to his bench, sat down and money changed hands.'

Boddy was teaching History of Theatre but was far more interested in arranging barbecues and other activities to amuse the students. He was a born rebel and would have been agin any establishment be found himself in. He was also looking for an outlet in writing. He compensated for his frustration with an inordinate amount of cooking and was no slouch as a chef. His wife, the painter Janet Dawson, seemed totally charmed by him and comfortable in his ample bosom.

Each year NIDA mounted a couple of productions of new Australian plays in a tiny wooden church in Jane Street, Randwick, a walk up the hill from the school. These plays were directed by members of staff and used the final year students, although leading parts were given to professionals. The Jane Street season had a sizeable reputation and had produced a couple of hit plays that had transferred to the Parade after an initial season of about six performances in this 100-seat space. It was the only showcase for new Australian drama in Sydney. A typical 'hit' by Rod Milgate or Tom Keneally would reach a total audience of approximately five hundred people.

To my great delight, John Clark offered me one of the Jane Street plays to direct and gave me a pile of unsolicited scripts to wade through. My initial delight turned to glumness as I discarded script after stodgy script—either dull domestic naturalism or pretentious retellings of Greek myths set in petrol stations in the outback.

One stipulation of the gig was that I was to utilise the current group of third year students. Now this was one remarkable group of people. At that time the NIDA acting course only went for two years, but these were all NIDA graduates who had been offered the opportunity to work together for an additional year on projects of their own devising. The acknowledged leader of the group was Rex Cramphorn, a disarmingly reticent figure with bright green eyes whose modest demeanour concealed an iron will and artistic ambition. The other eight were Robyn Nevin, Gillian Jones, Kate Fitzpatrick, John Paramour, Terry O'Brien, David Cameron, Nick Lathouris and Willy Young, who later changed his name to William Yang and is now one of our leading photographers. Willy/William was not yet approaching the identity/cultural crisis he so movingly describes in his one-man theatre piece *Sadness*.

When I was introduced to the group as their director for one of the two Jane Street plays, they eyed me off suspiciously. This was a tightknit, self-sufficient outfit. Nevertheless I tried to charm them over one by one, coming last to Willy.

'Well,' I said, surveying his long blue-black hair and decidedly Chinese features, 'Willy, you'll be able to bring to the production a whole other cultural influence.'

He stared me in the eye impassively. 'What do you mean, John? I'm Australian.'

'Oh yes,' I quickly recovered, 'but I mean, you know, going back a generation—or two . . .'

'No I don't know what you mean, John—my whole family's Australian.'

'Yes, yes, I know, Willy,' I flustered, sensing the rest of the group gazing at the floor and smiling tightly at my dilemma, 'but I mean—well, way, way back . . .' I finished, almost pleadingly. But Willy was implacable.

'No, John—we were always a hundred per cent Australian.'

So I gave up.

The group was busy working with Rex in devising their own show, which was to be the companion piece to whatever I ended up directing. They were working their way through a book by the Polish theatre guru Grotowski, of whom I hadn't heard at that stage, and were creating a piece called *Ten Thousand Miles Away*, which I presumed would be about travel and emigration.

I still couldn't find a script I wanted to direct and took my problem to Boddy, who suggested we lunch on it. We piled into his pink and white striped jeep and hurtled out to the Coogee Bay Hotel where we sat with our fish and chips and a couple of schooners gazing at the seagulls wheeling over a cobalt ocean.

'Why don't we make up something?' mused Boddy. 'I've been reading about this character named King O'Malley who founded Canberra and the Commonwealth Bank. He was a huckster, snake-oil salesman and evangelist from Canada—we could do the whole thing as a sort of revivalist meeting with Parliament as a circus full of clowns: a bit of melodrama, hymn-singing, music-hall and fart jokes . . .'

The thumbnail biography of O'Malley was not totally accurate, but the idea grabbed me immediately. Sorlies' tent show and Olivier's Globe rushed into my mind and we set about compiling ideas.

John Clark was not hard to convince but the Grotowski disciples looked at me askance—all except Robyn Nevin and Kate Fitzpatrick, who didn't seem quite at home with the monastic zeal of the Poor Theatre, and sensed a little relief in burlesque.

Boddy worked fast and audaciously. The show would begin as a revivalist meeting crossed with the Faust story as the devil in the guise of Nick Angel tempts O'Malley to fame and fortune in the Antipodes. Janet Dawson designed the show and turned the theatre into a traverse space with a long catwalk and a series of handsome backdrops painted in a romantic Arthur Streeton style. The melodrama and pantomime of the first half were easy-to-write pastiche but for the second act, mainly set in federal parliament, we needed the actors' help. For one rehearsal I dumped a heap of clothes from the NIDA wardrobe in one corner and a pile of props in the other. The cast spent the day trying on hats and coats, playing with props, each eventually creating an individual clown character, finding an appropriate voice and body language. Terry O'Brien turned into a lecherous prime minister, Billy Hughes, who conscripted the others into his army and put them through their drill.

From these improvisations Boddy built up the conflict of Hughes and O'Malley, and took a gallop through World War I and O'Malley's eventual apotheosis. As time ran short he called in Bob Ellis to help write lyrics for some of the music-hall numbers that peppered the second half. With accompanying piano and drums, bawdy adlibbing and a lot of interplay with the audience, the show had a contagious energy as well as a nod of deference to the grand old days of Australian popular entertainment—the Tivoli, Roy Rene, George Wallace et al.

I also got permission to include the second year NIDA students in the production and each of them devised a 'sideshow' character who worked the foyer during interval—the tattooed man, the fat lady etc. In my productions over the years I've often satisfied a yen to use the pre-show and interval times as part of the night's experience. Let's really give the audience their money's worth . . .

There was nothing new in *O'Malley*—it was all recycled gags, characters, songs and sentiments, but it did remind people that theatre didn't have to be formal or respectable. And it cocked a snook at the prevailing Old Tote repertoire: each year a Shaw, a Shakespeare, a Molière, a new West End or Broadway hit, all done within pretty safe, conventional bounds for a pretty safe, conventional audience in a tidy, comfortable space. Our gesture was directed more against house style than content. But the show proved extremely popular and after its Jane Street season it transferred to the Parade and was then taken up for a national tour and, later, a commercial season at the Richbrooke Theatre in Elizabeth Street. (It was originally the Phillip Theatre, home to revue. Then the Mandolin Cinema. Now it's gone.)

*O'Malley* could not have provided a starker contrast to *Ten Thousand Miles Away*, which featured a white cell of a set. The actors, barefoot in white pyjamas, talked and ran in a circle, nonstop, for over an hour. It was about travel all right, but an inner journey rather than an external one. All those months of Grotowski discipline paid off in what was essentially an endurance test, and an inspiringly original piece of theatre.

After an *O'Malley* performance I was approached by Ken Horler, my old mate from uni days and now a barrister: 'If I found a suitable space to make a theatre, how would you feel about coming in with me?'

'Sure, Ken, sure,' I said, virtually dismissing it as a pipe-dream. But I didn't want to go on teaching at NIDA. I had been there almost a year and felt I hadn't enough to offer yet. Now I had my first hit as a director I wanted to follow it up fast. But I needed a job. With two babies, the princely NIDA salary of $6000 a year meant security. So I fronted up to Robin Lovejoy, Director of the Old Tote which was then playing capacity business with *O'Malley* in the Parade. I explained that I wanted to move on from NIDA and wondered if there was any chance of a production with the Tote. Robin met my eye and said slowly and steadily: 'No, there's nothing.'

'Ah . . .' I was a touch disappointed. 'Well,' I said, 'after all my years with the RSC maybe there's an acting role for me in something.' A pause, then the same slow, steady: 'No, there's nothing.' Maybe he set no store by my one instant success — it could have been a fluke. Maybe there was a personal antipathy. Or maybe it was just that his books were full.

Right, I thought, my heart beating faster as I walked out. Stuff you, I'll start my own theatre!

I rang Ken Horler: 'You said you were looking around for a theatre space . . .'

'Well actually I've found something,' Ken replied. 'It's a bit of a dump, but worth a look. It's an old stable in Nimrod Street, Kings Cross. Let's go see it . . .'

# A stable in
# Nimrod Street

The stable in Nimrod Street, Kings Cross, was not a pretty sight. It was a small two-storey ruin of bare brick walls and rotting timber built in the shape of a narrow wedge. A rickety staircase gave access to the low room upstairs. There was one grotty toilet. It was hard to see even this much at first because the whole dump was full of rubbish, dirt and broken-down cars piled to the ceiling. I shook my head in disbelief but reckoned I had nothing to lose by devoting a few weekends to hurling out the junk and taking a better look.

Ken was determined it would be a goer and his wife Lilian backed him all the way. Ken and Lilian had sunk a lot of their own money into the venture and wrung financial support out of friends and acquaintances. There was one person on the payroll—me, at $6000 a year. We approached the recently formed Australia Council for the Arts for some funding. They said if we could survive a year without funding and produce an exciting artistic result, they'd consider a request for the following year. So we got on with it.

A small army of volunteers was rostered on, Ron Blair— future playwright—most prominent and consistent among them. Richard Wherrett lent a hand too. For months our weekends were spent hauling rubbish out of the stable, then bagging the walls with cement, painting and repairing. Lilian, besides shovelling cement, arrived each lunchtime with an enormous canteen of homemade fodder for the troops. There was recently arrived in town an energetic and disarming young Brit named Larry Eastwood, a close friend of Richard Wherrett since East 15 drama school in London. Larry was a dynamo of energy and ambition. He had obvious design talent and was a practical handyman as well. We asked him to take on the job of designing and building the Nimrod Street Theatre.

He came up with an ingenious design for the upstairs, which was to be the performance area. Keeping one corner of the room, he devised a triangular floor area with tiers of seats rising on two sides. He couldn't put in a centre block of seats because of a wooden post which held the roof up and would have obscured sightlines. So the post had to be written into every show. If you leaf through a few of those early scripts and come across quite arbitrary lines like 'Let's tie him to this post' or 'Just hang it on that tree' you'll know it's to explain the presence of that bloody post. (Incidentally, it's gone now. Refurbishment in the late eighties saw the post go, the ceiling raised and extra seats put in, plus air-conditioning, making the place almost palatial.)

Nimrod originally seated about a hundred people. I say 'about' a hundred because it was pretty arbitrary. There was no padding on the bare bleachers so it was bring a cushion or suffer a numb bum. If there was a big crowd, Lilian would unashamedly squeeze them all in: 'Come on, move up, there's room for a few more . . .' as the squashed audience groaned in protest.

The ceiling was corrugated iron and so low that in the back rows you had to sit with your chin on your knees. It was stiflingly hot and if we got too noisy the whores across the lane would hurl bottles onto the roof. Everyone had to push two at a time up the narrow stairs. There was no other exit except a hay-loft door halfway up the wall. We hopefully placed a FIRE EXIT sign above it, but if anyone had used it, it would have meant jumping twenty feet into the street below. Punters eyed it with apprehension. Downstairs was the bar and coffee area. Painted and well lit, in no time it became a social hub and the scene of many a late-night and drunken celebration. We opened for business without approaching the city council, knowing full well they would knock us back.

Larry had built the whole thing virtually single-handed, complete with lighting-box, electrical rig and dressing room. The dressing room was a bit of a tight squeeze for anything other than a one-person show. Most casts had five or six people. There was no toilet. You had to go before you came, so to speak. John Krummel, playing the title role in Ron Blair's *President Wilson in Paris*, used to get an attack of the nervous wee-wees just before his first entrance. He had no recourse but to piss into a paper cup and throw it out the window. One night, inevitably, he drenched two lovers snogging in the lane below.

Larry was production manager, designer and lighting designer for every show. In spite of the workload and emotional demands, his designs were always imaginative and ambitious. He achieved absolute wonders in that tiny space and one of the audience's chief delights was in seeing how the space changed for each production.

With the theatre under way our next decision was what to put in it. Our initial enthusiasm—'Hey, kids, let's do a show'—had paid scant consideration to what the show might be.

Richard Wherrett was now directing at the Old Tote, but had an interest in what was happening at Nimrod Street too. The excitement was pretty contagious. So we had meetings at Ken and Lilian's house to decide on our opening play or two. Ken and I were to be co-artistic directors, Lilian general manager, Richard an occasional director. Ron Blair was itching to get a play on but was untried as yet. The decision as to who should direct the first production was a delicate one. Ken, Richard and I all threw our hats into the ring, but I got the gig, probably because I was still riding high on the recent success of *O'Malley*.

I decided to try for another bull's-eye by teaming-up with Boddy and we had a few more meetings tossing around ideas for a subject. It was presumed from the start that the Nimrod Street Theatre would follow through some of the ground rules *O'Malley* had established. We would be first and foremost a space for new Australian plays (but not exclusively, because we all had other personal agendas as well). We would defy accepted conventions of theatre atmosphere, decorum and staging. As Anna succinctly put it, Nimrod allowed theatre to be 'silly'. We would create a house style that was informal, warm and welcoming. Our theatre space presupposed a remarkable degree of audience tolerance, discomfort and good nature in return for what we hoped would be a fresh and entertaining experience. Our aesthetic would honour the traditions of popular Australian show business, rather than the loftier shrines of high art. Hence we would draw material and techniques from vaudeville, music-hall, sideshows and fun parks. We would also be unashamedly nationalistic—it was okay to take shots at the Yanks and the Poms but also to ridicule the 'Ocker' image of the Ugly Australian. Direct confrontation with the audience, a degree of audience participation, and a bold, upfront playing style were to be encouraged.

We also decided from day one that no matter how 'rough' the presentational style, we would insist on the highest standards we could achieve in the areas of design, set and costume construction, lighting and of course acting talent. Everybody was to be paid above the award and we initiated the idea of rehearsal pay equal to performance salary. Some agents regarded this with suspicion, thinking we were trying to cut wages. We weren't—it just seemed the obvious and decent thing to do to make actors' lives easier. We were anxious to avoid any taint of amateurism, although we gratefully accepted volunteer services in areas such as front-of-house and bar duties. Anna organised a sewing-circle to make costumes.

In deciding on our opening production, folk heroes, comic book characters and great Australian eccentrics were all considered. We finally decided to base a show around the *Boys Own* hero, Biggles, the fighter pilot dreamed up by Captain WE Johns. Biggles was a well-known heroic icon ripe for toppling, a noble representative of all that was British, militaristic, and therefore risible. The first half of the show was a series of revue-type sketches of Biggles at school, giving us a chance to send up aspects of the English public school system. Song and dance and distorted versions of hymns and patriotic songs figured heavily. The second half of the show saw an ageing, clapped-out Biggles and his team performing the club circuit in Australia when his cred was shot to pieces, leaving the evening to finish on a rather sour note.

No great shakes as a show, it nonetheless contained some amusing sketches and a crack cast including John Hargreaves, Drew Forsythe, Peter Rowley, Jane Harders, Anna Volska, Ken Horler and Boddy himself playing the headmaster. It was colourful and amusing enough to launch the new theatre with great success. We opened on 2 December 1970 and the bright young, and not-so-young, things of Sydney, as ever greedy for novelty, crammed themselves nightly into our shoebox of a theatre. Except on Christmas Eve. I suppose it was silly to expect anyone really, but eleven people turned up, so we sang a few songs around the piano with them, gave them a drink and all went home early.

Whatever the shortcomings of *Biggles*, the press and media generally welcomed the new venture. Words like 'larrikin', 'irreverent' and 'knockabout' were applied immediately and stuck for the next five years or so, even when they were no longer relevant.

A short time after we opened we received notice from the city council that the theatre was to be closed down. It was a firetrap and it was unsanitary. We were devastated, yes, but there was no denying the council was absolutely right! Before they would consider allowing us to reopen, we had to put in a much wider staircase, provide an alternative fire exit and put in three toilets! We thought three toilets for a hundred people was luxury verging on deca-

dence, but the council held all the cards. The single dressing room upstairs was of no concern to the council and
retained its primitive character.

While the renovating went on we moved to St James Hall
near Hyde Park, where Ken directed Beckett's *Endgame*.
Three months later we moved back to Nimrod Street with
a much revamped theatre and renewed vigour. Anna, meanwhile, had scored a leading role in a long-running TV series,
*The Godfathers*. Thanks to this, we were able to put down
a deposit on a house. We could never have done that on
my theatre salary.

For the next three years Nimrod built its following and
attracted a little government funding. The emphasis was
still on informality and having a good time, but we began
to seek out scripts and writers of substance. So the mix was
a bit eclectic—'knockabout larrikin' shows like *Hamlet on
Ice* and *The Last Supper Show* (both pantomimes with
Boddy as chief collaborator); experimental and absurdist
pieces, often directed by Richard Wherrett, like Peter
Handke's *Kaspar* and *My Foot My Tutor*. These were two
particularly stylish and bold productions, designed by
Martin Sharp.

There were also classics adapted to the intimate space,
*Hamlet*, *Macbeth* and *Measure for Measure*; and substan-
tial new Australian writing including Ron Blair's *Flash Jim
Vaux* and *President Wilson in Paris*, Jack Hibberd's *Custom
and Excise*, and Alex Buzo's *Rooted*, *Tom*, *The Roy
Murphy Show* and *Coralie Lansdowne Says No*. Alma
de Groen contributed *The Sweatproof Boy*, Peter Kenna
*A Hard God* and Jim McNeill *The Chocolate Frog* and *The
Old Familiar Juice*. Rex Cramphorn directed for us too;
his gothic tales included *The Marsh King's Daughter* and

*Shadows of Blood*. Ken directed the McNeill plays and campaigned to get the author out of prison, where he was doing time for shooting a policeman. McNeill was released in 1974 and we continued to promote his work when we moved to our new theatre with *Jack* and *How Does Your Garden Grow?* Ken also conceived an Aboriginal revue entitled *Basically Black*; and in his legal capacity he helped settle any legal problems that might crop up.

The variety of both style and content in those first couple of years was remarkable. Sometimes people, especially journalists and bureaucrats, would try to pin me down with 'What is Nimrod's policy?'. It seemed flippant to reply, as I did, that it was whatever we felt like doing at the time. Of course, as time went on and we became more established, certain themes, concerns and attitudes tended to coalesce themselves into some sort of policy, but I think it's dangerous to pronounce a rigid policy statement because you then find yourself stuck with it, and having to rustle up material that conforms to it. Theatre is livelier than that. It changes all the time and it's very much the expression of whoever's running it, responding to current market demands or else creating new ones.

*The Last Supper Show* was a rather pale shadow of its hilarious predecessor, *Hamlet on Ice*, which epitomised all that Nimrod did best in the first year or two. The audience was encouraged to groan at the awfulness of the jokes; adlibs and comments on the tackiness of the scripts were de rigueur, but Aarne Neeme put together a zippy production with outstanding comic talent led by Graham Bond and Rory O'Donoghue, soon to become national TV icons as Aunty Jack and Thin Arthur. They were supported by Gary McDonald, Kate Fitzpatrick and John Wood. Not for years had Sydney seen anything as silly, as outrageously crude, as *Hamlet on Ice*, and it opened its heart to the production.

Ron Blair's *Flash Jim Vaux* also scored considerable success and enjoyed a number of revivals around the country. It was modelled on John Gay's *Beggar's Opera*, a celebration of a notable convict rogue with new lyrics set mostly to well-known folk tunes. Terence Clark collaborated with Ron and wrote some haunting original music as well as adapting period tunes like 'Lilibulero'.

Vaux, a dandy and con man, enjoyed the distinction of having been transported from England to Australia not just once but three times. He is chiefly remembered for his compilation of a dictionary of 'flash' or 'kiddy' language, employed by the criminal classes and still persisting today, with its rhyming slang: trouble and strife (wife), me china plate (mate) etc. John Gaden played Vaux with a seedy gusto, aided by Bob Hornery, Sheila Keneally, John Wood and Terence Clark himself at the piano. Ron's love of the eccentricities of language, his thorough research and sense of history were combined with an authentic theatrical instinct. He had already contributed ideas and sketches to shows like *Biggles* and *The Last Supper Show*, and was now finding his feet as a playwright. Our collaboration persisted over the next decade and I have directed, besides the original *Flash Jim Vaux*, premieres of *President Wilson in Paris* (with John Krummel, Anna Volska and Max Cullen), *Kabul* for the Old Tote, *Last Day at Woolloomooloo* at the new Nimrod in 1983, and his masterpiece, *The Christian Brothers*—a classic play with a classic performance by Peter Carroll.

# Nimrod in the ascendant

Macbeth and *Measure for Measure* were my first attempts at directing Shakespeare on a professional basis. At NIDA I had done *A Midsummer Night's Dream* with a cast of students that included John Hargreaves, Wendy Hughes and the glamorous Pamela Stephenson as a rather unlikely Snug the Joiner with a corked-on moustache.

With *Macbeth* I had been bitten by the Grotowski bug, Poor Theatre with a strong inclination to ritual. I had to do it within the tiny confines of Nimrod and I could only afford seven actors; even that number was a luxury! So I hit on the idea of doing the play as a kind of satanic black mass—the seven celebrants in simple black robes with the odd ecclesiastical embellishment—a mitre and stole for the king, for instance. As everyone from Rex Cramphorn's NIDA performance group was available, and since I had so enjoyed working with them on *O'Malley*, I invited them to join me for *Macbeth*. Nick Lathouris played the title role, Gillian Jones his Lady. Duncan (Terry O'Brien) was blindfolded and led to his sacrifice on the altar and the battle scene was performed as an exorcism with the cast chanting a *Dies Irae* as they surrounded Macbeth. This take on the play had been inspired by the Charles Manson Family's slaughter of Sharon Tate, the wife of Roman Polanski. I alluded to this by having the Porter (David Cameron) do a spoof on *Rosemary's Baby*, pushing a pram around the audience while playing 'knock-knock' jokes.

I'm quite certain that at the original performance of *Macbeth* the Porter would have played all that knock-knock stuff as broad pantomime with the audience responding 'Who's there?' to every cue. After all, knock-knock is the oldest comic routine in English. We can trace it back to medieval Everyman plays where the play opens with an ominous knock on Everyman's door. 'Who's there?' says Everyman. 'Death,' the visitor replies. And that's the significance of the opening of *Hamlet*. 'Who's there?' yells the soldier. And the audience already knows the answer— it is Death.

If *Macbeth* was experimental as a production, my next Shakespearean effort, *Measure for Measure*, was much more 'straight'. One can't claim that the play has had a great box-office record. For many theatre-goers it is too dour, dark and bitter. They find Isabella's insistence on her chastity as distasteful as Angelo's hypocrisy and the Duke's shameless manipulations. But I've always been greatly attracted to Shakespeare's darker comedies or 'problem plays' such as *Measure for Measure* and *Troilus and Cressida*. I find their cynicism, verging on nihilism, brave and stimulating. Catholic directors like Tyrone Guthrie have tried to turn *Measure* into a parable of Christian redemption, but to me it remains a sardonic and satirical commentary.

I wanted to highlight the hypocrisy and double standards of the characters by giving the play a mix of Victorian sentiment and sexual crudity. Leo Schofield designed it for me and loaned the theatre a sumptuous stained-glass window as a centrepiece of the set. Anna Volska's Isabella was pitted against the paranoid Machiavellism of a Duke played by Gary McDonald. One night when he was in full flight a black cat wandered up the stairs and strolled onto the stage. Without missing a beat, the Duke stalked across the stage, seized the cat and (I won't say hurled) 'ejected' it down the stairs from whence it had come.

I directed Anna for the first time in *Biggles*, but *Measure* was our first serious collaboration. We love working together, but in those early shows I tended to take out my tension and anxiety on her rather than anyone else in the cast. Naturally, she resisted—so we had the odd spiky moment.

For me the highlights of those years included working with Ron Blair, with Peter Kenna and the wonderful Gloria Dawn in *Hard God*, directing Reg Livermore and Chris Haywood in Sam Sheppard's *Tooth of Crime*, and playing Hamlet in a co-directing job with Richard Wherrett. The reason I asked to co-direct it was that I had such strong and clear ideas as to how I wanted the whole show to work, not just the role. Richard was a generous collaborator and the production proved mightily successful. One of the most pleasing comments came from the critic Katharine Brisbane, who mentioned how easily the Australian accents sat with the text. That took me by surprise. We hadn't intended to feature Australian accents—the question of accents never crossed our minds. This was a sign that some people, at

least, were getting over the cultural cringe. But it was surprising, when I launched the Bell Shakespeare Company
some twenty years later, how many critics still grizzled
about our playing Shakespeare 'with Australian accents . . .'.

*Hamlet* played a couple of seasons, toured to Melbourne
and was televised by the ABC. To exploit the commercial
potential of *Hamlet* in Sydney we moved it to a larger church
hall in Oxford Street, Paddington, while *Kaspar* played at
the home base. The same hall was used to accommodate
Richard's very successful production of *Summer of the
Seventeenth Doll* with a cast including Bill Hunter and
Melissa Jaffer.

My second Hamlet was some advance, I hope, on the
moody adolescent I had played for the Old Tote nearly a
decade earlier. This Hamlet was never melancholy or gloomy,
but a raging Freudian volcano, castigating hypocrisy and
'seeming', revenging himself on everyone except Claudius.
Anna's poignant Ophelia shocked the audience by appear-
ing for her mad scene with a shaved head, like someone
out of an asylum or concentration camp. There was a fair
bit of doubling, naturally, and Max Cullen played both
Polonius and the Gravedigger. We sought to capitalise on
this by not disguising him but simply having him look
ragged and dusty, so that when he popped out of the grave
tossing skulls about and singing 'a pick-axe and a spade,
a spade . . .' it was as if Polonius had come back from the
dead. And this gave Hamlet a bit of a turn . . .

Good old Max has given me many a laugh, on stage
and off; in *Hamlet* he surpassed himself: the grave was a
trapdoor in the centre of the raked stage. Max, having been
killed off as Polonius, did a quick change into his ragged
costume and crawled under the stage to await his cue for

the Gravedigger's surprise appearance. It was hot and dark under there and one night Max must have dozed off for a moment. Coming to, and noting a long silence, he thought, shit, I've missed my cue! So he flung open the trapdoor and popped up singing, only to find an astonished Claudius and Laertes, goblets in hand, plotting Hamlet's death, standing either side of him. Max was about three scenes too early. He sheepishly withdrew, pulling the trapdoor shut over himself . . .

For *Hamlet* we made the tiny Nimrod seem much larger by covering the walls with fragments of broken mirror. This also allowed the audience to observe themselves watching the play, like Claudius; it also gave us a few options for the Ghost. I was heavily into the psychological elements of the play and wanted to demonstrate that the Ghost was a figment of collective guilt and fear. It has a different manifestation for each witness: the soldiers, fearing invasion, see it as an armed, warlike premonition, but to Hamlet the Ghost has nothing to say of war; it is simply a confirmation of his deepest fears and suspicions concerning his mother's adultery and uncle's crime of murder. So sometimes I, as Hamlet, took the Ghost's lines, addressing myself in the mirror; sometimes they were spoken by the reflections of Claudius and Gertrude. I would play Hamlet every five years if I could, but even then I know I could never catch the whole of the character's potential in a single performance.

Peter Kenna had begun life as an actor and turned to playwriting with a couple of early successes such as *The Slaughter of St Theresa's Day*, which I had seen presented by the Trust Players at the old Elizabethan in Newtown in the early sixties. Small, ascerbic, passionate, sincere and generous, he was one of that generation who affected a Noel Coward-esque crispness of delivery and fondness for epigrams. Still a devout Catholic, he also suffered guilt and fear because of his homosexuality. At least in the theatre he was relatively safe from persecution and almost universally accepted, although looking back on it, I now realise how common 'poofter' jokes and 'poofter-bashing' (verbally, that is) were among the 'straight' acting fraternity. Along with jokes about dumb blondes, women drivers and 'coons', poofter jokes were a staple of Australian humour.

Peter had destroyed his kidneys early in life by an over-application of Bex tablets and spent most of the *Hard God* period on a dialysis machine awaiting a kidney transplant. It eventually came but he survived the operation for only a few years. His *Hard God* is largely autobiographical. The least durable part of it is the adolescent agonising about being gay and a Catholic. But the dialogue of the older characters, their reminiscences about the Depression, the drought, their painful search for the meaning of it all, is a triumph and a beautifully preserved piece of Australian folklore.

Gloria Dawn was a devout Catholic too, had endured a painful marriage and hadn't much to say in favour of the great vaudeville star Roy (Mo) Rene with whom she worked at the Tivoli. He worked 'blue' (which is to say, he told off-colour jokes) and Gloria wouldn't have a bar of that. Peter had been her lifelong friend and it was for his sake she agreed to play Aggie in *Hard God*. Hers was a classic performance of the Aussie battler, dry, stoic, but tremulously emotional.

In the early seventies the *Sydney Morning Herald* morning edition came out around 1 am. Theatre critics would dash off or phone in their reviews—sometimes they skipped the second act in order to make their deadlines. After a rousingly successful opening of *Hard God*, we partied on in the foyer until it was time for the morning edition. Then I drove Peter to Taylor Square to get the *Herald*. Haltingly I read out Harry Kippax's demolition job on the play while Peter's head sank onto his chest; he was devastated. Years later Kippax changed his mind and hailed the play as a classic, but Peter never got to hear that.

We toured the play to Brisbane and Melbourne and the ABC televised it. It was indeed an outstanding production with a cast including (besides Gloria) Frank Gallagher, Grahame Rouse and Gerry Duggan, with Tony Sheldon and Andrew Sharp as the boys. The highlight of the Melbourne tour for Peter was the night Stella Adler, the New York theatre guru, came to the show. I couldn't go to the performance but I saw Peter the next day and he was still glowing. 'Oh, John, she is wonderful! I escorted her to the theatre but was too nervous to watch the play with her so I waited outside. At the end the audience came out—but no Stella! I ran into the empty theatre calling out "Stella! Stella" and I heard this *sobbing*, so I ran down the aisle looking between the rows of seats and, John—there she was, spread-eagled on the floor in her black fur coat *heaving* with emotion. "Oh, Peter," she cried, her face *streaming* with mascara, "I have never been so overcome, so *overpowered* in all my life!" John, she's a wonderful woman— so sincere and so . . . so *unaffected*!'

But perhaps the most sensational hit I had in those early years was with a new play from Melbourne. By now scripts were pouring into Nimrod and we'd each take a pile home and dump them by the bed to read when we had time. We were all pretty busy and not well organised when it came to play reading. Some scripts languished for months, or got lost, and we were frequently bawled out by frustrated or disappointed playwrights. Anna helped me sort through the pile of scripts and one night yelled out (like Archimedes, she was in the bath at the time), 'Wow! Now here's a play!'—or words to that effect.

It was called *The Removalists* by a Melbourne writer, David Williamson. I concurred with Anna's judgement and read the play in one sitting. In fact I couldn't put it down. Here was an authentic Australian voice with a wry, mordant—and hilarious—sense of theatre. David's ear for colloquial idiom was uncanny and this explains the scale of his initial success, which he followed through with *Don's Party*, *A Handful of Friends*, *The Club* and others. Australian audiences were thrilled with the authenticity of his mimicry as well as the gallery of his most successful characters, all variants of the likeable arch-bastard along the lines of Barry Humphries' Les Patterson. David gave us Sgt Simmonds, Cooley, Jock, Mike Molloy and many others.

I went to Melbourne to see *The Removalists* at the tiny La Mama, where David himself was playing the Removalist. With him in the cast was his future wife, Kristin, while Bruce Spence and Peter Cummins played the two cops.

Naturally David was delighted that his play was to get an airing elsewhere than La Mama. In Sydney it caused a sensation. Thanks to the work done at the Pram Factory by the Australian Performing Group, Melbourne was well ahead of Sydney at this time in encouraging new Australian writing, especially of the earthy, confronting kind. Sydney had not experienced this sort of raw, Ocker colloquialism.

And in the close confines of the Nimrod theatre the violence and aggression were very much 'in your face'. We made the violence as convincing as possible. When Constable Ross beat Kenny to a pulp in the final scene, Kenny's body was hidden behind the kitchen counter while Ross kicked the shit out of a pumpkin (it sounded very like a head being kicked), and blood flew everywhere. Some members of the audience were physically ill.

My family, of course, never missed a show and announced they were coming to Sydney to see *The Removalists*. My heart skipped a beat. What would my mother think? She'd had a pretty easy run with my shows up until now, but this one was stuffed full of 'c' and 'f' words, blasphemies and profanities, 'adult themes' and two members of the Australian police force beating a man to death while he's handcuffed to a door. The whole family turned up for a matinee and Mum insisted on sitting in the front row, as usual. I sat next to her, nervously shifting from cheek to cheek. As the lights went down on the final tableau of the two cops punching each other over Kenny's bloody, battered body, Mum leaned close to me, touched my hand and whispered, 'Darling, that was lovely!'

*The Removalists* embodied much of what was good about the early Nimrod—vigorous writing and relevance in an intimate environment and some crash-hot performances from Max Phipps, Don Crosby, Kate Fitzpatrick, Jacki Weaver, Martin Harris and Chris Haywood. Harry Miller took up the production for a commercial tour. David and Kristin moved to Sydney soon after and I had the pleasure of working on several more of his plays—*A Handful*

of *Friends*, *Travelling North*, *The Club* and the not so hot
*Celluloid Heroes*. We took *The Club* to London and played
seasons at the Hampstead Theatre Club, then the Old Vic.
We also toured it all over Australia.

# Times out

Because of Nimrod's limited output in the early seventies, shared by three or more directors, I took occasional times out to work for the Old Tote, where Richard Wherrett was now on staff. He directed me in my first performance back in Australia, the title role in Brecht's powerful parable of the rise of Hitler, *The Resistable Rise of Arturo Ui*. It was the chance for a bravura display of clowning, parody and mock-Shakespearean rhetoric in George Tabori's excellent translation. It was certainly a great way to return to the Australian stage and must have impressed Robin Lovejoy—he offered me a twelve-month contract acting and directing for the Tote with time out to devote to Nimrod. Robin directed me as Petruchio in *The Taming of the Shrew* and I played the lead in Gogol's *The Government Inspector* directed by Phillip Hedley, who made a brief return visit to Australia.

I also directed a number of shows for the Tote—Ron Blair's ambitious fable of British Empire, *Kabul*, Brecht's *Good Person of Setzuan* and a Nimrod-style musical comedy spoof of Goldoni's *Servant of Two Masters*, an exercise in old-fashioned vaudeville featuring Robyn Nevin, Robin Ramsay, Drew Forsythe, Ron Haddrick and John Gaden, amongst others. We called it: *How could you believe me when I said I'd be your valet, when you know I've been a liar all my life*. It was unusual fare for the rather staid Tote audiences, but planted the seed for a later successful Forsythe–Goldoni collaboration, *The Venetian Twins*. It was also a part of my exploration of Australian popular culture and I preceded rehearsals with a two-week workshop for the cast to learn tap-dancing, slapstick and burlesque under the tutelage of a choreographer and old troupers like Gloria Dawn and Johnny Lockwood.

One of my most memorable experiences working at the Tote was when I took a role in *The Lower Depths*, directed by the Romanian Liviu Ciulei. This was his eighth production of the play, so his working knowledge was pretty secure. He directed in the classic old-fashioned European way: 'Copy me.' At first I rebelled against his directives: 'You walk three paces—longer steps—now, stick your chest out, stretch your arms wide—extend those fingers, further! Further! Now tilt back your head—further! Now say your line!' To me, this kind of direction was anathema—no discussion, no explanation, no investigation of character or motive, just: 'Copy me.' For a day I considered walking out. Then I thought, 'Hang on, he's done this show eight times, he knows what he's talking about. What he's doing is great—if I do that, I'll look bloody fantastic. All I have to do is do it with conviction.' So I did, and found I could inhabit the shapes he gave me. But I still don't like it as a way of directing. I much prefer collaborating with the actors, working as part of a team to get to the truth.

The set for *Lower Depths* was an elaborate rabbit warren of packing cases looking like a slum tenement, crammed with detail, idiosyncratic props and bits of furniture. Liviu took four days to light it (most lighting rehearsals take about six hours) and it looked fabulous—like a Rembrandt come to life. He contemplated the result and mused: 'Hmm . . . next time I direct it, I'll do it on a flat sheet of iron, like a hotplate. No props, no furniture, nothing.'

While at the Tote I was offered the opportunity to play in *Love's Labour's Lost* directed by Bill Gaskill, who had done some sensational work in England, both at the Royal Court and the National. I had seen and much admired his production of *The Recruiting Officer* with Olivier, Maggie Smith and Robert Stephens. His work had a distinctive sharpness and clarity. So I was eager to accept the opportunity to play Berowne for him. Anna was in the cast as well, playing the Princess of France, and Jacki Weaver was playing opposite me as Katherine. It was a good solid cast, including Alex Hay as Don Armado with Drew Forsythe, Ivar Kants and Shane Porteous as the other young men. The set was curiously old-fashioned and representational— a spreading oak tree on a very English lawn. The audience applauded it as soon as the curtain rose, but I was rather disappointed; I'd expected something more radical, more cutting-edge from him.

In a similar vein, Gaskill had chosen very conservative costumes—authentic Edwardian, because he saw the whole thing as a pre-World War I idyll. Similar thinking affected a disastrous *Hamlet* he directed a few years later for the Sydney Theatre Company. It had to be Edwardian, he said, because that was the last time people wore swords! What an unimaginative reason for determining your production design! How literal! For my money, modern productions of the classics have to reject that kind of pendantry.

I found nothing particularly inspiring or radical about this *Love's Labour's Lost*: sauntering around in tweeds, puffing pipes and being Oxford undergraduates made me feel as if we were playing Shaw rather than Shakespeare: all rather tea and muffins. Elizabethan gutsiness got gentrified. But Gaskill was ferociously demanding about the clarity of meaning and vocal delivery, and that was a valuable lesson. We rehearsed in a vast concrete warehouse in Alexandria and Gaskill would sit down one end with us at the other. So we had to project voices, diction and meaning over quite a distance—it demanded enormous energy and concentration.

'No, I don't know what you're talking about, do it again.' That was the most common direction; no pointers, no assistance, just, 'Do it again until I can understand you.'

After one gruelling session with the four young men, Gaskill concluded the rehearsal with, 'Yes, that will do. Thank you, gentlemen.' Then to himself, 'Tomorrow I'll give the ladies a bit of stick . . .'

But his insistence on putting Shakespeare productions into 'a period' grated with me. Of course every generation has altered the look of Shakespeare on stage. It seems quaint to us now, looking at pictures of Garrick or Mrs Siddons playing the Macbeths in periwigs, knee-breeches and panniers, but in fact they were only following Shakespeare's own custom of performing the plays in modern dress—that is, the clothes of the day. When Shakespeare's actors walked on stage they wore their own clothes, or else hand-me-downs donated by a wealthy patron. They might add some symbolic accoutrement to indicate rank or character—perhaps a crown for the king, a laurel wreath for a Roman emperor—but by and large they looked, dressed, talked and behaved like the members of their audience. So no matter what the title of the play or its supposed setting, the emphasis was on the issues being pertinent, close to home. 'The purpose of playing was, and is, to hold, as 'twere, the mirror up to Nature, to show Virtue her own feature, Scorn her own image, and the very Age and Body of the time his form and pressure.' Why else would Shakespeare have given that very significant (but dramatically unnecessary) speech to Hamlet?

Garrick was right in performing Shakespeare in his street clothes, as it were, aligning the characters and events as closely as possible to the familiar world of his audience. But when the theatre of the nineteenth century began to build its enormous auditoria, the new technologies in lighting and machinery coincided with two new phenomena—a Romantic retreat into medievalism (typified by Tennyson's *Idylls of the King* and the pre-Raphaelite painters) and archaeological discoveries, especially in Egypt, which fired the popular imagination with visions of ancient splendour. All these elements—machinery, artificial lighting, romantic medievalism and archaeological authenticity—conspired in the nineteenth and early twentieth centuries to make Shakespeare the raw material for spectacular display that was frequently bowdlerised, sentimentalised and light years away from honouring the intentions of the author.

London audiences flocked to Drury Lane or the Lyceum to see sumptuous recreations of ancient Rome or Egypt, scores of extras in authentic-looking armour cheering on Henry V at Harfleur, or real rabbits hopping about a very convincing Forest of Arden. The fact that the elaborate scene changes meant you had to cut great chunks out of the play didn't worry an audience who came essentially for the spectacle and the high points in the leading actors' performance—a bit like having only the arias in an opera.

The twentieth century saw a reversal in this approach and little by little productions made their way back to Shakespearean simplicity. Just as the camera freed up painters from the obligation to represent nature and drove them towards abstraction, the cinema took over the role of providing mass spectacle. By and large the theatre is still recovering from the advent of cinema, striving to reinvent itself, to redefine what is essentially 'theatrical' that the cinema cannot emulate. In this struggle some outstanding guides and prophets have emerged—Beckett, Meyerhold, Brook, Artaud, Grotowski and Brecht amongst them.

The essential job of a director and designer in tackling a Shakespeare play is to invent a world where the characters' speech and actions seem not only acceptable but inevitable. If the world you create is too literal, too prosaic, the language will sound inappropriate, and may cause additional problems—with a play like *Macbeth* or *King Lear*, for example, it leaves no room for the supernatural. If Lear's Storm is just a bit of bad weather, it can't suggest the moral chaos of his Kingdom. But if the world you create is too exotic, it will not touch the lives and experience of the audience. They have to be able to identify at least some aspects of what they see, so they can say 'it's familiar, a bit different to the world I know, but I can accept it as real.'

Every time you start directing a play and working with a designer, you start from scratch. What are the essential metaphors of the play? How can you bypass the audience's rational, critical faculty, sneak up on them and affect the subconscious, the visceral? Ignoring all that and simply putting the play into 'a period' is lazy and unproductive. It shuts the play in a box, and stops it reverberating. Shakespeare is, above all things, open . . .

I like playing him *now*, allowing him to reflect and ricochet off events happening in the world around us. That doesn't mean simply buying clothes off the peg and creating a set that is a literal representation of the street outside. The design must still be an abstraction, a reduction, an image that startles the observers and engages their complicity.

My *Richard III* for Bell Shakespeare (1992, 1993, 1994) was strong on metaphor, animal imagery and nightmare, but tipped into the bizarre to the extent that it lost any point of reference to the real world. I think I got it right in *Henry IV* where all the costume and scenic elements, as well as the music, were utterly contemporary; the continual reference to performance, extensive use of mime and direct address to the audience meant the audience was invited to share a theatrical game with the actors.

I couldn't crack the same result with *Henry V* the following season because I couldn't find a way to totally contemporise it. I got stuck in a World War I reference where 'God, king and country' patriotism worked for the last time. This meant that despite all my efforts to keep the production non-representational, it came across as a 'period piece' and was therefore less confronting than it should be.

The cast of *Biggles*, Nimrod, 1970: front, Michael Boddy; back row (left to right), Jane Harders, Peter Rowley, Drew Forsythe, John Hargreaves and Anna Volska.

Directing Mel Gibson (Romeo) and Kerry Walker (the Nurse) in *Romeo & Juliet*, Nimrod.
*(Photo Robert McFarlane)*

*Overleaf*: Anna Volska as Ophelia, *Hamlet*, Nimrod, 1972.

Photographers always say 'Do
something interesting with your
hands'.

*Previous page*: Anna at our home
in Surry Hills. *(Photo John Bell)*

Playing the title role in Brecht's *The Resistable Rise of Arturo Ui* (Old Tote, 1972), with
Reg Gillam and Darlene Johnston. *(Photo Robert C. Taylor)*

As Hamlet, with Margo Lee as Gertrude, Nimrod, 1972.

As Prince Hal, with Frank Wilson as Falstaff (*Henry IV*, Nimrod).

Directing *Much Ado About Nothing*, Nimrod, 1975. *(Photo Robert McFarlane)*

Peter Carroll (Benedick) and John Walton (Claudio) in *Much Ado About Nothing*, Nimrod, 1975.

Demonstrating against the Fraser Government's proposed cuts to arts funding, Sydney Town Hall, 1980.

In *Cyrano de Bergerac*, directed by Richard Wherrett, in the Sydney Theatre Company's first season.

*Overleaf*: Hilary and Lucy with our pet dog Lottie, in our garden in Surry Hills.
*(Photo Anna Volska)*

A final word on 'period' Shakespeare: 'period' is not the same thing as 'authentic', and therefore no guarantee that you are 'getting it right'. 'Period' is a fabrication. It's only in retrospect we can generalise about the spirit of a time in history. You don't feel it while you're living through it. You're just aware of people being at different phases of their life. We're always living in a state of flux and things are changing around us all the time. Any production of a Shakespeare play should note how Shakespeare's worlds are always in a state of flux, the younger generation shouldering their elders aside. This generation gap should be stressed in clothes, body language and behaviour rather than attempting homogeneity.

Alongside my work for the Old Tote, I was still putting in time at Nimrod. My performance as Arturo had attracted a few fans, amongst them an enthusiastic and energetic businessman named John Mostyn. He was a bit of a mover and shaker in opera circles and now began to attend shows at Nimrod. He was pretty shocked at the fiscal differences between the opera world and that of live theatre: 'Do you know,' he said to me, 'Joan Sutherland gets $14 000 a performance of Lucia—what are you getting as Hamlet?'

'Three hundred dollars, John.'

'That's outrageous!' he fumed. 'Only three hundred dollars a performance?'

'No, John, three hundred dollars a week—for eight performances.'

He was struck dumb.

# The move to Belvoir Street

John Mostyn was firmly of the opinion that Nimrod had outgrown the old stables venue and deserved something bigger. In this he was right. By 1973 we were ready to double or treble our audience capacity, and the present Nimrod was severely limited in space and facilities. So with indefatigable energy, Mostyn set about procuring us new premises and came up with an enormous factory site bordered by Elizabeth and Belvoir Streets, Surry Hills. The whole block was occupied by the defunct Cerebos Salt–Fountain Tomato Sauce factories and had been purchased by developers Sid King and Gary Bogard.

The local council would permit them to build high-rise apartments on the site only if some cultural amenity was provided. So Mostyn talked Gary into giving Nimrod (for $1 a year in rent) a whole corner block to convert into a theatre. After the deal was signed, the council reneged on the plans for high-rise apartments, Gary retired to the

Riviera, and the rest of the site remained a wasteland for the next twelve years. But we had our building and invited architect Viv Fraser to convert it into a theatre. His achievement provided a model for many other new theatres around the country and he was employed to do a similar makeover on one of the Walsh Bay wharves for the Sydney Theatre Company in the mid eighties.

Our opening show was a rushed job. We had announced an opening date and were now building the theatre and rehearsing the show against a deadline. We sought something popular in tone and ambitious in scale and settled on *The Bacchoi*, a rock musical based on Euripides by Queensland pair Bryan Nason and Ralph Tyrrel. Larry Eastwood designed the set and lighting, Kim Carpenter the Felliniesque costumes and the cast included such pop icons as Jon English and Jeannie Lewis. We held our final week's rehearsals on stage with the theatre literally being finished around us. Rain poured through the partially constructed roof, sending the cast skidding across the stage and threatening to electrocute the rock band who were wired for sound, trying to be heard over the electric drills and power saws.

By the time opening night arrived the show was by no means ready. All around us workers were finishing off the building, connecting wiring, painting and sweeping—it was chaotic. The night before we opened I sat with Larry in the stage manager's box trying to light *Bacchoi*. He was utterly exhausted, having designed and built the set, rigged the lights and done a thousand other jobs. Dog-tired, we plodded from cue to cue, testing out the new lamps and lighting board, shouting over the din of hammering and sawing while people finished the set. We got about a third of the way through the lighting and it was well after midnight.

I called a cue number and nothing happened. I looked beside me and there was Larry, collapsed over the lighting board, fast asleep. Obviously there was no point persisting. I shook his shoulder and said: 'Larry, go home. We're not going to finish lighting the show. Get a good sleep, come in tomorrow night and ride the board—improvise, just throw up any lights that come to hand.'

Since the show was a rock'n'roll musical, the lighting didn't need to have an obvious logic or consistency. The next night was a bit of a wild ride. Amazing lighting effects came up in the strangest places—sometimes appropriately, sometimes not. I kept glancing at the box and saw Larry, pale-faced and wild-eyed, trying to keep pace with the show, throwing switches and fading dimmers with all the desperate concentration of a racing car driver battling out the Grand Prix in a cyclone.

Despite the hype we were concerned that our old audience might not follow us to the new venue with its three hundred seats that we had to fill, but those anxieties were soon assuaged and the new Nimrod foyer and bar became another Sydney social hub, especially as we turned on free drinks every Friday afternoon for any actor who cared to drop in.

The opening of the new Nimrod Theatre in Surry Hills coincided with a boom time for arts funding in Australia. The great example set by Don Dunstan in South Australia was followed through by Prime Minister Gough Whitlam, newly come to government, who had taken unto himself the arts portfolio, as had New South Wales Labor Premier Neville Wran.

Gough set about patronising the arts in a Medici-like manner, giving special attention to writers. Nimrod fared well in this new climate, and Gough and Margaret were frequent first-nighters, trudging unattended by lackeys or security through the weeds and rubble up to the theatre.

That first season in 1974 included a popular production of *The Seagull* by Richard Wherrett and three new Australian plays, Michael Cove's *Kookaburra*, *Well Hung* by Robert Lord and Jim McNeill's *How Does Your Garden Grow?* The following year was notable for Richard's stylish production of *The Ride Across Lake Constance* by Peter Handke with a cast including John Hargreaves, Kate Fitzpatrick and Anna Volska; a revival of Romeril's *The Floating World* directed by Ken Horler; Ron Blair's masterpiece of a monologue, *The Christian Brothers* (a great vehicle for Peter Carroll); and two Shakespeare plays on an adaptable set—*Much Ado About Nothing*, which I directed as a kind of Italian circus, and Richard's production of *Richard III*, in which I had my first crack at the hunchbacked villain. Not all the new Australian plays did good business, so Shakespeare paid the bills and kept us solvent. We began to hive off his 10 per cent author's royalties to commission new works.

*Much Ado* was probably my most popular success since *King O'Malley* and shared much of the same carefree spirit. We played capacity business and after a tour to Adelaide, did a return season at Nimrod. If we'd had the resources, we would have mounted a national tour and cleaned up at the box office. This was my most determined effort so far to earmark Shakespeare as both popular entertainment and a part of Australian theatre—not a British cultural appendage. I was determined to stop the actors putting on the plummy 'Shakespeare' voice we had been brought up with. I suggested we rehearse the play with mock-Italian accents—

a parody of the Australian/Italian 'greengrocer' voice. This immediately took the preciousness out of the acting and made the language more volatile and expressive. But it wasn't enough; the physical part of the acting didn't match up—some people still adopted 'Shakespearean' poses and gestures.

I invited a group of actors from the Australian Theatre for the Deaf to come and work with us. Deprived of vocal language, they had a rich repertoire of body language, signing and mime. They also had enormous powers of concentration and an urgent need to watch each other closely—so they were far more sensitive to physical nuance than hearing actors tend to be. They were an inspiration to us and we adopted some of their signing as well as inventing a signing vocabulary of our own, which meant that the actor's body was never static but always alert and expressive.

I had wanted the whole production to be 'Italian', mainly to get away from those ersatz English classical affectations, but also because the play makes more sense when you see it in its Italian context: these people are obsessed with vendetta, male pride and military honour. They are sensual, passionate and explosive. There is nothing polite or stitched-up about them. Setting the play in a circus tent with costumes a cross between Garibaldi's soldiers and circus performers (lion tamers, acrobats and so on) liberated the actors. It also allowed us to employ that strain of Australian popular entertainment (yes, back to Bobby le Brun and Roy Rene) so dear to my heart.

As opening night drew near, I said to the cast, 'Okay, it's time to drop the rehearsal Italian accents and just play it straight.' But we realised this was impossible: the sounds and vocal energy were now totally integrated with the physicality and couldn't just be 'dropped'. Audiences were delighted with the result, but one or two critics had to carp. They assumed that I was out to 'send up' or trivialise Shakespeare. The battle still goes on, thirty years later. Any unusual treatment of the classics has to endure a period of hostility before it is accepted, is absorbed into the mainstream and, in its turn, becomes passé.

We used the same team of actors in both *Much Ado* and *Richard III* with the addition of myself in the second play. Kim Carpenter designed the clothes for both, Larry Eastwood the sets. By pulling down *Much Ado*'s colourful canvas wraparound and lifting off the stage floor, we exposed the metallic structure of the set—scaffolding and steel grilles—which served for *Richard III*. The costumes for *Richard III* were based on the tough clothes of a factory—overalls, welding masks; the weapons were metal pipes. Again anxious to avoid 'Shakespearean' elocution, I persuaded Richard Wherrett to let us invent a kind of rough, rustic Elizabethan dialect, based on what we know of Shakespeare's own Warwickshire accent.

Both productions made much use of direct audience contact; in the case of *Much Ado* the actors actually sat amongst the audience, crawled between their legs, clambered in the lighting-rig over their heads. (My experiments with actor/audience interaction found further expression in *Tristram Shandy*, where seven small stages were placed throughout the auditorium and linked by catwalks; and in *The Speakers*, the actors stood on soapboxes, like the orators in Sydney's Domain, and the audience wandered around the space, choosing which speaker to attend.)

In 1976 I had my one and only crack at grand opera. The Australian Opera offered me a production of *Don Giovanni*, which I asked Peter Corrigan to design. I was determined to knock what I perceived to be the stuffiness out of operatic performance. I insisted it should be sung in English (no surtitles in those days) and devised a new translation with the help of the renowned and somewhat irascible Jani Strasser, the Australian Opera Company's chief répétiteur. He taught me a lot about Mozart's skill in uniting music and libretto.

Corrigan's set was defiantly abstract—a lot of doorframes standing in a pink desert—and I found some of the older singers both baffled and enraged by my approach. I treated them as I would actors, and kept talking about motivations and intentions. Most of them just wanted to stand down-stage centre and sing. Younger principals like John Pringle (the Don) and Eileen Hannan (Zerlina) were a delight but I fell foul of the conductor, John Pritchard, who decided that I was desecrating a masterpiece.

The last straw came when I flew in a Brechtian placard over the finale, with the text which the performers were singing: 'Thus do all deceivers end . . .' Pritchard snorted, 'That is the final insult to your audience,' and stormed out of the rehearsal. Interestingly, Ingmar Bergmann used the same device a few years later in his charming film of *The Magic Flute* and everyone loved it. Oh well. I quite enjoyed the experience and loved the music, but I should have moved more slowly and diplomatically in what were, to me, totally uncharted waters.

# Upstairs,
# Downstairs

Now that we had secured our new theatre in Belvoir Street, Surry Hills, I was concerned that not many new plays were drawing crowds into the upstairs three hundred-seat theatre. We were mostly dealing with first time playwrights and many of the plays didn't warrant an expensive production and a five-week season. So we decided to convert the downstairs rehearsal room into a performance space where developing work could be given a window. We opened it in 1976 with a production of Heathcote Williams' *The Speakers*, featuring a number of soapbox orators scattered through the space. Downstairs produced much exciting work over the seasons that followed, sometimes making Upstairs look a bit conservative by comparison.

Although primarily intended as a try-out venue for new Australian plays, Downstairs played host to good new American writing, including David Mamet's *American Buffalo* and *Sexual Perversity in Chicago*; Eric Bentley's *Are*

*You Now or Have You Ever Been?* and the popular *Kennedy's Children* (the latter two directed by Ken Horler). George Whaley gave us an excellent production of Dario Fo's *Accidental Death of an Anarchist* and Aubrey Mellor introduced Vaclav Havel to Australian audiences with his *Protest* plays. This was timely and significant political theatre.

But the bulk of the Downstairs program was new Australian writing. I directed *Inner Voices*, Louis Nowra's debut in Sydney; Neil Armfield directed David Allen's portrayal of DH Lawrence and Frieda in Australia (*Upside Down at the Bottom of the World*) and Stephen Sewell's *Traitors* with Barry Otto, Max Gillies and Colin Friels. Janis Balodis's play *Backyard* proved a strong vehicle for Bryan Brown and Joan Sidney. Ken devised a colourful cabaret piece called *Kold Komfort Kaffe* as a showcase for Robyn Archer and John Gaden. For this show, the seating was replaced by tables and chairs, wine was served and Martin Sharp painted the whole venue beautifully. The show was an outstanding success, but the all-time winner as far as Downstairs was concerned was *The Elocution of Benjamin Franklin* by Steve J Spears, directed by Richard and marking a wonderful comeback for that great comedian Gordon Chater. The production went on to enormous popular and critical success throughout Australia, then to London and New York.

Always full of ideas, Ken devised a production of *Treasure Island* which ran successfully every Christmas holidays on Shark Island in Sydney Harbour. Half the fun was the ferry ride to the island with pirates swarming over the ferry. Another highlight of the show was the moment Jim Hawkins (aka Simon Burke) shot the villainous Israel

Hands, who plummeted off the set into the drink. This always caused a stampede of tots to the sea wall, no doubt in the hope of seeing the pirate devoured by sharks.

Ken's production of Stoppard's *Travesties* and *Jumpers*, both vehicles for John Gaden at his best, were sell-outs Upstairs, as was Steve Spears' *Young Mo*, a tribute to Roy Rene in which Gloria Dawn appeared opposite Gary McDonald, suppressing her dislike of the original Mo himself. This show gave us Martin Sharp's brilliant poster, which became Nimrod's logo—Mo's black and white makeup with his trademark leer achieved a kabuki icon's power in an image that was simultaneously grotesque and refined.

Ken's productions in the Upstairs venue also included Brecht's *Galileo*, with Gaden giving a sterling performance, and Alex Buzo's *Martello Towers* and *Makassar Reef*. Anxious to have a serious go at the Greeks, in 1980 I directed Aeschylus's *Oresteia*, with designs by Kim Carpenter and a strong cast that included Colin Friels, Ralph Cotterill, Kris McQuade, Anna Volska and Carol Burns.

During 1976 I took off alone around the country in a one-man show written for me by Ron Blair. It was called *Mad, Bad and Dangerous to Know* and was based on the letters and diaries of Lord Byron. For my taste, Ron was too faithful to his sources, left little room for his own invention and the whole thing remained a bit of an English Lit exercise. Worse, I could not empathise with the character. Initially, Byron presented a romantic, heroic image, but the more I researched him, the less I liked him. I detested his treatment of women, especially his abandoned daughter Augusta. I fell into the old acting trap of judging a character. Unless you can empathise with him you'll never play him well. I knew I wasn't giving a compelling performance when my director, Richard Wherrett, kept falling asleep in rehearsal—and there were only the two of us in the room! 'Psst . . . Richard, wake up!'

I've rarely felt so miserable as the opening night of *Mad, Bad* at the Adelaide Festival. I was alone on stage in my opening pose with my toes almost touching the curtain. On the other side of it I could hear the dull roar of the audience coming in and taking their seats. I looked over my shoulder and the Stage Door Exit sign beckoned. 'Just leave now—simply walk off stage, out the door and down the street. Go on, do it now . . .' I was about to obey when the curtain slowly began to rise and there I was staring into the footlights and the void.

After playing *Mad, Bad* in Adelaide and Sydney I toured a pleasant series of venues stretching up north—Brisbane, Townsville, Rockhampton, Cairns—tropical paradise in glorious sunshine. In Townsville I was urgently requested for a publicity interview on radio and took a cab to the remote station manned by one announcer who rang his own gongs and threw all the switches. We were going to air live and he frantically beckoned to me through the glass panel as he finished the news. He had my press release in his hand but something had got lost in the transmission. 'And now, listeners, it is my pleasure to introduce Mr Eric Bell from the Nig Nog Theatre Restaurant in Sydney, who is here in town with a play about Shelley . . . Isn't that so, Eric?'

In Rockhampton I had the bizarre experience of playing bad Lord Byron to an audience of eight hundred very young school kids at 11 am in the Town Hall. This building was all glass on one side looking out onto a wide footpath lined with trees covered in red berries. It was impossible to get any sort of blackout as the sun streamed in and about half an hour after I started, flocks of noisy parrots began to arrive, cavorting in the trees and screeching with delight at the abundance of fruit. But these same berries had a formidable alcoholic content and soon after they had gorged themselves, the parrots began to sway and sing drunkenly before plummeting to the ground with hideous yells and splatting on the pavement. The kids seemed quite used to it, but I was transfixed and could hardly remember what line came next as I gazed sidelong at this panorama of pissed, nose-diving parrots littering the ground like one of the plagues of Egypt.

One of the happier aspects of this tour was that Anna and the girls could join me for a brief tropical holiday. During those Nimrod years Anna had done a fair bit of work in television and film as well as stage plays for other companies. But a lot of her time and talent had been devoted to Nimrod. Amongst her outstanding performances were Beatrice in *Much Ado*, Olga in *Three Sisters*, Nina in *The Seagull* and roles in *The Ride Across Lake Constance*, *Tales form the Vienna Woods* and *Women of March the First*.

By 1978 the Old Tote was in serious trouble and its director, Robin Lovejoy, resigned. I was asked by the New South Wales arts ministry if I would take it over. I was very torn between Nimrod and this new challenge, but I entered into negotiations. Talks failed when I said I must have authority over the general manager and be solely responsible for the choice of repertoire. The Tote's chairman, Dale Turnbull, and his general manager, Ken Southgate, rejected this demand and I withdrew my interest, even though I was

warned by the ministry that if I did so the Tote would probably be denied funding. The Tote board then offered the
job to Sir Robert Helpmann, who accepted it and gave a
press conference outlining his plans. It was then that the
government refused funding and the Tote collapsed—
a rather embarrassing debacle.

Shortly afterwards Premier Neville Wran announced
plans to form a new Sydney theatre company to replace the
Tote and applications for the role of director were invited.
Richard, Ken and I all thought we should throw our hats
into the ring, just so we couldn't grizzle later if someone
we thought unsuitable got the gig. Again, my heart wasn't
in it and I gave a lacklustre interview. I had even said in
the press before my interview that I was in two minds about
it. I insisted that the company should not perform in the
Drama Theatre of the Opera House—an auditorium I have
always hated. That was an absurd demand, of course. The
premier had to have his state company resident in the
Drama Theatre. But above all, I was reluctant to leave
Nimrod and all I had helped to build up there. I felt duty-
bound to serve Nimrod's long-time supporters; I felt bad
about deserting them. So I was negative and uncooperative
with the selection committee. The job went to Richard,
which I think was a very good thing. He was ready for it,
he wanted it and he made it work in a way that was stylish and popular. He gave Sydney what it wanted. I think I
would have stuck too much to the Nimrod recipe, whereas
something new was needed, and Richard provided that for
the next eleven years.

In the year's interim before the Sydney Theatre Company got under way in 1980, each of the local companies
was invited to contribute a play at the Opera House. Nimrod

chose a musical version of Goldoni's *Venetian Twins*, with script and lyrics by Nick Enright and music by Terence Clark. It was devised mainly as a vehicle for the comic genius of Drew Forsythe, but I felt one of my chief contributions in directing it was subverting the ghastly Opera House Drama Theatre. To counteract the deadly impact of that letterbox of a proscenium, I placed a tiny stage in the middle of it with scaffolding all around for actors and audience to sit on. The little stage had a steep rake and thrust out over the front rows of seats. Carnival lights replaced the dreary house fluorescents. It was no wonder some people thought the Drama Theatre was still under construction.

*Venetian Twins* was one of those riotously enjoyable shows to direct. The actors' adlibs and inventive comedy all became part of the finished script, just as they had with *O'Malley* and many a Nimrod show. I directed it again some years later at the Seymour Centre and it has had a number of subsequent productions around Australia.

For all its gags and slapstick nonsense, I see *Venetian Twins* as having an important function: to remind us of the joys, the spontaneity, the human contact of live performance—theatre as a shared experience.

While maintaining my presence at Nimrod I played a number of roles for the Sydney Theatre Company over the next decade. In his first season, Richard offered to direct me in Louis Nowra's witty new prose translation of *Cyrano de Bergerac*. Film actress Leslie Caron came to see it twice and said to me: 'Oh, it's so much better in English—all that French poetry—eet ees so boring!' *Cyrano* was a lavish, big cast show and after a sell-out season in the Drama Theatre we transferred it to the much larger Opera Theatre. I had two delightful Roxannes, Helen Morse and Robyn Nevin, and a wicked cast including Peter Whitford and Stuart Campbell, who was playing one of my offsiders. I think Stuart had a bit of a crush on the lad playing the sentry, but as said lad didn't reciprocate, Stuart bore some malice. One night, on cue, the sentry called: 'I see a man running away!'

'Who is it?' I cried.

'It's his agent,' Stuart whispered in my ear, leaving me unable to speak for the rest of the scene.

*Cyrano* is a skilfully constructed tear-jerker, but not much more; a confection and a romance—but it provides a good show-off role.

I always seemed to have more success playing grotesque characters: Arturo, Cyrano, Richard III, the extravagant, theatrical ones. As a young actor I felt more comfortable when I could hide behind a role rather than speak through it, though I have found myself in later years saying a lot about myself through roles like Lear, Astrov and Shylock. Were I younger, I'd jump at the chance to play Hamlet again and again. That's one part you can totally personalise.

It never crossed my mind to seek a career in movies or television. I assumed that for movies you had to have good looks and sex appeal, and I was convinced I had neither. I liked the makeup, the disguise, the being someone else. And that suggests a deal of personal insecurity. I suppose I must have a pretty healthy ego, looking back on things I've done; but it's balanced by an uncertainty as to what *right* I have to be doing it at all. This has resulted, at various times in my career, in my not assuming authority when I could and should have done so, waiting for someone else to call the shots. At the age of sixty I began to understand this, just as I began to understand (vaguely) what acting and directing are all about.

I think I was led up something of a blind alley by a lecture given by Jerzy Grotowski in Sydney in 1971 in which he claimed that acting is a form of confession—in the Polish Catholic sense. This is to say that in performing, you should reveal your deepest, darkest secrets, just as you do to the priest in the confessional. People don't go to theatre to see people *pretend*, Grotowski argued; they go to see truth. So get rid of all makeup, disguise and 'acting'—reveal your innermost self through the role. This theory appealed to me greatly and seemed to endow theatre with a new and profound purpose. So for the next twenty-odd years I did my utmost to put that theory into practice—trying to find the Macbeth, the Lear, the Prospero within me. But in doing so I experienced a deal of frustration and incompleteness.

In the generation that followed the English greats like Olivier, Gielgud and Richardson, it was fashionable to knock their preoccupation with 'technique', as if that signalled a facile, hollow approach, lacking 'sincerity'. But I am convinced that the right answer is to weld together both schools of thought. Of course you have to be prepared to delve into your innermost self and reveal to an audience what you find there. But I think Olivier was right in saying that if all you do is try to find the part *within yourself*, you limit all roles to that one small frame of reference. You must also invent a persona outside yourself, find *yourself in the role* rather than *the role in you*.

No matter how much 'sincerity' or 'feeling' you have to offer, acting is also a craft, a game, a play—you *create* something. It's surprising, when you do this, how much of yourself you reveal anyway. Olivier's own Richard III is a good example. Throughout his life, he publicly denied any suggestion that he was other than heterosexual. Yet various biographers have documented his bisexuality, along with observations about his 'flirtatiousness' as a theatre manager. He had a high degree of sexual ambivalence on stage and off, and used it to great effect as Richard—even flirting with the *camera* in his film portrayal. Yet it was a part of himself he strenuously denied and attempted to conceal.

I think it was Picasso who said 'Art is made up of lies that tell the truth.'

After Cyrano I played other roles for the Sydney Theatre Company including Macbeth (again with Richard directing and opposite Robyn Nevin), and leading roles in David Williamson's *Emerald City*, *Shadowlands*, and Stoppard's *The Real Thing*, the latter two with the adorable Jacki Weaver. *Shadowlands* was one of those boffo box-office hits, but I felt uncomfortable with its Christian piety. And of course all those plays were in the Drama Theatre, which I loathe as a performer and as an audience member. The Playhouse has its limitations too, but at least you can see your audience and sense their reactions. On the Drama Theatre stage you stare into a void utterly bereft of personality. Each night before the performance I would go into the lighting-box at the back of the auditorium so I could watch the audience coming in. I would study their faces and say to myself, 'Right, tonight I'm doing the play for you . . . and you . . . and you . . .'

# Nimrod: decline and end

1980 saw the beginning of Nimrod's decline. Lilian had given up the post of general manager and Paul Iles, a bright young Englishman, took her place. Paul had a great nose for marketing and publicity but worked on a grand scale. On his initiative we twice imported Berliner Ensemble star Eckhardt Schall along with his wife Barbara Brecht (daughter of the great Bertolt) to do a one-man show at Nimrod Upstairs; and we produced the Peter Brook triple bill of *The Ik/Ubu Roi/Conference of the Birds* at the Seymour Centre. Great theatre, but very expensive and a big cost to Nimrod. And when our board abandoned our previous salary structure and paid commercial star salaries to Warren Mitchell and Mel Gibson in *Death of a Salesman*, we were entering murky waters.

The new Australian plays—apart from Williamson's—were losing money. Government subsidies were not keeping pace with rising costs. Every few months we'd go cap in hand to funding authorities, tugging our forelocks, confessing our sins, and promising to try and do better. As we shuffled along the corridors of power and sank into the luxurious sofas of the ministry, it often occurred to me to ask some of these bureaucrats a simple question: 'Do arts companies exist to keep you in a job, or do you exist to help us?'

Ken Horler resigned as co-artistic director in 1979 but stayed on the board. In his place we took on Neil Armfield and Kim Carpenter, but Kim soon found that the management component of the job was not to his taste and that he'd rather concentrate on designing and directing alone, so he left. To replace him I inveigled Aubrey Mellor to leave the safe confines of NIDA and join us. He soon showed himself to be an inspiring director, especially of Chekov. His *Three Sisters* and *Uncle Vanya* were outstanding. Besides the Australian plays he directed, he introduced local audiences to the work of Canadian writer George Walker with *Zastrozzi* and *Beyond Mozambique*. 1980 and 1981 also saw David Hare's *Teeth'n'Smiles* directed by Neil Armfield and Aubrey Mellor's highly entertaining *Cloud Nine* by Caryl Churchill. Steve Sewell got exposure in the larger venue with Neil's production of *Welcome the Bright World*. Paul Iles left us to run the State Theatre Company of South Australia.

But the changes in staff and administration saw factions forming, each wanting to pull Nimrod in a different direction. The weekly company strategy meetings became inflammatory and divisive, proposals increasingly wild and irrational. In moves to 'democratise' the company, it was proposed by someone that all members of staff should have a vote in the choice of repertoire and that selling tickets

was 'elitist' and that the seats should be free. Neither proposal was adopted. I believed strongly in trying to maintain
a degree of democracy in the company, but we hadn't
thought through how to implement it. I saw increasing evidence that 'democracy' was simply creating power blocs.

Relations between the staff and the board became
increasingly strained until the board directed the new general manager, Bruce Pollack, to put the house in order and
that meant sackings and resignations.

Throughout all of this I found myself buffeted between
the staff and the board, but my main concern was to prevent the company sinking into chaos. Bruce Pollack
resigned and a pragmatic numbers man, Michael Donovan,
was appointed in his place. Faced with growing financial
problems, chairman John Mostyn proposed that Nimrod
should endeavour to be a national company, touring
Australia and thereby attracting major funding, and that
we should sell the Nimrod building, which we now owned,
and do a deal with Sydney University whereby we became
the resident company at the Seymour Centre. All this could
possibly have worked if only the Seymour Centre was a
more popular venue. But in spite of having three workable
auditoria, the right number of seats (800, 600 and 200
respectively), spacious foyers and good facilities, the place
has never taken off, even though it packs out for one-off
events and festivals. Geographically it's in a dead spot and
its image is blurred in the public eye—neither quite on or
off the campus.

We'd had some previous successes there: I saw Warren
Mitchell's marvellous performance in *Death of a Salesman*
at the National in London and invited him to re-create it
for us with George Ogilvie directing and Mel Gibson as

Biff. The show played capacity business. I also directed
*Candide*, one of my favourite musicals, in a popular pro-
duction featuring Philip Quast, Jon Ewing, Tony Taylor and
John Hannan.

Before the move could be effected, our financial crisis
came to a head and I went to Premier Neville Wran to dis-
cuss a rescue package. He agreed to bail the company out
as long as I stayed on as an artistic director (with Aubrey
Mellor) and gave the company my best shot. But the board
would have to go and be replaced by one made up of his
nominees who would supervise the company's financial
renewal. It was tough on the old board members who had
striven so hard and given so much—particularly John
Mostyn, Justice Robert Hope and Tony Gilbert; the latter
two had been directors since the beginning. Mostyn had
been the driving force in establishing and sustaining the
new Nimrod. It was galling for him to be dumped so un-
ceremoniously. Despite my continuing public recognition
of his contribution, he has never spoken to me since.

With a new board in place and the experienced arts
troubleshooter Ken Tribe in the chair, we transferred to the
Seymour in September 1984. The university gave us a good
financial deal but would not come at some radical cosmetic
changes we thought were vital to popularise the venue—
such as knocking down the surrounding walls and providing
taxi ranks; neon and other signage on the outside of the
buildings; and inside, a breaking up of the cavernous foyers
with more bars, coffee lounges and a major paint job on
the raw brick walls.

*King Lear* opened our new season, directed by Aubrey
Mellor, with myself as Lear, Judy Davis doubling as Cordelia
and the Fool, and a strong cast including Colin Friels

(Edmund), Robert Menzies (Edgar), John Howard (Kent),
Jon Ewing (Gloster) and Gillian Jones and Kris McQuade
as Goneril and Regan. Michael Gow played Oswald. Since
the play was on the Higher School Certificate syllabus we
preceded our metropolitan run with a season at the
Bankstown Sports Club. The club offered us the venue
because it was out to lift its image. We drew in thousands
of kids from the western suburbs and it was a bit weird
seeing them marching through the bar past the pokies.

We struggled on for two seasons at the Seymour, doing
our best to keep the Everest and York Theatres fully occupied while encouraging the university students to utilise the
downstairs space. But we were running out of puff. Fourteen years of slog, of financial anxieties, funding crises,
searching for new plays, acting and directing with rarely a
break, plus the burden of trying to bring the Seymour
Centre to life, had left me exhausted. Aubrey was feeling
much the same, so in 1985 we tendered our joint resignations and set about helping the board find replacements.
It was with much relief and few regrets that I handed over
the reins to Richard Cottrell. The original Nimrod spirit
had evaporated some four or five years earlier but I had
ploughed doggedly on in an attempt to keep the company
alive, even though I was sometimes programming works I
had no faith in.

It was a relief to escape, for a while, the claustropho-
bia of the theatre industry. I avoid opening nights whenever
I can, my own excepted. I prefer to slip in to a show when
there's a paying audience there, and hear a genuine reaction.
Opening night hype was typified for me by the late Bill
Ball, one-time director of the Actors' Conservatory Theatre

in San Francisco, whom I had met when he was here for a playwrights' conference in the early seventies: 'I always hire *two* claques for opening nights,' he told me in all serious- ness. 'One to do all the yelling and screaming and one to rush down the aisles and clutch the actresses' ankles. No matter how lousy the show, people walk out saying, "But wasn't the reaction fabulous!"'

'What's your next project, Bill?' I asked him.

'*The Three Sisters* starring Kathy Crosby.'

'Kathy Crosby?' I raised my eyebrows.

'Bing made it worth my while.'

I spend most of my life with actors and love the com- pany of whichever group I'm working with at the time. There are few things I enjoy more than rehearsing or having a beer in the foyer with a bunch of actors after a show. Actors tend to be generous in a way that isn't shared by other elements of the theatre industry. Theatre directors rarely have a good word to say of each other. Playwrights are better, but jealousy and envy are common. I remember going to an opening night of a play by Barry Dickins at the Courthouse in Carlton. The audience was sparse. 'Where are all your mates?' I asked. 'In the pub across the road,' Barry replied. 'They don't want to come in case it's a success.'

In a way the Nimrod I had helped create, along with Ken, Richard and many others, had served its turn. We set out to make theatre less stuffy, more confronting and more Australian. Drawing on old popular traditions of music-hall, vaudeville and pantomime we encouraged the cheeky, irrev- erent aspect of the Australian character to invade the temples of high art. Along with Melbourne's Pram Factory we helped encourage the emergence of a new generation of Australian playwrights and with them provided opportunities for

Australian performers. Nimrod presented over one hundred productions of Australian plays. We helped popularise the notion of an Australian theatre, an Australian voice, and this in turn had a positive impact on the fledgling local film industry. We raided the classics and lassoed them into our cause, demonstrating that they could be as funny, as dirty, as confronting and relevant as the latest Australian play. And we left behind two excellent theatre venues (now known as the Stables and Belvoir Street) to carry on the work we had started; venues we'd helped build with our own hands and which absorbed our joy, as well as our sweat and tears. It was a relief that when we vacated the Nimrod building, it was taken over by a syndicate of artists from which Company B emerged.

I remember when Olivier was appointed head of the National in London, he was quizzed by some journo about his qualifications. 'Well, I've failed with running several other companies,' Olivier replied, 'and I think I've now learned enough to run the National.' That's called putting a positive spin on it. But likewise, the hard lessons I learned at Nimrod stood me in good stead for later. I've learned to do only the things I believe in and never do things to fulfil someone else's agenda.

I learned that you can't run an arts company by com-mittee. It needs one person's vision to drive it and that person is where the buck stops. I now have around me at Bell Shakespeare a devoted and marvellous team of people in all areas of administration—management, finance, mar-keting, production etc. They are mostly half my age and that keeps me in touch with what the next generation wants and thinks. I consult them on everything and listen to all they have to say. I do the same with my board of directors (who seem to be getting younger by the year). But in the end I carry the can.

Every major business and marketing decision (every press release, brochure, flyer, newspaper ad) needs my scrutiny and careful weighing of consequences. When I'm directing a play now, I go into each day's rehearsal with a hundred ideas which I keep to myself until I've heard everybody else's. If better ideas come up, I throw mine out the window. But I never walk into a rehearsal room or a meeting without a very clear idea of what I want the outcome to be. So lobbying and fall-back positions are fundamental.

The director's job, in part, is to provide clear parameters, to build the playground and then let free and joyous play happen inside. From that the director will select, carefully and ruthlessly, only what is useful to the end product. And that will be done without anyone feeling resentful or aggrieved.

Things have changed enormously in the arts scene in Australia since the heady days of the seventies and Whitlam's largesse. For an arts company to flourish in the first decade of the second millennium, expertise must be devoted to the areas of corporate sponsorship, public relations and a nonstop, shameless campaign of networking . . .

The last few years of the Nimrod saga had taken their toll on me. I found it very easy to identify with Dr Astrov in Aubrey's production of *Uncle Vanya*—a man prematurely worn out, exhausted and clinging to his ideals by his fingertips. Fortunately, through it all, the family hung together and that gave me enormous emotional support. Anna acted with me in both *Three Sisters* and *Uncle Vanya*. Hilary was now twenty, toying with art school but on the verge of discovering her great talent as a poet and playwright. Lucy was eighteen, graduating from Sydney Girls' High and experimenting with Sydney University and SUDS before throwing her hat in the ring and enlisting in NIDA. Both girls had literally grown up in Nimrod: sleeping under the bleachers at the old Nimrod while Ma and Pa rehearsed; later watching rehearsals and putting on their own shows at the new Nimrod. Their stellar teeny-bopper casts included Miranda Otto, Felix Williamson, Emily Russell and a few more, so that the Sunday afternoon audience of proud parents looked like a who's who in theatre.

Whenever I go back now to any of those one-time 'Nimrod' venues—the Stables, Belvoir Street, the Seymour Centre—I find it a bit hard to cross the threshold. Something pushes me back. I think it's a great wave of exhaustion, the ghosts of so many heartbreaks, heartaches, triumphs, late nights, frantic excitement, disasters, rave reviews, lousy reviews, production meetings, funding crises, explosions of temperament, tears and laughter all summed up in one word—STRUGGLE!—Fourteen years of STRUGGLE . . .

Occasionally a return to the source is a joyous one, though; none more so than when Hilary was commissioned by Ros Horin to write a play for the Stables 2000 season. She wrote a surrealistic comedy-melodrama called *The Falls* and asked me to direct it.

It so happened that I could shuffle dates at Bell Shakespeare to make it fit. The budget was minuscule, so I directed it for nothing. It was not only the thirtieth anniversary of my first theatre venue, I was being *offered* a play by my own daughter! I would have moved heaven and earth . . . I auditioned a number of actresses for the leading role, but everyone agreed (as impartially as they could) that Lucy was made for it. This was the second (professional) collaboration between Hil and Luce at the Stables. Two years earlier Lucy had triumphed in Hilary's superb *Wolf Lullaby*, which has subsequently been produced in Paris, London, New York and by the Steppenwolf Company in Chicago.

*The Falls* is about lies, deceit, self-deceit and fraud, and ties together a number of famous historical hoaxes. Every good play is autobiographical, and underlying *The Falls* is Hilary's abiding concern: 'Unless I tell myself I'm a brilliant writer, I can't get up in the morning.' This is not self-deceit; it's the humble integrity that makes Hilary's art so affecting. To work with *both* of them on the one project was three months of unalloyed bliss, pride and gratitude. One of the highs of my life.

*The Falls* marked a happy return in 2000 to the original Nimrod site and it aspirations. But back in 1984, I was determined never to run a theatre company again. Fourteen years in harness at Nimrod had worn me out; the political squabbles within the theatre, the continuing financial crises, the ongoing battles with funding bodies, the sheer effort to find and produce a dozen plays each year, every year, as well as direct and act in several of them—all this had left me dried up, exhausted and disenchanted. So, by 1985 I had left Nimrod and found myself freelancing as an actor and director again—my time and my life were my own and I found I could double my income.

My career took an unexpected turn when impresario John Frost rang me to ask if I would be interested in being in a musical. I told him I'd never been in a musical and couldn't sing or dance to save my life. But he was quite insistent: 'It's more of an acting role,' he said, 'you can almost *talk* the songs.' The musical was called *Big River* and was based on one of my favourite childhood books, *Huckleberry Finn*.

I bowled up to meet the director, young New Yorker Michael Greif, who I liked immediately. The music by Roger Miller was a clever mix of bluegrass, gospel and Dixieland, and I faked my way through it with a lot of help from the musical director. My dancing was less successful and had the choreographer doubled over, in pain and laughter alternately. So I just grinned and waved my hands a lot, to distract. My partner was one-time protégé and old buddy Drew Forsythe. We played a couple of con men on the run. They called themselves the King and the Duke and had some lively song-and-dance routines. We shared the stage with the appealing young Cameron Daddo, playing his first big stage role, and a team of black Americans with rich, thrilling voices. I stayed with the show for nine months and enjoyed every minute of it, tingling with excitement each night behind the curtain when the pit band struck up the overture.

Anna and I had bought shares in the new Company B at the Nimrod, now renamed the Belvoir Street Theatre. Neil Armfield invited me back there to play Prospero in *The Tempest* and Pastor Manders in *Ghosts*. I've never been crazy about acting in Ibsen; I always feel like a mouthpiece for his attitudes rather than a human being. Manders was quite enjoyable, but the part is almost too much of a caricature. I preferred Judge Brack, which I played for the Melbourne Theatre Company with Helen Morse as Hedda Gabler and Peter Carroll as her husband. Brack has a touch of complexity and ambivalence about him; Manders is little more than the expression of Ibsen's loathing of the Church's hypocrisy and repression.

*The Tempest*, on the other hand, was a joy to be in—
a thoroughly satisfying production. The stage floor was deep
in sand, with a simple white curtain at the back. Prospero
looked like an old beachcomber in his ragged clothes and
wildly overgrown hair and beard. Gillian Jones was a
detached, pained and ethereal Ariel, Max Cullen a sullen,
sly Caliban filled with inarticulate fury. Alan John's music
score for string instruments expressed the freedom and
lightness that characterised the production. Jennie Tate's
sea-stained costumes were beautifully appropriate.

I played Prospero again in 1997 for Bell Shakespeare
with Jim Sharman directing. This time Paula Arundell
played Ariel as a sexy, endearing Girl Friday to the ageing
magus. It was easy for me to see her as the muse and inspiration for a lonely old man . . .

Prospero loves extravagantly and is nearly always disappointed when his love is not reciprocated. His love of
both Antonio and Caliban has been betrayed, and Ariel
cannot return his love. He must lose his beloved daughter
Miranda to Ferdinand. He imposes love on people. They
can't cope with the burden of it. He expects too much and
tries to bully, to demand love and loyalty. His way of creating an emotional bond is always that of the martinet,
schoolmaster, taskmaster.

Prospero has neglected his duties to pursue his studies.
He is consumed by his 'Art'. What is his Art? It sounds like
nuclear physics ('the strong based promontory have I made
shake') or black magic ('Graves at my command have
opened'); but it also takes in theatre, music, pageantry and
spectacle. When he says 'This rough magic I here abjure',
it sounds like Galileo's recantation, or Einstein or Oppen-

heimer after Hiroshima. He seems to reject pagan science for something closer to Christian orthodoxy.

And my ending is despair,
Unless I be relieved by prayer,
Which pierces so that it assaults
Mercy itself and frees all faults.

But the 'revels now are ended' speech is closer to a Buddhist concept of dissolution into chaos and cyclical rebirth—it is not a Christian speech.

Our revels now are ended. These our actors,
As I foretold you, were all spirits and
Are melted into air, into thin air;
And, like the baseless fabric of this vision,
The cloud-capped towers, the gorgeous palaces,
The solemn temples, the great globe itself,
Yes, all which it inherit, shall dissolve
And, like this insubstantial pageant faded,
Leave not a rack behind. We are such stuff
As dreams are made on, and our little life
Is rounded with a sleep.

He has to let go of his inspiration (Ariel) at the end, but he'll never shake off Caliban ('This thing of darkness I acknowledge mine'). I felt that in his isolation he shouldn't touch anybody except Miranda (a little too much perhaps?).

While rehearsing *The Tempest* it struck me how the play is full of references to imprisonment versus freedom: Caliban is kept in a cave; Ariel was imprisoned in a pine; Prospero threatens to pin him in an oak; the mariners are locked under hatches; the comic plotters are trapped in a bog; the evil plotters are trapped in a spell; Ferdinand is made a slave; Caliban enslaves himself to Stephano and Trinculo, while singing of freedom; Prospero and Miranda were prisoners on a leaky boat and are now trapped on an island.

How often does Prospero refer to his 'cell'? Even before the play begins Prospero imprisons himself in his library. His last words in the play are: 'Set me free.'

Like Hamlet, there is something enigmatic about Prospero. Is this because the role is so autobiographical? Whence his rage, his melancholy?

Prospero plays at being God in his punishing, judging, forgiving his enemies. He realises his own mortality and that he has wasted his life, alienated or lost those he loved. He realises how far short his 'rough magic' falls of 'heavenly music'. Shakespeare is obsessed with the fragility of life, the transience of beauty, the brevity of love.

It was with mixed feelings that I had trod the boards again at Nimrod—now the Belvoir Street Theatre. Memories had flooded back—both painful and exhilarating. I was glad that *Ghosts* and *The Tempest* were both popular and artistic successes that vindicated my return. I was proud to see the venue still operating successfully. Whatever else we achieved, Ken, Lilian, Anna, myself and others had bequeathed Sydney two new theatre spaces (the Stables and the Belvoir) which we'd helped build with our bare hands. Most of all, the Nimrod years had taught me lessons that would be invaluable in my next incarnation as an actor-manager.

# Manning Clark's
# History of
# Australia,
# The Musical

I 988 was Australia's Bicentenary and all sorts of celebra-
tory events were in the pipeline. In mid 1987 I was
approached by Melbourne mate Tim Robertson, who had
written and performed in a rather anarchic version of *Tristram Shandy* I had done at the Nimrod in 1982. For four
years he'd been working on a stage version of one of the
icons of Australian literature—Manning Clark's *History of
Australia* (Volumes I–VI). Only someone as brilliant and
perverse as Tim could even think of such an idea (who else
would have dreamed of staging *Tristram Shandy*?). It was
so outrageous, so impossible, that I leapt at it . . .

I very rarely keep a diary but when I started working
on *Manning Clark's History of Australia, The Musical*
I decided to keep some daily jottings for interest's sake. I
describe the whole saga here in some detail because it docu-
ments the challenges in mounting a new work of any scale

and because the whole episode was such a glorious and—
to me—significant 'failure' . . .

Tim had been working on the project with another brilliant mind—Don Watson, the historian who was soon to
come to prominence as Paul Keating's speechwriter. Along
the way they had taken John Romeril on board as co-writer
and had got a script together. They also had some music
by George Dreyfus, set designer Shaun Gurton, costume
designer Annie Marshall and producer John Timlin. They
were looking to get the show up for 1988 and wanted to
know if I was interested in either playing Manning Clark
or directing it. I couldn't see myself in the role, but the idea
of directing it really grabbed me. The question was how to
do it—on what scale, in what form, and how to make it
commercially viable?

We decided to conduct a workshop on what there was
of the script and I brought in Dennis Watkins to assist and
advise, because he was someone with a nose for popular
taste. Given the scope of the work, the daunting aspect was
that, stylistically, the script belonged to that raffish, almost
undergraduate mode of theatre—erudite and irreverent—
that would go down very well at Nimrod or the Pram
Factory, but wouldn't attract the coach parties from the
suburbs. Yet to get it on at all required a big investment.
Our choices seemed to be keep it small and rough, or think
big and turn it into a popular musical.

Dennis Watkins persuaded us to go for the second
option. George Dreyfus's music was not my idea of popular musical material so we brought in Martin Armiger and
later David King, who'd had years of experience conducting the big commercial musicals and composing a lot for
theatre.

The almost insoluble problem was the book—how to fit six volumes of Manning's history of Australia into a two-and-a-half-hour musical along with the ideas and commentary of Manning Clark. Given the amount of stage time taken by song and dance, the book had to be kept fairly minimal and the lyrics simple enough to be comprehensible at first hearing.

With the number of characters to be fitted in, every song tended to be of the 'Oh me name it is Ned Kelly' variety and characters tended to introduce themselves and be off again before you had a chance to know or care much about them. Moreover, Don and Tim, in their charmingly perverse way, tended to highlight some of the lesser-known figures of Australian history rather than the predictable icons. So a good deal of time was devoted to Frank the Poet (the first recorded Irish convict versifier), Quong Tart (the Chinese merchant who got around in a Scottish kilt), Louisa Lawson (Henry's mother) and Joe Byrne of the Kelly Gang, rather than Ned himself. Any one of their stories was sufficient material for a play or musical, so to try and cram the whole lot into one evening seemed virtually impossible.

As Dennis pointed out, if you're going to do a musical in the traditional sense, there are a couple of indispensable ingredients: you need a hero or heroine with whom you can empathise, whose journey you go on. You need a love story. You need a few good thumping tunes you can reprise occasionally, and you need lyrics that might be clever but can't afford to be too highfalutin. (As it turned out, the lyrics tended to be brilliant but too clever by half. Don in particular was averse to dumbing them down.)

So we decided to make Manning himself the hero of the story. His journey would be his quest to tell the story of Australia and understand its meaning.

> I want to write the final chapter
> I want to be there ever after
> I want to drink the living water
> When at last we understand this history of ours

The love interest would be the romance between Manning and his devoted, supportive wife Dymphna, whom he met while an undergrad at Oxford.

Many different formats were presented, worked on and finally rejected. I was unhappy with the device for Act I, which showed early Australian history, or infancy, being done as a kid's play with Manning and his school friends performing it. I thought it was too cute. It infantilised the colonisation story and presented huge stylistic problems, such as how to stage a really sophisticated song and dance number or utilise professional design, lighting and musical complexity, while retaining schoolyard naivety.

Another proposed opening was to have Manning present at Kristallnacht in Germany, shocked by the barbarity into questioning 'the meaning of it all'. Or else open with Manning at his favourite fishing spot, communing with his dead poet mate David Campbell. Or watering the garden of his suburban bungalow, and a car pulls up with Ned Kelly, Captain Cook, Nellie Melba and Billy Hughes. Manning asks them in for a drink and the history kicks off. This last idea came closest to what the show needed—not a sequential re-enactment of historical events, but a dreamscape where iconic figures from different eras could intermingle, argue, tell their stories and express contrary points of view.

Philip Quast (centre) as Candide, Seymour Centre.

John Bell as Lear and Judy Davis as the Fool in *King Lear*, Nimrod, 1984.

As Judge Brack, with Helen Morse as Hedda Gabler, Melbourne Theatre Company.
*(Photo Jeff Busby)*

Tony Gilbert, the beloved godfather of the Bell Shakespeare Company, and feisty chairperson, Virginia Henderson. *(Photo Anna Volska)*

Launching the Bell Shakespeare Company in 1991. Left to right: Michael Scott Mitchell, Paul Bishop, Susie Dogherty, Marco Chiappi, Simon Arlidge, Marian Dvorakovsky, Carol Woodrow, Susan Lyons, John Polson, John Adam, James Wardlaw. Anna is in front, I'm at the mike.

Directing *Hamlet*, Bell Shakespeare Company, 1991.

As Richard III, with Sean O'Shea as Tyrell, Bell Shakespeare Company, 1992.
*(Photo Sesh Raman)*

As Shylock, *The Merchant of Venice*, Bell Shakespeare Company, 1991. *(Photo Branco Gaica)*

The Bell Shakespeare Company actors in 1994 (*Macbeth* and *The Taming of the Shrew*): standing centre, Sean O'Shea; back row, Simon Arlidge, Dmitri Psiropolis, Chris Stollery; third row, David Fenton, Daniel Lapaine, Gary Cooper; second row, Achilles Lavidis, Heather Bolton, Brandon Burke, James Wardlaw, Grant Bowle and me on the end; front row, Patrick Dickson, Anna Volska, Tammy McCarthy, Marian Dvorakovsky, Essie Davis. *(Photo Branco Gaica)*

The Macbeths
at home, 1994.
*(Photo Adam Knott)*

As Malvolio, with Lucy as Viola, in *Twelfth Night*, Bell Shakespeare Company, 1995.
*(Photo Branco Gaica)*

Hilary and Lottie watch a rehearsal.

With Mum on her eightieth birthday.

One of the most successful sequences in the finished show was set in a mythical outback pub. The drinkers included Daniel Mannix, Melba, Tom Roberts and Ned Kelly. This 'figures in a landscape' concept allowed more imaginative freedom and evoked more resonances than a sequential narrative.

But we were still tearing out our hair as to what we could afford to omit. The more we looked into it the more stories there were to tell, the more fascinating characters kept popping up. Apart from anything else, working on the project was a wonderful education in Australian history. I was shocked to discover how little I knew.

The final format agreed upon, we opened with an ensemble number representing all the explorers, prior to Cook, who had touched on the Great South Land—the Chinese, the Dutch, the Spanish. Cook, Joseph Banks and company paid tribute to the Enlightenment and then, ironically, we were plunged into the abyss of the transport hulks, the Irish convicts, the Flogging Parson and the miseries and deprivations of the early colony. This was thankfully not presented in tragic mode but through stirring rock music (courtesy of Armiger) and exuberant pantomime.

The following scenes included a lively rhumba led by Willy Wentworth, the Gold Rush, Henry Parkes and Federation, the Kelly Gang's last stand, Louisa Lawson's campaign for women's rights, Henry Lawson touring the country with Melba and Tom Roberts, Billy Hughes and the conscription campaign, Gallipoli and, as a grand finale, the opening of the Palais de Danse at St Kilda, where the devil danced with Samuel Marsden, Ned Kelly with Queen Victoria, the Unknown Soldier with Billy Hughes, and so on, in a dance of celebration and reconciliation. Interspersed with the historical vignettes were episodes in the life journey of Manning and Dymphna as they strove to unravel and comprehend the events happening around them.

I kept a rough diary part of the time, except when things got too fraught.

### Melbourne

*I told the company on day one of the workshop that the whole point of the exercise was to test the product, to decide whether or not we had the makings of a commercial musical on our hands. I had chosen some people from Sydney, but most were locals to cut down the costs. The Australian Bicentennial Authority (ABA) had shown scant interest in the project but put $2000 towards the workshop.*

*We worked in a church hall off Parkville for two weeks, Monday to Friday 10 am to 5.30 pm. We had three rooms to work in: in Room I the actors learned songs, in Room II actors worked on the text, while in Room III the three writers and their helpers rewrote, cut-and-pasted and provided us with new material.*

*The amount achieved in the two weeks was phenomenal and the actors were inventive, especially Bill Garner, Terry Bader and Rob Meldrum. Chris Harriot was very helpful with the music—at least when working with Martin.*

*By the end of workshop we had cut and reshaped the piece considerably and Martin had provided four new songs. We had a showing on the last Friday for about 100 backers, investors and nabobs like the fence-sitters from the ABA. The hour's presentation went down well, the actors performing valiantly, especially Tyrone Landau at the piano—he has proved himself a gem over the two weeks. It was great to have Manning and Dymphna there and we all felt in high spirits when it was over. We decided to proceed with plans for a production and put our heads together next day to consider the feedback. We decided the show should be two acts, not three, and it would be much more of a musical—cut dialogue or turn it into libretto. Manning's part needs building so that we understand the passion that drove him to write the history, as well as the enormous sacrifices and effort he had made.*

*Romeril spent many hours sticking sheets of paper round the hall with all sorts of cryptic guidelines, mottos and ideological pointers.*

*While in Canberra with* Emerald City *I rang Manning and he invited Anna and me to Sunday lunch. Manning and Dymphna pottered around hospitably. Lunch was basic and homely and it was a treat to see Manning's study (or rather attic at the top of a vertical ladder—Robin Boyd had tacked on the study as an afterthought). I marvelled at the layout of steel-nib pens with which he had written the six mighty volumes.*

*Some good things came out of the conversation—Manning stressing how much he had travelled to write the history—not just all over Australia but England and Ireland as well, saying that basically what he wanted to do was tell a story, and how hard that was to do. Under some interrogation from me Dymphna admitted that parts of the book made her angry and that if she had been writing it, it would have been from a woman's point of view. She was at pains to say she'd had no part in the work and he was at pains to acknowledge her contribution and support. They drove us home, he wearing his ubiquitous Akubra, and then chugged off into the grey Canberra twilight.*

***Meetings: Melbourne, 21 and 22 July at John Timlin's
Almost Managing office***

*We decided to bring in David King as musical director and
musical collaborator, ie third composer. He and I met with
the writers, Timlin and Martin Armiger. All went well. Then
George Dreyfus arrived. David clearly and simply sketched
out what he thought about the show and how he saw his
job as MD. But there was a right old blowup between
David and George and I thought we'd lost David then and
there. George left, and David went for a walk round the
block to cool down and think it over. I said to the others,
'I think we've lost him—let's try to get him back.' So Tim
and I had dinner with him and took him to see Nine, a
lacklustre production but David was in good spirits at the
end of the evening. Tim and I had spent all our time re-
assuring him and he rang Timlin two days later to say he'd
take it on. Phew!*

*That means David and Martin working round the piano
with the writers, cutting text and putting a lot more of it
to music. David can orchestrate and arrange Martin's music
but George won't let a bar of his stuff be touched. So we'll
just settle for the few bits we've got from him. Pity, because
some of his stuff like 'Reedy River' is good.*

*Talks with Shaun Gurton resulted in a starcloth, a desert
floor and a gantry or crane that flies in and out. I like simplicity but am wary about monotony, lack of flexibility and
also the mechanical and engineering expertise to utilise the
gantry properly . . . But it's a start.*

***1 August 1987, back in Sydney***
*We must create half a dozen scenes in this show that are
breathtakingly beautiful. Went to Nielsen Park this after-*

noon and watched the boats on the water. There's an opening number! Sydney Harbour ... the brilliant impact of
light on water, the sun, the big sky and the marvellous mess
of boats, sails big-bellied, then tacking about and coming
at you head-on.

'Reedy River' should be redolent of Roberts and Streeton—
Golden Summer. There must be a stark and bitter beauty
too, the beauty of ugliness—Gallipoli, the Depression (see
Blackman and the war artists).

Talked to Shaun tonight. He hasn't done much since our
last talk. I told him how I'd like at least two gantries rather
than just one ...

Dave King rang me and is anxious about tying all the
music together in a particular style. He thinks at the
moment it lacks character. 'Anyone could have written it.'
I'm encouraging Martin to cooperate with him as fully as
possible.

We need a motorbike, a Baby Austin, an FJ Holden and
the Endeavour. How? Pedal-cars maybe.

### 4 August

The set Shaun and I have gotten so far solves a number of
problems, but basically it doesn't mean anything—just a
starcloth, a raked desert floor, a gantry or two, a couple of
trucks, a few swings, maybe a couple of traps. All this provides some acting spaces and some nifty exits and entrances
but what does it amount to? What is the metaphor? You
look at it and what does it mean? Nothing yet ... unless a
set has a wholeness about it, an image, it cannot be beautiful. And until I know what that reference point is, what is
the motor image for the whole show, I can't make any of
it work.

*I've suggested Sylvia Jansen for the poster and insisted on the title being* Manning Clark's History of Australia, The Musical—*at least they'll know what they're coming to see.*

### 5 August

*I'm worried about how heavy those gantries will be and how limited in what they can do. I'm also very worried about a set that I can't get to rehearse on until production week.*

### 8 August, Melbourne

*Three good days with Shaun talking set. We considered setting the whole piece in a library but finally hit on a couple of tall mobile towers and some trucks, all pushed around by the actors. This is flexible, I can adapt it even to last minute changes in the script and I'm not too dependent on machinery, which is expensive, time-consuming and often unreliable.*

### 9 August

*Casting. Spent a couple of hours with Geoff Rush yesterday, playing him the music and gently enthusing him about the project. He'd be a good Manning—eccentric, unpredictable, inventive and flamboyant. The last thing the part can afford is a stitched-up pomposity. Needs to be . . . Quixotic.*

*Keen for Nancye Hayes, John Biggins, Valerie Bader and Terry Bader too. Tomorrow I start auditioning in Sydney— over 100 in the next three days.*

*Three days of auditions and three of callbacks. Max Lambert (very good bedside manner) at the piano. He can play almost anything and we were polite to everyone.*

*A lot of Aboriginal performers had their names down
but it seems they've decided to boycott it.*

*Could cast the show twice over in Sydney; slim pickings
in Melbourne. Timlin will be hopping mad about the living
allowances. Have written to Ivar Kants in LA offering the
role of Manning.*

### 24 August

*Rang Timlin with offers on all sixteen in the cast.*

### 25 August

*Don and Tim arrived in a towering rage about Sylvia
Jansen's poster—their opinion was that it was 'circus-like—
a travesty, everything they'd wanted to avoid, every
Australian cliché'. They rampaged around a while and
couldn't be placated . . . I think it will be fine—huge and
full-colour and yes, pretty populist. But I think we're going
to have to pull out every stop to sell this show—an eso-
teric poster is the last thing we need. [We eventually had a
different poster—I forget who by, but I hated it.]*

*They sat and drank coffee and fumed and rejected all
the work we'd done yesterday. They had stewed all night
and no longer wanted the opening they'd devised—the cast
doing a ghastly foxtrot, with Manning, up a tower, shining
a spotlight over them.*

*So we spent most of the day reworking that bloody first
scene AGAIN! I went off to see Peter Sara of the ABA and
agreed to go to Melbourne to launch* History *as part of the
Bicentennial. We're hoping the ABA will cough up a sub-
stantial amount to help with the touring costs.*

When I got back Don, Tim and I ploughed through Act I, cutting and reshaping. Romeril had slipped a lot of his own stuff back in on floppy disc, so we cut it out again.

Timlin rang to say that things look like coming to a head with George; he wants to come in and take over as MD for part of the rehearsal period; I won't have it.

First half looking reasonably okay. Second half still about twenty pages too long and will need heavy pruning.

### Wednesday 26 August, Sydney

Got my daughter Hilary a dogsbody job on the show so she can watch rehearsals and trace the show's development. She's keen on writing musicals.

Took her to Dave King's this morning and he played us an idea for the opening of the London scene—five-part harmonies and Christ knows what. Hilly's eyes shone and she told me later in the Pandora pie shop, where she's working, that she was INSPIRED . . . I'm thrilled.

Don and Tim look a bit nonplussed but appreciate a new discipline. Dave asks them to articulate exactly what each song is about, jots down the points, decides how many lines of lyric are needed to express the ideas, allocates a dummy lyric and gets them to rewrite. Then we read each scene, time it, cut every extraneous word and line, time it again and calculate how long a scene will run with music. So far it's just over one minute per page—so, more cuts ahead.

### Thursday 27 August

Don and Tim pretty tense today, gritted teeth about more cuts and the translation of arcane phrases. Erudite Don just couldn't believe that if you sang very fast the phrase 'Broach a cask of porter', the audience wouldn't under-

*stand it; 'Open a barrel of wine' he thought just too banal. Dennis Watkins is a cheery soul and a conciliatory presence—I'm glad I have him as my assistant director.*

*Dropped in to see Hilly at the pie shop again and was distressed to see her working so flat out and entirely on her own till 9.30 pm. Oxford Street, Darlinghurst, can turn nasty at night—not safe for a young girl alone in a shop.*

### Friday 28 August, Melbourne

*Had to fly to Melbourne for the ABA launch—a drab affair but lots of press and TV people (looking pretty bored). I did a big pitch for the show and thanked the ABA for their $45 000 and told them we needed another half a million to get the show outside Victoria (lots of nervous laughter). Timlin and I gently monstered Sara afterwards, hoping more dough would be forthcoming, but I suspect Sara only got us there to give the ABA something to show off.*

*Timlin threw lots of figures at me and is genuinely worried about getting the show on in Sydney. On present budget, even at 80 per cent capacity, it loses close on $490 000.*

### Monday 31 August

*Big drama. George Dreyfus has produced a letter of agreement and insists there must be no more than two composers on the show. Impossible. David has already written a lot and he and Martin are collaborating well. Timlin and the others are in a lather but they'll simply have to come up with some formula like 'Additional Music By . . .'. I told David that if he goes, I go, and I told Timlin the same. They don't realise that the MD is the director's right hand, more crucial than the designer.*

### 1–4 September

*Due to the delay in offering contracts, we're losing quite a few of our first-choice cast to other productions. Worked hard on the phone wooing Ivar Kants, Michelle Fawdon, Linda Nagle, Tina Bursill, John McTiernan, Bob Hornery and others. All wanting to know 'How many good parts do I get, how many solo spots?' Put lots of offers out to second choices.*

*Timlin going berserk about the Sydney figures. It looks as if we can't afford to play at all. The Australian Elizabethan Theatre Trust is charging us $55 000 a week for the Maj in Sydney, compared to $19 000 a week for the Princess, or $9500 for the Seymour Centre. I suggested to Timlin that we play outside Sydney, maybe the new theatre at Parramatta.*

*Meeting with Scandred and Co. to plan and budget the sound design. Shaun has done bugger-all on the set (still doing five jobs at once).*

*Did an enormous amount of work on Act I and half of Act II with Tim, Don, Martin and David. No sign of George. Romeril keeping a low profile—just as well, really. I like Romeril enormously, such a sweet, generous nature—but the kitchen's getting a bit crowded with cooks.*

*It's a funny situation whenever I walk into a script meeting now—you've got to be very quick to work out whose turn it is to feel insecure and chuck a wobbly. Yesterday it was Martin's turn. He'd just seen* Rasputin *which he said was lousy but full of pop stars who got a warm reception from the teeny-boppers. So he suddenly starts on about our production being too 'safe' and where are the pop stars? Well, with a title like ours, 'safe' is one thing it's not, and it's going to need the most adroit and expert cast we can*

muster to save it from going down the gurgler. I pointed
out to Martin (and to Don and Tim who were in glum
agreement with him) that the pop stars he named can't act
for nuts and our show is not Rasputin. After a while he
calmed down but I am constantly amazed at the emotional
tangents people go off on. As Sondheim said, the hardest
thing is to get all your collaborators round a table and agree
what show you're writing. It's an exercise we're having to
perform about three times a week!

Anyway we cut about 20 more pages of Act II, totally
rewrote the Gold Rush, Eureka, all the Louise Lawson
stuff, rearranged the entire sequence of events in Act II.
I left Melbourne feeling wrung out but happy with two
days' productive work ... Timlin looked a bit happier by
the end of the day and turned on French champagne. I do
enjoy the Melbourne camaraderie and generosity. Its down
side is dogged old-mate loyalty and ideological stubborn-
ness. Very tribal. I hope I've convinced Timlin to take on
Annie Hoban as stage manager. She'd be invaluable. And
I'm pleased Martin is weighing in with so many good ideas
about dramatic structure. David King is pure gold—his
presence has galvanised the whole proceedings ... We
might have a musical on our hands.

Anna came to Melbourne with me and had a couple of
good days—it was wonderful to have her there.


### 10 September, Sydney

It all seems cast except for our producers making the frightful gaffe of telling the agents we're rehearsing in Sydney
now (because it's cheaper) before they told me or before
they'd checked on the actors' availability. So John McTiernan (for one) is working at the MTC for the first three

weeks of our rehearsals, and since I want him and Shana-
hans regard the offer as binding, he'll have to be flown to
Sydney and back two or three times a week!

Nor had our producers considered the making of set and
costumes in the same town where the actors will be. Thank
God Annie Hoban's on board as stage manager. Hope she
can prevent future cock-ups.

### 26 November

Shaun now six weeks late with model and working draw-
ings—and I'm dissatisfied with the finish and lack of detail.

### Rehearsals Week Two: 3 December

Peter Kenna's funeral this afternoon. Lacklustre service but
a good turn-up and Nick Enright gave a fine eulogy. I
couldn't bring myself to mouth any of the nonsense prais-
ing the Lord and glorying in the Life to Come.

Worked on Heaven and Hell all morning (ironically) and
it started to come good when played very seriously—the
Irishman's fantasy of eternal reward for his suffering here
below. Bob Hornery very moved by the biog of his
character, Frank (the poet) McNamarra. You can see Goat
Island from the rehearsal room—the real Frank was
chained up there for months on end in the open air.

### 7 December

Into week three and a lot of the show now blocked and
choreographed. Not much time for the acting yet—have to
keep discouraging them from caricature. Not everyone's a
hero—keep the gold-diggers predatory, not heroic. Keep
Dave King away from the beautifully sung chorale; hit
those strine vowels harder.

*Company morale is very high despite chaos and confusion in management. People in wardrobe haven't been paid for up to three weeks and work in horrendous conditions. Publicity and bookings all in hopeless disarray. They've stuffed up the Qantas deal.*

### Showing on 18 Friday

*Showing for about 90 industry people—Meg Fink, Nancye Hayes, Sheldon, Tony Taylor, Gillies, Ed Campion, Martin Portus etc., Manning and Dymphna too, a nice surprise. Cast all shitting themselves understandably. Pretty good, if nervy, run and it soon became clear where the dull bits are.*

*After lunch about half the audience stayed on for feedback time and took their role very seriously. Anna one of the most vocal and sensible. Decided to cut (as a result of the showing) Ivar's big number at the end of Act I, big nips in the rhumba, the Irish sequences, and rethink Federation completely. We cut ten minutes of Act I (at least five more must go) and ten from Act II.*

*Stopped rehearsals lunchtime Xmas Eve with Bob Hornery as Santa Claus doing the Grab Bag. Morale high and four days off will recharge my batteries.*

### 1 January 1988

*Have really overhauled all of Act I, putting Manning into centre of every scene rather than watching from the sidelines. He is now pivotal and either initiates all the action or is affected by it. Changed the end yet again. No-one wants the Palais de Danse but I'm sure it's the right ending.*

*Now the Kelly scene looks bad again—the song has nothing to do with the rewritten dialogue. So I've asked*

*Martin to come up with new lyrics by tomorrow—the three writers have shot through: Don to Tasmania, Romeril to Thailand and Tim to Violet Town. So Martin has to write it. It should be a simple rock lyric: 'When You're a Jet' sort of thing.*

*Dress parade tomorrow and I'm dreading it. Only about half the stuff is ready and I think they may have made some disastrous fabric choices. It will be a revelation—for better or worse. The props are appallingly badly made and we've had to cut or remake most of them. Gearing up for production week and move to Melbourne.*

*Had a really pleasant little New Year's Eve party at home—twelve people, candlelight, champagne. Fred and Ginger music.*

*Quiet sunny day today and at 5 pm will go to Centennial Park for opening of the new Pavilion and Beethoven's Ninth at sunset. I'm looking forward to a great 1988 . . .*

*It pissed with rain and the orchestra packed up after the first movement. It somehow seemed right and exhilarating . . . you had to laugh—it was so Australian.*

### Saturday
*Dress parade went better than I expected. What there is looks pretty exciting and some of the fabric choices are really witty. Not brilliantly made but the men's tailoring is terrific. Props on the other hand are shithouse. The Explorers' banners the latest disaster. Scrap them.*

### Bump-in: 4–15 January
*Nightmare bump-in. Took days longer than it should have, everybody busy blaming everybody else. The overtime*

*wages for the first week were $40 000. Set wouldn't fit in the wings, stuff was too heavy to fly and when Ned Kelly's FJ Holden finally arrived it was too small for him to get into! Production manager McGill and Shaun shrugged, and Shaun said, 'Oh well, he'll just have to walk behind ...' Like hell he will! 'Stick on a running board! He can at least ride shotgun!' I fumed ... (Actually it gives Ned a better entrance.)*

*Another choice moment was when the whole bloody set was finally up in time for the first preview, and a team of workmen arrived and announced cheerfully, 'We've just come to pull down your set—it hasn't been fireproofed.' I rushed around and found McGill—it had been fire-proofed, he'd just stuck the wrong labels on everything.*

*We couldn't have the corrugated iron wall for Ned Kelly because it was so heavy it took six stage-hands to fly it and was dangerous. I got them to knock off the top seven panels so we got it for opening night. Nigel [Levings] got no time to light the show so had to plot it blind on computer and adjust during the preview.*

*Wardrobe frantic all week. Anna [Volska] volunteered her services and they got in a lot of extra help. Finally the costumes look terrific. Annie Marshall is a crash-hot designer.*

*Previews went well. No major cock-ups. Stifling heat, no air-conditioning. Big audiences, good response.*

*First night packed to the rafters, Bob Hawke and John Cain were there with Manning and Dymphna. Response pretty tumultuous.*

*Stretch limos to Town Hall for party. Hawke and Manning made speeches and Manning cut the giant Akubra cake. Huge crush and deafening rock band. Couldn't hear myself shriek over the din and left early.*

### Monday 18 January
*Reviews are just out and are devastating. Don rang me, pretty shaky, sniffing 'conspiracy'. Might be in for a short season.*

### Tuesday
*Spent most of last two days discussing strategies with Timlin. If we can survive two weeks we can get into Sydney. Airwaves running hot with Clarke Forbes (the Sun) and Leonard Radic (the Age) rubbishing the show. Timlin taking them on. Good stuff. But box office appalling. We're cancelling Saturday matinee and next Monday and Tuesday because of triple time holiday loading, and both matinees next week. Last night's house small but very warm. Leigh Davis sent two crates of champagne backstage, so Don and I chewed the fat with the cast until 3.30 am. Cast very emotional and supportive and keen to keep hacking away.*

*I'll go in today and cut the Gallipoli sequence, trim Hell a lot, restage 'Nance the Ferrett', find a new segue into the finale and do a new curtain call reprising 'Sons of the South'. May be only cosmetic changes. Perhaps the real problems lie much deeper. Press on.*

### Thursday
*Up until 2 am last three nights, reworking the show. Bookings nil. We've lost $1 million and are losing $80 000 a week.*

## 6 February

*Press onslaught continues—largely political: the* Sun's *Clarke Forbes calls it 'left wing cant spewing over the footlights'; the* Herald's *economics writer, Terry McCrann, prays for the demise of this show by 'left wing intelligentsia'.*

*Hoyts have said they'll bankroll the show into Sydney.*

## Thursday night

*Timlin called. 'We close Saturday. Hoyts have done their figures again and won't back us.'*

## Friday night

*I'm in Sydney, rehearsing* Ghosts *at Belvoir.*

*11 pm Hilly rang from Melbourne to say the show had been packed, people queueing for tickets, huge response. The actors took their curtain calls and went to their dressing rooms to change but were called back on to find the house lights up and the whole house standing, clapping, shouting for encores. Cast wept. During the show the crew made a formal offer to work for nothing next week to keep the show on. Front of house staff and musicians follow suit. Unheard of!*

## Saturday

*Very good matinee and evening show packed again and another standing ovation—the whole house, prolonged cheering. The lyric 'It's knockers that we hate' drew prolonged applause, cheers and laughter.*

*Manning and Dymphna were there again with family. Ivar made an emotional curtain call speech, thanking the staff and crew (another standing ovation just for them). He*

thanked Hoyts for paying for next week's ads and Mariner
for giving us the theatre for free.

I asked the crew why they'd made their generous offer
and they replied, 'Because it's an Australian show and we
want it to work.'

There is also an extraordinary degree of fraternisation
between cast, musos and crew. The Princess is not blessed
with an after-show bar, so the crew run their own bar in
the basement. The cast and band stay back and drink every
night. This wonderful architectural oversight has meant
great camaraderie and egalitarianism. 'No prima donnas in
this show,' the crew remarked. A very heady night. I was
thrilled that Anna was with me and we shared this remarkable experience—an extraordinary ovation. I went over to
Manning at the interval and said, 'Do you believe in the
Resurrection?' He clasped my hands and murmured, 'I have
a shy hope.' The cast wanted me to drive Manning on in
the Baby Austin at the curtain call but I thought that would
have been too cute for words.

The creditors had been in and ripped down all our
posters from front of house, so I scribbled a big one saying
'History has a Future. We are NOT closing tonight. Book
NOW for next week.'

It's only a week's reprieve and it will be hell trying to
keep the cast and band together much longer, but even if
we close next Saturday, the last two nights have been a
total triumph and proved Melbourne has a soul after all.
How I love this bunch of people!


### 13 February

I got the next Friday off Ghosts rehearsals and zipped down
to Melbourne. Worked with Watson and Romeril all Friday

*morning and we came up with a new opening and a new close. We'll put the show into Kinsellas in Sydney if there is a Melbourne turnaround. Timlin a bit tight-lipped about the possibility of losing his agency and going bankrupt while Kinsellas picks up the show.*

*I hear we owe Scandred $60 000 for sound, but Starlight Express owes him $300 000. Timlin drove me home. I stayed at his house and we had a good, long relaxed talk. He was in again next night with Di Gribble and Don with Hilary McPhee AGAIN! Those women sure are loyal, but none more loyal than Anna.*

*I came back to Sydney on Sunday reeling a bit from the strange mix of continuing saga of hate in the press and audience euphoria. Total strangers grasp me after the show or are waving and calling out to me from all over the theatre. An old lady there for the seventh time. The press, TV and radio full of the show's fortunes every day since we opened! Barry Dickins' review ecstatic!*

### Week 5: 15–20 February

*Houses disastrous so far this week . . . about 200 a night and one packed, noisy school matinee. This means we might finish on Saturday. It also means there has been no turnaround—just a flourish of interest from a minority audience.*

*Then again, we did not advertise this week, Bass had no tickets, we had no TV ad, and Hoyts reneged on their offer of newspaper ads. So all we have is one little ad in the Age . . . no way to sell a Big Musical!!*

Working on *History* was one of the most important and
satisfying things I've experienced in theatre and, at times,
one of the happiest.

It brought me into contact with a dedicated, talented
group of people I might never have worked with otherwise.
And we tried to tell the greatest story of them all—the story
of our country and who we are.

There were gaps, of course. There were no Aboriginal
people in the show and scant mention of them. The role of
women in shaping Australia's history was undervalued. But
these are gaps in Manning's original work too, as he later
admitted; and we were, after all, doing Manning Clark's
history through his eyes and inevitably with the perspectives of the time when he was writing.

We couldn't do much to redress the absence of Aboriginal people in his account, but we did try to beef up the
women's contribution, partly through the emphasis on
Louisa Lawson's feminist campaign and also by giving
Dymphna a song where she asks for acknowledgement of
all the people in the shadows, the ones whose stories never
get recorded by the historians.

*History* was a monumental labour of love. It was an
audacious, impossible, foolhardy undertaking. It should
never have tried to be that kind of 'commercial musical';
we should have workshopped it again and again; we should
have had an out-of-town try-out; we should have had at
least a three-month advertising and marketing campaign;
and we shouldn't have opened in a disused derelict theatre
in the middle of a heatwave. Oh yes, there are endless
lessons to be learned. But if I could have another go at it
tomorrow, would I do it? You bet. Because if *History* was
a failure, it was worth a dozen ordinary successes.

With this project and in my acting roles, I was certainly enjoying the sweet breath of freedom and vowed I'd never run another theatre company. Then came an offer I couldn't refuse.

*Part 4*

# THE BELL
# SHAKESPEARE
# COMPANY

# 'You have to start a theatre company'

In 1990 I got a call from my old friend Tony Gilbert, the one whose fan letter I'd responded to when I played Giovanni in *'Tis Pity She's A Whore* at Sydney University in 1961. Fifteen years older than me, bespectacled, tidily groomed and grey-suited, Tony seemed the antithesis of my scruffy self, but a common passion for literature and theatre kept us in touch, and when the Nimrod Theatre was set up in 1970 and we were looking for some worthy citizens to make up a respectable board of directors, I called upon Tony's goodwill and accounting skills. He served the Nimrod board loyally for ten years.

Now, twenty years later, he came to me with a proposition. He had set a little money aside which he said he'd like to see used to promote the cause of Shakespeare. Appalled at the prospect of Shakespeare being phased out of the education curriculum and dissatisfied with both the limited amount of Shakespeare being performed and the general standard of performance, he was willing to put up a bit of money to stop the rot. But he was unsure as to the best course of action—whether to institute some sort of scholarship or finance a conference. My immediate reaction was that the only real answer was to finance Shakespeare in performance, perhaps even establishing a permanent company specialising in the work. 'You have to start a theatre company,' I told him.

'No, no,' Tony replied. '*You* have to start a theatre company!'

Tony had already had a conversation or two with Adam Salzer, the chief executive of the Australian Elizabethan Theatre Trust, and now we went off together to see him. Adam offered to help us by giving me an office space, a phone, a mailing list and some secretarial help to start raising money. Tony's contribution would be the seeding money, but he couldn't be expected to foot the whole bill.

Adam threw himself into the project with zeal and energy. In truth, I think our proposal came at a good time for him. The Trust, established by the federal government in 1953 as the official conduit for funding to arts organisations, had been overtaken by the Australia Council and was searching for a reason to exist. The idea of a Shakespeare company touring all over Australia appealed greatly to Adam's sense of adventure. A board of directors was quickly assembled to oversee the activities of this company as a subsidiary of the Trust. Tony was a director, of course, Adam was chair and I was artistic director. Other directors included Lady Primrose Potter, Dr Rodney Seabourne and Virginia Henderson, whom I met at one of our fundraising lunches, generously provided by Rex Irwin in his Queen Street Gallery, Woollahra.

We quickly set about organising a series of dinners and lunches at which Adam and I enthused about the idea of the company and encouraged people to put their hands in their pockets. Within nine months we had raised our half million dollars. It wasn't quite enough to kick off the first season, but we thought that if we delayed too long the whole thing would lose momentum. I contributed six months of my time without pay, but we did pay one of the Trust's employees, Warwick Ross, to look after finances. I had an office space and some part-time secretarial back-up.

For several reasons we were determined not to go to the state or federal funding authorities to ask for help. There was enough of a dogfight going on already among theatre companies scrounging for money. To have a newcomer enter the field seeking funding of the order we needed would only send the funding agencies into a spin and enrage the rest of the industry. We wanted to attract the goodwill of the industry at large and hopefully demonstrate how much could be achieved without government assistance. Ironically, this stance was read by the funding bodies as arrogance and some kind of snub. That wasn't the intention, although I had been down the miserable path of begging for assistance so often that the thought of not being a mendicant was a blissful one.

The thing I was most keen to pursue was the setting up of an acting ensemble of young performers of various ethnic backgrounds who would bring a fresh energy to performing Shakespeare, as well as a frame of reference that was not merely Anglo-Celtic. I was well aware that our potential audiences, especially school audiences, would be composed of many people from non-English-speaking backgrounds, and I wanted them to feel that this kind of theatre was theirs too. So in the first two years cast names included: Marian Dvorakovski, Marco Chiappi, Carla Aquilia, Dmitri Psiropoulos, Ira Seidenstein and Achilles Lavidis. This concern for a rich ethnic mix was by no means exclusive to our company, but I did pursue it with vigour despite constant criticism that some actors couldn't handle Shakespearean language. But the same was true of actors who had a purely Anglo-Celtic background.

Although my casting in recent seasons has had a greater Anglo-Celtic bias than I would ideally like it to have, I keep trying to redress the balance. This isn't because of political correctness or tokenism; I just find that a racial mix is more exciting to watch and more representational of the society we live in. One frustration is the tiny number of Asian and Australian Aboriginal students coming through our drama schools. Many Asian parents (perhaps prudently) seem to discourage kids from hazarding a life on the stage. Aboriginal students do not apply for entry into drama schools in significant numbers, and those who do enter the profession are often attracted to work with companies specialising in indigenous repertoire.

Problems also arise with the gender imbalance in Shakespeare's plays. The usual mix is something like thirteen men to three women. One can do an exercise in cross-casting, but I often find the result less than satisfactory. So many of the plays are about male power bases from which women are deliberately excluded, and sometimes this point is lost when female actors are allowed to assume the symbols of male authority and play judges, officers, dukes etc. If they are relegated to minor roles and functionaries, tokenism has triumphed again. I hope that we will continue to break down existing conventions and expectations, to evolve a new theatre language in Australia that is colour blind and gender blind. But all these considerations aside, when the show goes on the most important thing is to see sixteen actors up there who, whatever their gender or racial background, are the best possible actors for the play, the most exciting, articulate and accomplished.

A major challenge I set myself and the company was trying to find ways to make 'Australian' Shakespeare. I don't mean a parochial outlook that seeks to play up anachronisms and force local references; I mean to find ways to rescue Shakespeare from the deadly perception that it is a British appendage to Australian culture, that the English do it 'the right way', that there is some kind of tradition in performing Shakespeare that, like the apostolic succession, is sacrosanct.

I am not dismissing or denigrating the heritage of Shakespeare performance in England, which I find a constant source of wonder and admiration. The three years I spent with the RSC was a time of great inspiration and invaluable education.

When I first started acting in the early sixties, there was no doubt about it: English theatre was considered the real thing and the best we colonials could do was to imitate it. That perception has changed over the last twenty years or so. At first it necessitated a bit of obvious vulgarity—broad Aussie accents and corks around the hat—just to break the British grip on the windpipe. But more importantly, we have begun to look at Shakespeare's plays as a fundamental part of Australian cultural life, examining the ways they both shape and reflect our own thoughts and behaviour. Most directors nowadays seek out and attempt to play the political subversion, irony and moral ambiguities in Shakespeare which previous generations ignored.

Australian accents are taboo for some critics and audiences when it comes to playing Shakespeare. They still hanker after the 'proper' Shakespeare sound they've heard so often from the BBC. I agree that there are various problems Australian actors have when it comes to speaking Shakespeare. Accent isn't one of them. If we could hear the voices of the original performers at the Globe, we'd be shocked by the rich but barbarous mix of dialects: cockney, Somerset, Northumbrian and, of course, Shakespeare's own Warwickshire burr as well as a dozen others. There was no such thing as a homogenous London accent—they were still inventing one.

Nor is there one uniform Australian accent. I know at least a dozen, and they vary from state to state, suburb to suburb, job to job. Long regarded as something to be ashamed of and dispensed with as soon as possible, the various Australian accents are in themselves no better or worse than anyone else's. They are simply geographical and sociological indicators, of which people are sometimes self-conscious. I frequently hear an Australian voice that convinces me there is no more pleasant accent in the world— open, relaxed, confident and generous.

Where Australian actors currently have a problem (and it's one they share with their contemporaries through the English-speaking world) is with scale of expression, with the art of rhetoric, with colourful, emotive and sensual speech, an appreciation of the musicality of language. Since the advent of cinema and then television, our actors have been painted further and further into a corner where the blank look and monosyllable are meant to say volumes.

Masters of this ultra-naturalistic style of acting, like Robert de Niro, are regarded as 'good' actors because they are so convincing, and anything stylised or formalised is therefore categorised as bad or 'hammy' because it places itself outside the bounds of naturalism.

Combined with Australians' traditional preference for laconic understatement and unwillingness to display emotional sensitivity, this has led a generation of actors to despise full-blooded declamation. Now the wheel is turning again. There is an awareness that cinematic naturalism is not the only kind of truth. Since the 1970s the impact of directors like Jerzy Grotowski, Tadeusz Kantor, Tadashi Suzuki and Peter Brook has combined with experiments in video and performance art to excite a new generation of actors with alternatives to cinematic naturalism. This has led to a flurry of imitations and our stages have seen an excess of conch shells, chanting and stomping. 'European' is the epithet of approval applied to anything mildly incomprehensible. But these are only growing pains. Inspired by the achievements of major foreign companies on our ever-increasing festival circuit, and the dynamics of a recently developed racially diverse society, Australian actors and directors are beginning to look for theatrical modes that are bolder and richer in expression than are mere reproductions of everyday life.

Today's actor needs not only a lively imagination, but an extraordinarily expressive voice and body as well as the courage to extend him/herself way beyond the demands made by a television camera. At the risk of looking absurd, an actor must seek ever-new ways to penetrate our dulled senses, our pedestrian expectations, our conventional definitions of what is appropriate or 'real'. We cannot shackle

Shakespeare within the narrow confines of our current performance conventions or assessments of what is good taste
or politically correct. We have to stretch ourselves a long
way, physically, vocally and spiritually in our attempt to
embrace the universe he offers us.

So that was the charter I wrote myself in setting up the
Bell Shakespeare Company—a national touring company
of mainly young actors with open minds and unlimited
energy, specialising in performing Shakespeare in productions that seek to relate the plays as closely as possible to
the life experience of audiences young and old, and pro-
claim Shakespeare to be a vital force in contemporary
Australian culture.

# Why
# Shakespeare?

Shakespeare not only had the largest vocabulary of any good English writer, he also had the biggest emotional vocabulary, and his work is a gigantic trove of emotions that, but for him, we might not now still know of, nor feel so keenly even yet. Courtly love. The love, not necessarily homosexual, of man for man. The scalding envenomed love of old lovers when they meet again. The radiant sorrows of kingship. That sense of honour that is worth dying for, by one's own hand. Ambition that will dare all, defying the gods. Young love so strong it must, like Juliet's, end in death. The love of a man like Antony for a dead ally he must cruelly avenge. The desire to howl and curse under bad weather. The welling fear of madness in oneself and others. The guilts that materalise as ghosts over dinner.

And so on. The list is large; he gave us a Sistine-size canvas of emotions that without his word music might now be lost to us, a tonal range of emotional melody we might otherwise be deaf to. It's fair to say I think (and this is not a long bow either) that people unacquainted with Shakespeare live starved and meagre lives.

Some schools would ban him for political incorrectness, but they miss the point, which is that with his great enlargements of those fitful things we sometimes feel— in the cool of the night, in the stirrings of youth, the carps and cussings of age, he maps and enumerates our species as no other.

Bob Ellis, *Sydney Morning Herald*, 6 May 1998

Every time I launch a season or give an interview, journalists are bound to ask 'But why Shakespeare? Why is he important? Is he still relevant?' These questions have become so predictable they have become Dorothy Dixers, but they do prompt me to get my thoughts in order.

The continued popularity of Shakespeare so far beyond that of any other writer is, at first sight, somewhat puzzling. His plays are over four hundred years old; the language in which they were written is largely archaic in its vocabulary and syntax; his writing is studded with references to classical literature, to the Bible, to historical events unfamiliar to the majority of today's population. And yet his plays are now performed more than at any other time, including his own lifetime. They have been translated over and over into many languages and seem to exert a universal appeal. In 1994 I attended the Shanghai Shakespeare Festival where I saw eleven productions in Chinese. On the way home I dropped into Tokyo to see their Globe Theatre and do a workshop with one of Tokyo's four Shakespeare companies.

The cinema has thrived on Shakespeare even before the talkies and television, and directors such as Orson Welles, Olivier, Zefferelli and Kenneth Branagh have delivered whole series of plays from the canon. And that's only in English. The Russian and Japanese cinemas have also notched up a series of Shakespeare masterpieces.

Academia has turned Shakespeare into an industry and the various schools and departments of English literature continue to bombard bookshops with a never-ending avalanche of theory. If you add up the academics, theatre companies, actors, directors, publishers and others hanging on to Shakespeare's coat-tails you understand why Dame Judi Dench respectfully refers to him as 'the gentleman who pays the rent'. Despite years of appalling teaching at both secondary and tertiary level, despite thousands of ghastly or inadequate productions, despite attacks from various ideological camps, Shakespeare is holding his own, even burgeoning in popularity. Why?

At one level he was simply a superb entertainer and storyteller. He rarely bothered to invent plots of his own — that was not required. Audiences wanted to see stories they were familiar with — the tragedies of King Lear or Julius Caesar, the conquests of Henry V, a national hero. The plots and even characters of many Elizabethan plays were familiar.

Shakespeare's characterisation is another reason for his enduring popularity. An actor himself, he knew what actors needed and how much to leave out. Dialogue is only part of the character — a good writer leaves room for interpretation, ambiguities and hidden motives, room to move and make choices, so that no two Hamlets, for instance, can ever be alike. He provided more great roles for actors than any other playwright has done: Richard III, Malvolio, Hotspur, Iago, Lear, Hamlet, Othello—the list goes on; roles that you can make your mark in, roles that will make you famous. And not just male roles. Although severely handicapped by the fact that women were not allowed to perform on stage, he created for his adolescent male actors an astonishing repertoire of the greatest female roles: Cleopatra, Lady Macbeth, Rosalind, Viola, Portia—it's a tribute to the talent of those young players that Shakespeare entrusted them with such treasures.

Another unique attribute of Shakespeare's talent was his versatility—the fact that he could turn from comedy to tragedy to farce to historical chronicle to mystical fantasy, and carry all of them off triumphantly, is astonishing. Most playwrights excel in one or other genre; none has the range of Shakespeare's technical expertise. This enables the theatre industry and public at large to go on endlessly recycling the plays. If we've had too much of the tragedies lately, suddenly it seems appropriate to see the world through the bittersweet prism of the comedies. At other times the dark plays and satires like *Measure for Measure* or *Troilus and Cressida* seem best able to reflect the mood of the time. Theatre needs great stories and actors want to play great roles, so it is the theatre that is mainly responsible for keeping Shakespeare alive.

Another accidental historical factor that worked in Shakespeare's favour was the very nature of the Elizabethan theatre itself. For a start, the physical shape had been determined by necessity, not some imposed aesthetic. It grew from the inn yards with an open space surrounded by galleries—a natural meeting place for people to hear a proclamation or watch an entertainment. The communication

Putting some grunt into it as Coriolanus, urged on by Steven Berkoff, Bell Shakespeare Company, 1996. *(Photo Tracey Schramm)*

As Prospero, with Paula Arundell as Ariel, Bell Shakespeare Company, 1997. *(Photo Marco Bok)*

*Previous page*: With Lucy during rehearsals of *Pericles*, Bell Shakespeare Company, 1995.

*Opposite*: With Barrie Kosky during *King Lear* rehearsals.

The French cavalry take a stirrup cup before the battle of Agincourt, *Henry V*, Bell Shakespeare Company, 1999. *(Photo Jeff Busby)*

Joel Edgerton as Prince Hal with Richard Piper as his dying father, *Henry IV*, Bell Shakespeare Company, 1998. *(Photo Branco Gaica)*

*Opposite*: *Portrait of John Bell* by Nicholas Harding, which won the Archibald Prize in 2001. *(Private collection, courtesy the artist and the Art Gallery of NSW)*

*The Falls* company at the Stables, 2000. Back row (left to right): Barry Otto, Jennie Tate (designer), Jennifer Hagan, Kevin de Silva (stage manager), Jackie Weaver, myself, Brett Graham (lighting designer), Tim Hansen, Guy Freer (musician). Front row (left to right): Angus King, Hilary (usurping the wheelchair), Phillip Johnston (composer and husband of the author), Lucy and Peter Cousins. *(Photo Tracey Schramm)*

Bill Zappa and Paula Arundell as Antony and Cleopatra, Bell Shakespeare Company, 2001. *(Photo Heidrun Löhr)*

With an aspiring young actor at the John Collet School, Sydney.

Introducing grandson Moss to the world of puppetry, 2001. *(Photo Anna Volska)*

*Overleaf*: As Richard in Michael Gow's production of *Richard 3*, Bell Shakespeare Company, 2002. *(Photo Tracey Schramm)*

between actor and audience was total and unapologetic. There was no attempt at illusion—the actor stood on a scaffold in broad daylight and told a story to people standing on the ground in front of him, or leaning over the gallery railing. The reconstructed Globe on Bankside is teaching us a lot about the direct actor/audience dynamic and shows us what we lose by putting Shakespeare indoors under artificial light, and smothering the plays with excessive technology.

The fact that the actor was standing there in broad daylight in his everyday clothes meant he had to work hard to transport you to the midnight battlements of Elsinore, a moonlit wood outside Athens, a magic island or a blasted heath. But he had two great things working in his favour: superb descriptive, evocative poetry and a predetermined contract with the audience who had come to *hear*, not *see*, a play, who had no expectations of illusion and were prepared to accept whatever you told them:

'How sweet the moonlight sleeps upon this bank.'

'Light thickens and the crow makes wing to the rooky wood.'

'Now entertain conjecture of a time when creeping murmur and the pouring dark fills the wide vessel of the universe.'

Such a simple and universally accepted contract allowed the writer unlimited freedom to create what world he chose, merely through the power of language. It allowed Shakespeare to create one of the great metaphors for the power of theatre itself.

Peter Brook has pointed out that in *King Lear*, Edgar— disguised as a mad beggar—leads his blind father Gloster to a desert place. The old man, exhausted by his suffering, exhorts the stranger to lead him to a cliff top so that he may fling himself over and end his life. In broad daylight the Elizabethan audience watched Edgar lead the blind man along a perfectly flat floor, all the while assuring him he was climbing steeply to the cliff tops. When they reach 'the summit' the old man takes leave of the stranger, topples over and believes he has fallen an enormous distance. He is then congratulated by Edgar for his miraculous survival. The scene is at once absurd, almost slapstick, and intensely moving. It is the ultimate metaphor for theatre itself—a triumph of the imagination and the willing suspension of disbelief.

But something more than its rough potency made the theatre a vital organ of Elizabethan life. We still hang on to a rather rosy picture of Elizabethan England with its sonneteers, the exquisite miniatures by Nicholas Hilliard and the plaintive airs of John Dowland. We envisage gallant courtiers in lacy ruffs or sturdy yeomen and wenches cavorting on the village green. We tend to forget the dank misery and poverty, the religious persecution, the prevalence of disease, the cruel 'entertainments' of animal baiting, public mutilation and horrific executions. We overlook the rigid censorship of those celebrated songbirds, the poets and dramatists. Writers of pamphlets, ballads or plays could have their ears, noses or hands lopped off if they offended the court or the Church.

The theatres were located outside the city limits, in the so-called 'liberties', along with the more disreputable pubs and brothels by the waterside. This meant that the theatres, along with the pubs, brothels and bear pits, were crawling with low life, thieves, prostitutes and pickpockets, as well as sailors, merchants, apprentices and aristocrats slumming it. They were also crawling with secret police, spies and informers, because theatres were convenient meeting places for plotters and subversives. Theatres were dangerous because of their very nature: here were large gatherings (two thousand or so at any one time) to hear plays that could be construed as blasphemous, seditious, satirical or critical of court, Church and state. Ben Jonson was jailed for a joke that offended James I, and Shakespeare and his players were in fear of their lives when Queen Elizabeth took great exception to the deposition scene in *Richard II*.

But in spite of all its perils, the theatre was the one place you could speak your mind and get away with it, as long as you located your play in some other time and place. It was permissible to say 'Something is rotten in the state', as long as you added 'of Denmark'. Hardly any of Shakespeare's plays are set in his contemporary England. From the safe distance of ancient Rome or medieval England he could pose pertinent questions about republicanism, the office of kingship, the workings of the law, the basis of authority, and accepted values pertaining to nationalism, class, honour and nobility.

Far from being a bourgeois or conservative apologist, I see Shakespeare as subversive, sceptical, agnostic. This flirting with danger and saying the unspeakable reminds one of the significance of the theatre behind the Iron Curtain during the Soviet era. New plays were virtually forbidden unless they were frivolous. To engage with serious content theatres had to fall back on the classics. But through the great plays of the past, especially Shakespeare's, Soviet actors and directors found they could communicate messages of protest and subversion to their audiences. Through costume, makeup and props, these tyrants and usurpers could resemble figures close to home. When Hamlet, the eternal student rebel, enters reading a book there would be excited consternation in the audience: what is he reading? Is it a book or journal that has been banned?

In 1974 I saw the great Ramaz Chkhivadze playing Richard III with the Rustaveli Company of Georgia, USSR. He was made up like Napoleon, Russia's nemesis, with kiss-curl, tricorn and greatcoat. When I saw the production again in Adelaide in 1994, he bore a striking resemblance to Stalin, with his crew cut and military uniform.

When I met him I quizzed him on this point he laughed: 'Well, Stalin's dead! We can get away with it now, but we had a hell of a time with Edward IV, Richard's brother. We had him resembling Brezhnev—the makeup, the costume, the medals all over his front and a few down the back as well. The censors came to see a dress rehearsal before giving us permission to perform. They looked at this Brezhnev figure and squinted their eyes: who's that supposed to be? We shrugged innocently and said, Edward IV, of course. Are you *sure* it's Edward IV? Sure we're sure. They couldn't actually pin anything on us, so the show went ahead.'

As Jan Kott has pointed out in *Shakespeare Our Contemporary*, the sense of menace, suppression and brutal tyranny that pervades Shakespeare's tragedies and history plays touches a familiar chord with anyone who lived in the Eastern Bloc during the Cold War. Those Europeans were much closer to Shakespeare's world than any modern westerner.

Theatre was a vital part of life experience for the intelligent Elizabethan—a platform for debate, ideas as well as poetry. Add to this the raw face-to-face intimacy and feeling of community as you packed around the thrust stage in broad daylight, with the audience as much a part of the show as the actors, and add to this again that you were seeing all these plays for the first time, hearing this extraordinary language for the first time, and it's no wonder the playhouses attracted such large audiences and gave headaches to the Puritans and the civic fathers.

Try as we might, there are factors of that Elizabethan experience we can never recapture. Four hundred years have driven a wedge between the Elizabethans and us. The language has changed and evolved, and continues to do so at a steady rate. The sense of danger and subversion has disappeared (unless we fall victim to some future totalitarian regime). But we can try to recover the sense of roughness, intimacy and community. We don't have to reproduce the Globe on Bankside, but we can learn a lot from it. The semicircular space makes us aware of each other. As long as we sit in darkened theatres, with our backs to the people behind us, staring at a picture frame stage, we'll be stuck with theatre that is a pale imitation of the cinema. That's why I think what happened by accident in the construction of Nimrod's two theatres (now the Stables and Belvoir), utilising what already existed, had some beneficial spin-off in influencing theatre architecture.

I'd prefer to do all my work in rough, flexible, unglamorous spaces, maximising actor/audience interplay and exploiting the sense of community. But given the touring schedule of Bell Shakespeare and the venues we go to, I find my work stuck most of the time behind a proscenium with an audience sitting somewhere out there in the dark, an anonymous, faceless mass.

If you ask most people what Shakespeare is notable for, they will reply 'his language'. This is the lesson drummed

into them at school and university and has led to generations of dreary analysis in the classroom, a grappling with
archaic words, expressions and syntax. It's true that Shakespeare's language is one of the glories of English, perhaps
its crowning glory; and as an actor it gives one enormous
satisfaction to speak it in public, to exploit its rhythms and
musicality. But for all its beauty, the language is slipping
from our grasp and becoming increasingly incomprehensible to each succeeding generation. The day will come when
we'll have to translate Shakespeare, not just the odd phrase,
but the whole box and dice. This won't be altogether a bad
thing, if it's done, say, with the skill of Seamus Heaney's
translation of *Beowulf*. It will need a major poet to do it,
but the result could be electrifying.

One reason for the lasting success of Shakespeare in
Russia, Germany and other parts of Europe is that he has
constantly been translated into modern idiom. These trans-
lations inevitably lose the exotic qualities of Shakespeare's
poetry, but meaning can be translated, and the meaning of
Shakespeare's plays is at least as important as his poetry.

Shakespeare has come to mean a lot more than the substance of any one of his plays, or even his whole body of
work. The word 'Shakespeare' carries a lot of baggage—
memories of great performances, ideology and controversy,
a sense of history and traditions that alter with each new
generation as it rediscovers and reshapes 'Shakespeare' in
its own image. As the scholar Stanley Wells puts it:

> Shakespeare is an ever changing and ever fluid concept.
> A ballet based on Shakespeare for example is still somehow
> imbued with Shakespeare. Shakespeare is in the water
> supply, and even a very diluted Shakespeare nevertheless

is still part of what Shakespeare set going those 400 or so years ago.

Speaking of ballet reminds one that Shakespeare also includes all those spin-offs based on his plays or inspired by them, from the operas of Verdi to musicals like *Kiss Me Kate* and *West Side Story*, to films like *Ran* and *Shakespeare in Love*, to dozens of plays, novels, even comic books, based on Shakespeare's life and works. The influence goes further than just adapting or reworking material. Says Michiko Kakutani:

> In fact his influence on other writers has been so pervasive that he has become part of the very literary air we breathe. Dostoyevsky, Kierkegaard, Nietzche, Freud, Baudelaire, Ibsen, Strindberg, Pirandello—to name just a few of the authors and thinkers indelibly shaped by Shakespeare is to rattle off a litany of the makers of modern Western culture. Nineteenth century nihilism and twentieth century psychology, French existentialism and Emersonian self-reliance—all could be said to have seeds in Shakespeare's art.
>
> The fact that such crucial writers and philosophers responded so ardently to Shakespeare, however, suggests that there was something in the playwright's work itself that was in tune with the modern Zeitgeist. The very style and structure of his work—mixing and remaking genres, fusing highbrow art and popular entertainment, breaking the fourth wall of the stage—prefigures our post-modernist outlook, just as his work's ambiguity and pursuit of plural truths resonate . . . with our age of relativity.
>
> The game-playing of Shakespeare's characters, their gender confusion, their romantic and familial disputes,

their efforts to grapple with the contingency of reason and love, all seem peculiarly modern. Such spirited, independent heroines as Beatrice and Rosalind appear to have more in common with today's feminists than the circumscribed women of Elizabethan England, while his questioning heroes like Hamlet, so skilled in irony and self-dramatisation, reflect the preoccupation with the self manifested by both the Reformation and contemporary America.

In his bestseller, *Shakespeare: The invention of the human*, the scholar Harold Bloom argues that the playwright was the first writer to give us portraits of human beings capable of change and growth. He brought psychology to the fore, Bloom suggests, while laying out an unsentimental, even nihilistic vision of a world of loss and flux.

Peter Brook, one of the greatest directors of the last fifty years, called Shakespeare 'a great School of Life'—and he has been that for every generation. They have each understood him differently, but they have each used him as a reference point in struggling to answer the two most important questions we'll ever have to ask ourselves: who are we, and how should we live? As we enter the twenty-first century we are as intent as ever on answering those questions. And as the various churches and religions lose their authority for many of us, we turn elsewhere for inspiration and guidance. In the twentieth century it was the artists who shaped our consciousness and our consciences, who gave us a new view of the world—Picasso, Shostakovich, Arthur Miller, James Joyce, Judith Wright and Sam Beckett, to name a few at random.

And the great artists of the past—Dante, Michelangelo, Bach, Goya and Shakespeare—provide us with an inexhaustible well of wisdom, beauty and knowledge from which we can continually draw to refresh and renew ourselves.

But Shakespeare is not the Ten Commandments. He is not dogmatic, not judgemental. He gives us no quick fix, and not much reassurance. He does not give answers—he simply holds the mirror up to nature. A mirror can't give advice—it just reflects what's there. But if we study our reflection we may get to know ourselves better, and the better we know ourselves the better we can tackle that other question: how should we live?

Shakespeare's view of the world is complex and contradictory. His comedies are shot through with the sadness of the passing of time, the brevity of youth and the folly of mortals; his tragedies are not about heroic archetypes but very recognisable human beings—people of great potential who carry some seed of self-destruction, a scenario familiar from our observations of private and public life. His history plays are a merciless analysis of political machinery. He seems fascinated by the personalities and private agendas that shape historical events and directly affect each one of us. But while he is detached and enigmatic, Shakespeare is never a cold or aloof observer.

The tantalising thing about him is that you feel he's always hiding just around the corner, ready at any moment to throw his hat into the ring. Take *The Merchant of Venice*—a romantic comedy with one of the great stage villains, Shylock the Jew. But in the middle of the play, Shylock suddenly turns on his accusers (and the audience) and asks:

> Hath not a Jew eyes? Hath not a Jew hands, organs, dimensions, senses, affections, passions? Fed with the same food, hurt with the same weapons, subject to the same diseases, healed by the same means, warmed and cooled by the same winter and summer, as a Christian is? If you prick us, do we not bleed? If you tickle us, do we not laugh? If you poison us, do we not die? And if you wrong us, shall we not revenge? If we are like you in the rest, we will resemble you in that.

Now what is that speech doing in the play? It has no right to be there. It doesn't advance the action of the drama—in fact it holds up the action. And if Shylock is meant to be the villain, then the speech subverts the author's intention. Why is it there? Because it's Shakespeare. Because he couldn't help himself putting those words into the character's mouth in that situation. And, of course, in doing so he forced the play to transcend its formula and take on new levels of ambivalence and humanity. It shocks and confronts our preconceptions. We thought we were seeing one kind of play and suddenly it charges off in a new direction. Shakespeare is important because he keeps reminding us that art is not just a diversion, a distraction from everyday life. It's more than just escapism. What are we trying to escape? Art is not an escape from life but an engagement with it in all its aspects—the good, the bad and the ugly. And art has to tell the truth because if it doesn't, it's worthless. Art has to be heretical, always questioning given 'truths'. Art has to be radical because it's about life, and life is about change; change is the very essence of our existence. Art is about evolution.

People say we have evolved from the apes. Looking around the world today and the things we are doing to each other, I think that statement's a downright insult to many a fine ape I know. But if we are going to evolve to something better, to realise our spiritual potential, art is the way we're going to do it.

You may remember Stanley Kubrick's movie *2001: A Space Odyssey*. In that movie you see a large black monolith spinning through outer space. Occasionally it lands on the earth or the moon, and if people come into contact with it they are suddenly catapulted forward in time. They make an evolutionary leap. I think there are people like that monolith dropped amongst us from time to time, and if we come into contact with them we can make an evolutionary leap. Shakespeare is such a person.

# Back to the circus

Having set up my new company, one of the first formalities was finding a name for it, and I put forward names like the Australian Shakespeare Company and Southern Cross, but the first had been claimed some years before and the second was the name of a commercial rural windmill! So after much tossing about of brains, the board decided that the company should bear my name, so long as I would commit myself to a lengthy period of involvement. The commitment was no problem for me, but I shied away from the apparent grandstanding of naming a company after myself. I was persuaded by the argument that many performance companies found it advantageous to be identified with an artistic leader. It made it easier to establish an image and attract support, by putting up a face for the public to relate to.

We decided to launch our first season in January 1991. One factor I considered vital was that we should not perform in conventional proscenium-arch theatres. I've always found Shakespeare most exciting when played in 'rough' conditions, on a thrust stage or unusual space where the actors have maximum contact with, and access to, the audience. This allows them to create the kind of unique personal experience that cinema cannot ever compete with.

Rumour had it that I wanted to build a mobile Globe Theatre and tour it around the country. That was not so; I see no virtue in trying to replicate Shakespeare's playhouse for the sake of nostalgia or 'authenticity'. But there are features of the typical Elizabethan playhouse that are not only appealing but practical, as the plays were written for specific buildings. Once you recreate some of those original conditions you understand a lot better how the plays work: the nature of 'asides'; the importance of direct address to the audience (not only in soliloquies but throughout much of the performance); the relative unimportance of scenery and props; the requisite size of performance to inhabit the language; above all, the sharing of the play with an audience pressed close all around you in broad daylight.

So, with some of the features of the Elizabethan playhouse in mind, we started to design our touring theatre. An old mate from Sydney Uni days, Laurie Neild, was now Professor of Architecture, and set his final year students the project of designing a touring playhouse. At least six of the final proposals were very exciting, some involving a couple of semitrailers whose trays came together to form a stage. But what with lighting, sound, seating etc., none of them came in under two million dollars.

As rehearsals began in a studio at the University of New South Wales, the idea of our own theatre receded. Whatever money we had must go to the actors and the productions.

The theatre building would have to wait. As it turned out, we played our first season in a circus tent because I was still unwilling to occupy conventional theatre spaces.

Michael Scott-Mitchell designed a series of ramps and platforms that could be rearranged for each play with the 800 seats also adjusting to various configurations in the tent. The staging was fine, the seating less so, because we could not afford to rake it in tiers. So the 800 blue plastic chairs all sat on floor level, which made the environment far more pedestrian.

As with my production of *Don Giovanni* for the Australian Opera, I bit off more than I could chew in trying to rewrite the rulebook all in one go. I was creating not only an unconventional space and seating, but also a young company, for the most part inexperienced, playing Shakespeare in modern dress with Australian accents. Today none of that would raise an eyebrow, but in 1991 it raised some cries of outrage. Were I repeating the exercise today, with the benefit of hindsight, I wouldn't do it any differently except in one regard: I'd use a few more experienced, heavyweight actors in some of the major roles.

I was probably too keen to avoid predictable casting. But it was overstretching some of the younger actors to expect them to learn their craft while giving eight shows a week in a difficult space—the tent, for all its charm and novelty, had lousy sightlines and worse acoustics. Temperature control was nonexistent, so in Sydney an audience drooped in a heatwave while a few weeks later in Canberra they shivered under blankets. By the time we were ready to go to Melbourne, we decided to ditch the tent altogether, especially when we discovered it was going to be smack next to a racing-car track. So we played the first Melbourne season in the grubby, rundown Athenaeum, Melbourne's most neglected (and potentially beautiful) little theatre.

Our first two plays were *Hamlet* and *The Merchant of Venice*. I directed *Hamlet* and played Shylock in *Merchant*. To direct the latter I chose Carol Woodrow, a Canberra director whose work I admired and who brought to *Merchant* an intelligent and intense feminist perspective. Portia, the woman imprisoned by her father's will, denied any choice in who she will marry, finally has her day in court when she impersonates not only a male, but a judge at that; and reclaims the spouse of her desire by breaking the nexus of male bonding that holds him in thrall. Does Bassanio win Portia fair and square by his prescience in choosing the right casket? Or does Portia help him out a little by singing (while he ponders his choice), a song that goes: 'Tell me, where is fancy bred? In the heart or in the head?' Is it just a coincidence that every last word rhymes with 'lead'? Portia is no slouch when it comes to bending the law a little to get what she wants.

Carol's production certainly made no bones about Antonio being violently anti-Semitic and punitive, especially in his vile demand that Shylock must save his life by converting to Christianity. The production was also explicit in making Antonio's attachment to Bassanio a homosexual one; an attachment Portia realises for what it is—hence her test of loyalty with the wedding ring, and her forcing Antonio to act as celebrant of her match with Bassanio. The final act of *Merchant* is not a romantic coda but the resolution of a love triangle.

The production opened in a bathhouse with Antonio and his coterie clad only in towels and the scene concluded with a full-on kiss and grope between Antonio and Bassanio.

At a packed school matinee in Newcastle, this caused pandemonium and an entire Christian school contingent was marched out of the theatre straight onto the bus. The publicity we got from this was wonderful: front-page news for three days, plus the letters page of course; we were on every TV and radio report and consequently the queues for tickets stretched around the block.

I have always regarded Shylock as the most sympathetic character in the play—the victim of bigotry, harassment and discrimination. When his daughter robs him and elopes with a Christian she ceases to be a Jew; she is dead to him. His grief tips him into a temporary insanity of messianic zeal so that when the opportunity arises to take revenge on Antonio (who personifies the persecution of all Jews), Shylock sees himself as father Abraham, wielding the knife of righteousness on behalf of Israel.

That's only the half of it, of course. Shakespeare's major characters are always complex and ambivalent. Shylock is not a 'good' Jew. He has not an ounce of spirituality. He is materialistic and self-centred. But he is also sharp, witty, passionate and courageous. I wanted to get under his skin and avoid theatrical cliché. I was fully aware of the dangers an actor (and producer) face when presenting this play—charges of anti-Semitism in particular. So I researched the role for six months, studying the history and culture of Judaism, dining with Jewish families, attending synagogue and other Jewish social occasions. The hardest thing was trying to get someone to explain to me what being Jewish meant. 'Oh not them—they're not *real* Jews,' one family would say of another. The various racial strains, degrees of orthodoxy and diversity of opinion had me quite confused. It was well summed up in a joke I heard: 'A Jew gets wrecked on a desert island; he's there on his own for ten years and builds two synagogues. When he's rescued they ask him: "Why two synagogues?"'

'"Well," he says, jerking his thumb at one of them, "I wouldn't go into *that* one."'

I found myself at dinner one night with a Lubavich family, extremely orthodox. Herta wore a wig and they wouldn't even answer the phone on a Saturday. We discussed Shylock for a bit and I finally asked: 'What's the best way to understand the Jews?'

Herschel thought hard for a moment then said: 'Get out the video of *Fiddler on the Roof*—that's pretty accurate . . .'

I ended up modelling myself on the Jewish businessmen I observed in the coffee shops around Bondi and St Kilda. I used the black suit and briefcase, the reddish beard, long black coat, black hat and fairly broad Australian accent. I decided he was an Ashkenazy, one of those of German or European background, specialising in the arts and commerce rather than the more exotic Sephardic Jew so often seen on stage. In this way I got around Anna's initial reaction when I told her I wanted to play the role: 'You can't play Shylock!' she retorted. 'You're the most Aryan-looking person I've ever met.' Happily my research showed me there's no such thing as 'Jewish looking'.

After the first performance of *Merchant* a number of my Jewish friends came backstage. 'What did you think?' I asked.

'Well,' said one of them sheepishly, 'we think you were a bit tough on the Christians.'

I was heavily influenced by the statement made by John Middleton Murray:

> Shylock is given his human shape by the noblest imagi-
> nation of Humanism. Shakespeare could not help himself.
> The terrible caricature of the Jew created by medieval
> Christianity . . . was turned by Shakespeare into the fierce
> Accuser of Christianity which, by conceiving him, had
> forced him into existence, and made him the scapegoat
> of its own inhumanity . . .
>
> In Shylock are combined, in a mighty, imaginative
> creation, the passionate determination of revenge, the
> secular wrongs of Jewry with a scorching and irrefutable
> indictment of the Christianity which inflicted them.

Shylock is a loner. Nobody speaks well of him, all detest
him. I didn't want it to be easy for the audience to do this,
so at the start I made him as affable as possible. I empha-
sised his love for Jessica. Her betrayal and elopement drive
Shylock to a frenzy. He has no private life—he is 'the Jew'
and nothing else. He has no spirituality, he is the slave of
money. Compare this with Portia's boundless liberality,
Antonio's rash generosity, the profligacy of Bassanio,
Lorenzo and Jessica.

I wanted to show a Shylock who is dignified, canny, a
leader of his community, but who, underneath, is seething
with rage and resentment. Why does he propose the bond
of a 'pound of flesh'? Some Shylocks play it as a murder-
ous trap, others as a joke. I see it more as an insult to
Antonio: 'I despise you . . . I don't want your dirty money.
Are you man enough to risk your life? I dare you!' I see it as
Shylock contemptuously demonstrating that he can afford
to lose three thousand ducats; he wants to see Antonio
crawl . . . But when the Christian layabouts steal his daughter
and she betrays him, he tips into temporary insanity—all

his fury is unleashed, and he acts with an Old Testament vengeful wrath. His defeat is inevitable—those wily Christians can always twist the law. He accepts his defeat with a 'patient shrug' as his tribe has always done. Olivier exited with a howl of despair—that is pure bathos and not justified by the text. Shylock will live to fight another day.

Getting the season launched was a big stretch. I was directing *Hamlet* and rehearsing Shylock simultaneously as well as having to cope with management and publicity. And our facilities were pretty limited. We occupied a couple of rooms in an old house in Redfern leased by the Elizabethan Theatre Trust and we had a skeleton staff and crew.

Had I known we'd be playing in a circus tent, I probably would not have chosen *Hamlet*, or else I would have devised a *Hamlet* that was appropriate to a circus tent—something robust and colourful—but the production I had conceived was deliberately downbeat, colloquial and contemporary—street clothes, grim and quite drab. By the time the tent was decided on, the production was fully in place. I was looking at the breakup of the Soviet empire, the corruption, despair, the search for a new spirituality now that the old ideologies had been devalued. John Polson played Hamlet as a young, angry and confused rebel without a cause. With Claudius and Gertrude (Marco Chiappi and Anna Volska) I wanted to depict the cynical exploiters of a totally corrupt political machine. Patrick Dickson's Polonius was a trade union opportunist who had wheedled his way to the top, but still had the air of the shop steward about him.

When Chris Stollery took over as Hamlet the following season he showed Hamlet escaping the straightjacket of conformity by adopting the disguise of the lunatic—

a shaven-headed jester with licence to say and do outrageous things.

The advent of the company was widely welcomed in the media and the honeymoon lasted through our initial season, despite a disastrously hot first night in our packed circus tent. Sydney really knows how to turn on a January heatwave, and I am eternally grateful for the sight of Gough Whitlam in the front row, perspiring and purple as a plum in his black tie, applauding valiantly at the end.

Another distressing factor contributed to our first-night nerves. The talented Marian Dvorakovski was both Ghost and First Player. His Polish accent and the lousy acoustics combined to make him inaudible. He battled through the two previews but I was entreated by my board and chairman not to let him perform on opening night. I resisted until the last moment, but was finally convinced it would be detrimental to both Marian and the show were he to play the Ghost. (The First Player was less crucial to the plot of the play.) So about an hour before curtain-up I announced to the company that I would be going on as the Ghost. Most of the cast were sympathetic, though one or two were outraged for Marian's sake. Luckily I knew the lines and moves well enough to wing it and I played the Ghost for the rest of the run. Marian was generous and understanding. He stayed with us for two more seasons.

There is a strong military presence in *Hamlet* and I wanted the soldiers to have a bit of grunt, so Victoria Barracks loaned me a drill instructor sergeant major for a week. He put the lads through their paces and taught them to smarten up. On the first morning he lined them up and asked their names.

'James, right . . . Simon, right . . . what's your name, son?'

'Marian, sir.'

'What?!'

'Marian, sir . . .' Stunned silence.

'All right, well I'm going to call you George.'

When performing any Shakespeare play, you keep colliding with moments of topicality. While we were playing *Hamlet* the Gulf War broke out, and that night the following words from *Hamlet* struck a chilling chord:

> We go to gain a little patch of ground
> That hath in it no profit but the name . . .
> I see the imminent death of twenty thousand men,
> That, for a fantasy and trick of fame,
> Go to their graves like beds, fight for a plot
> Whereon the numbers cannot try the cause,
> Which is not tomb enough and continent
> To hide the slain . . .

After our Sydney season we moved on to Canberra, where the site offered to us for our circus tent was at the National Aquarium. Punters had the rather unique experience of boarding a toy train and chugging between rows of fish tanks to get to the performance. Despite—or perhaps because of—this novelty, Canberra welcomed us and numbers were healthy. But this was deceptive: the cost of maintaining the salaries of fourteen actors plus the crew, the touring expenses, marketing and publicity were devouring our slender resources and box-office takings could not keep pace with expenditure. By the end of our Melbourne season in March 1991 the financial strain was

showing. To make things worse, our mother ship, the Elizabethan Theatre Trust, went into liquidation, though not
because of us. It had been sailing close to the wind for some
time but, naturally, kept it quiet. So we had no home, no
board of directors, and—worst of all—no tax-deductible
status. If we couldn't offer tax breaks for donations we
were sunk. Some of the Melbourne press confidently
announced that the Bell Shakespeare Company was
finished.

Nearly all our board of directors (including chairman
Adam Salzer) were also directors of the Trust, so had to
resign. The only remaining directors were myself, Tony
Gilbert and Virginia Henderson. Virginia sniffed the scent
of battle and determined that the company would not go
under. She immediately took over as chair and the next day
she and I went to Canberra to plead for the company as a
new independent entity, to retain its tax-deductible status.

We were to spend many dreary hours over the next
seven years trudging the corridors of power and cajoling
arts ministers, both state and federal, to keep the company
alive. My diary note of 4 December 1993 describes a typical meeting:

*Most exasperating meeting with X and Y (New South Wales
Ministry for the Arts). For a start we arrived on time but
were kept waiting the obligatory fifteen minutes. X was
downright insulting—so switched-off and noncommittal—
fiddled with papers, hummed and hah-ed, stared at the
ceiling and twiddled his thumbs, while Y gave us reasons
Why We Can't Fund You:*

*'You are doing too well with your fundraising and cor-
porate sponsorship.'*

'*Oh,*' *I cracked,* '*so we get penalised for hard work and success?*'

'*Oh no, no, no,*' *puffed X,* '*my government, my minister would* never *penalise success.*'

*Says Y:* '*You have survived, and that is a problem for us. It means that if we give you money* this *year, you'll probably survive and come back for more* next *year! It's called "the lock-in principle"* . . . *we'd be* locked *in to supporting you, leaving no money for the little companies who rise up and die each year.*'

. . . *So we can't win any way. If we get no support we die. If we get support, we are too successful, and if we survive we are an embarrassment and an encumbrance* . . .

Anyway, we survived our first year, recruited a new board and set about fundraising in a big way. Government support was pretty minimal. Little by little we squeezed money out of the Australia Council for 'special projects', but there was no guarantee of ongoing commitment. State government support came only from New South Wales, although we were working just as much in Victoria as well as touring, at our own expense, to Brisbane, Adelaide, Canberra and Perth. The state government support was pretty minimal too, so we depended heavily on box office (which brought us approximately 63 per cent of our revenue), private donors and corporate sponsors. But chiefly we owed our continuing existence to the generosity of Tony Gilbert who remained, for ten years, our major financial supporter. Without him the company would never have happened, and without him it certainly would not have survived. Quiet, retiring and hating public 'fuss', Tony had a steely nerve and an acute eye on the balance sheet.

Whenever it came to the crunch, as it did many a time, he showed his true grit by bailing us out.

On one occasion when we were looking down the barrel and the federal arts ministry needed persuading that they should come to the party, Tony, Virginia and I made one of our many trips to Canberra to see Labor Arts Minister Bob McMullan, who proved to be a true arts enthusiast. But he wasn't going to simply throw money at us, he needed convincing. Tony faced him across the table and stated: 'The company will fold without half a million dollars right now. I'm prepared to put down two hundred and fifty thousand if you'll do the same. But if you don't nor shall I.'

Bob looked a bit stunned but he wasn't going to be held to ransom, not right then and there anyway. He'd have to think about it. Within a few days he'd made his commitment and we were on our way to receiving annual government support. Still, as the company grew and extended its activities, government financial support could not keep pace. By the end of nine years our government support (both state and federal) amounted to no more than 6 per cent of our income. Private support grew slowly, and thanks to Virginia's tenacity (and charm), and the aid of her hard-working board, we built up and maintained an extraordinary degree of corporate sponsorship. We had learned good house-keeping the hard way and had never taken financial support for granted, but scrounged and fought for every cent while continually reining in expenditure. Throughout most of our first six years, emergency board meetings were frequent, always addressing the same ominous questions: 'Can we pay the salaries next week? Can we open in Melbourne next month? Because if we're going to, we have to commit now . . .'

From the Nimrod experience I had learned that if a venture is going to work, you have to devote yourself to it 100 per cent. Balancing that with home and family takes a bit of doing. While Hilary and Lucy were growing up, Anna and I toured as little as possible. We tried to ensure that weekends were a time we all spent together and got out of town to the beach and bush. Once the girls left home we felt free to go on the road and now, if one of us is touring and the other is at home base, Anna and I make sure we spend time together at least once a fortnight.

# Actors at Work

As our first season finished mid year, I was determined to find a way to keep at least some of the fourteen actors together as a company, so I devised an education program which I called Actors at Work, designed to play sixty-minute shows in secondary schools, demonstrating actors' approaches to bringing Shakespeare to life on stage. The concept was deliberately non-academic, a counterblast to those who pronounced that there was one 'correct' interpretation of any Shakespeare play or character, one that would satisfy examiners. Our show set out to demonstrate that any play or character is subject to multiple interpretations; moreover, that Shakespeare is dirtier, more radical in his thinking and more fun than you ever dared hope from studying his texts in the classroom.

In the first year I led the team of seven myself. My two favourite performances of the sixty or so we did were in disadvantaged schools. One was in a collapsing boatshed

that served as the school hall. The kids were barefoot, unin-
hibited and totally delighted. The other was in a western
suburbs school that had an inflatable dome as the all-
purpose gym/school hall. The kids looked desolate and
miserable, the teachers disinterested. When I thanked one
snotty-nosed youngster for helping arrange the chairs he
replied, 'That's the first nice thing anyone's ever said to me.'
My least favourite shows were at some North Shore estab-
lishments where the staff actually processed to chapel in
academic gowns and the bored gilded youth merely endured
our performance, stretching out their grey flannel legs and
staring at the ceiling.

One of the most revealing, at least of the Australian
male persona, took place at Christian Brothers, Waverley.
The sixth-formers, hulking rugby players most of them, sat
glaring at us with folded arms. Not a flicker of interest or
emotion showed on their sullen faces. 'Oh well,' we said
to ourselves, 'that one was a write-off . . .' Next day we
played to the sister-school, St Catherine's, down the road.
The girls greeted us enthusiastically: 'Our boyfriends from
Waverley rang us and said "Make sure you see the show—
it's fantastic!"'

Actors at Work has now been going strong since 1991
and at present consists of two teams of four actors with a
director who devises the various programs aimed at upper
and lower secondary schools. The unit has been through
several directors, but has always retained an accent on audience involvement, highlighting the themes and dilemmas
close to adolescent hearts. The actors do up to three shows
a day, driving themselves to each school and conducting a
dialogue with students backed up by extensive teachers'
notes and study plans. The actors work solidly throughout

the school year in every state—metropolitan, regional and outback. We are always booked out a year in advance and are now expanding the tours into South-East Asia, with an office in Singapore. Apart from anything else, Actors at Work is a marvellous apprenticeship for actors. It has had several incarnations since I devised and led it in 1991: Mary-Ann Gifford has given it a solid text-base, Jenny Lovell a playful degree of audience participation and Des James a highly inventive intermeshing of themes such as homelessness and child–parent conflicts.

Already a number of actors have moved on from Actors at Work to roles in our 'mainstage' productions. I see the exercise as being fundamental to our mission and am delighted that Actors at Work has been hailed as one of the most popular and successful theatre-in-education ventures ever undertaken in Australia.

Education should enable us to create values to live by and distinguish what is worthwhile and what is not. I was talking recently with someone involved in executive search (or head-hunting, as it is more popularly known) who was describing the degree of despair and confusion amongst many of the people he interviewed. Mostly men, mostly in their fifties, high achievers who have devoted their lives to getting to the top but who now, due to reorganisation in the corporate world, find themselves redundant, expend-able. Bang goes their self-esteem and, shortly after, bang go their marriages. They no longer know who they are or what they're worth. They have no spiritual resources to fall back on, no frame of reference other than the one which has dumped them. The suicide rate in this group of people is significant.

We may be able to learn something from people who create for the sheer joy of it, who find a deep meaning in working and playing as part of a community. While holidaying in Bali in 1976 I was invited to a 'gamelan contest'. The gamelan is that wonderful percussive ensemble that provides the musical accompaniment to most Balinese dramatic and dance performances. The contest was held late at night and in a remote location. The open air space was packed with local people—I was one of the few foreigners present. 'Why so late and so remote?' I asked. My host replied politely but firmly: 'This is not for the tourists—it's for us.'

For the next two hours we were treated to a succession of brilliantly dressed performers and glowing brass instruments. The dancing and singing were as exquisite as the music was thunderously rousing. During a short lull between bands I asked, 'Are all these performers professional?'

'Professional?' queried my puzzled host.

'Do they get paid?'

A look of horror crossed her face. 'Oh no!' she exclaimed. 'We do this for the gods!'

Suitably chastened I said no more until the end of the performance. The last notes of music were met with generous applause and the satisfied audience got up to leave.

'Is it over?'

'Yes.'

'But I thought it was a contest. Who won?'

'That band over there!' said my host, pointing confidently at the ones in blue.

'But where is the announcement? Where are the judges?'

'Oh,' she replied casually, 'we all know who's best.'

A far cry from the hype and rampant commercialism of the Oscars.

In my desire to build an acting ensemble, I attempted early on to keep most of the same actors from season to season, and to keep plays in the repertoire so we could go on exploring and improving them. My experience at the Royal Shakespeare Company and observation of European companies convinced me that an ensemble and long-term repertoire were the keys to artistic excellence. Robert Strurua, the director of the Rustaveli *Richard III*, told me, 'We've been performing this for thirteen years . . . of course it's good.'

In 1992 we remounted *Hamlet* (with Chris Stollery replacing John Polson in the title role) and *Merchant*, while adding *Richard III* to the mix, playing all three in repertory. Because of our limited funds I felt it incumbent on me to direct and perform as much as possible. So in 1992 I directed *Hamlet*, played Shylock in *Merchant* and directed *Richard III* as well as playing the title role. I was using my dressing room as an office, making phone calls, sending faxes and puzzling over finances whenever I was off stage. And while I was on stage I was too busy making mental notes to give to the other actors to concentrate on my own performance.

During our 1992 season at the Theatre Royal in Sydney, the great Georgian actor Ramaz Chkhivadze came to the theatre and gave us a three-hour master class. I had seen him in the superb production of *Richard III* by the Rustaveli Company at London's Roundhouse in 1974 and again at the Adelaide Festival ten years later.

Ramaz told us: 'We rehearsed *Richard III* for seven months and it was a disaster. So we put it away for a couple of months . . . but in that time something was ticking over; so we started working on it again and in three weeks we had a production. We've been playing it now for thirteen years and we're still working on it . . . You can't get Shakespeare right at a premiere, it takes four or five weeks of playing in front of an audience for a Shakespeare play to start to work.

'Start with psychology in Shakespeare,' he advised us. 'Understand the role that way; but then start responding intuitively, play hot, then cold, whatever he gives you; play the actions, don't try to connect them or find any transition. Play the moments, the extremes. Shakespeare doesn't work from logic.'

I asked him what he wanted audiences to take away from *Richard III*. He replied: 'There will always be Richards, and they get worse as history progresses. Richard III wasn't such a bad fellow after all: he only killed fifteen people. Stalin killed twenty million.'

I saw *Richard III* as a nightmare poem (so much happens in terms of dreams, prophecies, omens, curses and nightmares) rather than a 'history' play. Much comment is made in the text about characters' animal characteristics — the dog, the rat, the wolf, the hog and the bottled spider feature in the menagerie. So rather than search for a historical reference I chose to set the play in a kind of vertical sewer-pipe (the Tower) with the characters as feral animals scrambling for survival and supremacy. Sue Field's costumes used fur, feathers and claws to help each actor find a physical shape and appropriate body language. James Wardlaw saw Buckingham as a panther, whereas Marian

Dvorakovski said: 'I see Lord Rivers as a rooster who thinks he's a peacock.'

Nigel Westlake provided a powerful music score and Michael Scott-Mitchell's set proved versatile enough (with a few bits added or taken away) to accommodate *Richard III*, *Hamlet* and *Merchant*, so we could play all three in repertory with a daily turnaround. All three productions proved popular enough to warrant return seasons in Sydney, Melbourne and Canberra. We played *Richard* and *Hamlet* for three seasons, and *Merchant* for two.

Richard is one of my favourite roles. I decided to depict him as the product of civil war and family feuding of the bloodiest, most treacherous kind, like some kid brought up in Belfast or Beirut. He is despised for being crippled and deformed . . . what kind of hatred and resentment might that breed? He has no conscience and no pity. He has always been hated, even by his mother, so has developed no empathy, no sense of self, no social sense. He is a complete *loner*.

I sought advice from a medical specialist who, after a close study of the evidence in the text, diagnosed scoliosis. This meant a side hump with one shoulder up and forward. He added: 'There is probably also a touch of polio in one leg and arm and some breathing difficulties.'

Richard is an actor, a performer. He can 'change shapes with Proteus for advantages'. (Not many Richards I have seen use that.) I did a lot of reading about serial killers and mass murderers to try and understand their thinking patterns and asked myself, 'What is his *inner* deformity?' It's more important than the physical one. Richard is still a medieval man, almost on the verge of humanism, but subject to superstition: he *believes* in ghosts, curses, heaven and hell.

In *Hamlet* the only people who are not pretending are the Actors. They are the only ones you can trust because you *know* they're acting. But acting can also be seen as a false existence: one is always feigning, getting out of touch with one's real feelings. Cedric Hardwicke said that by middle age most actors have forgotten who their real selves are. Joan Plowright said she didn't really *know* her husband, Olivier—he was acting all the time. This is the reverse of Grotowski's dictum that acting is 'confession', a revelation of one's real self. Most of the actors I know are reasonably well-balanced people. You come across the occasional ratbag, but you get them in any profession. Many actors lead a precarious financial existence and can suffer bouts of low self-esteem. But all that creativity, exercise and cameraderie seem to encourage both happiness and longevity.

My first Richard, at the Nimrod in 1975, was a fallen angel with long blond hair, a birthmark on his face and a rough rustic accent. Peter Kenna remarked: 'It's as if they sent the idiot son out to chop the wood and he came back with the axe . . .'

My second Richard, for all my research, was too stylised, too abstracted. In my attempt to realise the play as a nightmare, I sacrificed some of Shakespeare's essential earthiness and humanity.

I was quite delighted, therefore, when in 2001 Michael Gow, artistic director of the Queensland Theatre Company, rang to ask if he could direct me as Richard in a joint production between our two companies in 2002. I hadn't contemplated playing Richard a third time but relished the opportunity for one more crack at this great role. Back in early 1992 I also got a directing gig of a very different flavour. I was in Brisbane playing Shylock when I got a phone call from my old mate Don Watson, who was now Prime Minister Keating's speechwriter.

'Can you come to Canberra for a day, say, next Saturday? Paul's got this election coming up and a few of us are worried about his speech-making. He needs a bit of help.'

'Hang on, Don,' I said, 'I'm not a public speaker or speech therapist. What use can I be?'

# A day with
# Paul Keating

'What Paul Keating lacks,' Don Watson had told me on the phone, 'is a bit of confidence in his presentation. He's suspicious of acting and showmanship—he thinks it's all bullshit. So even though he's saying some great things, he doesn't sell them well. Maybe you can just give him some reassurance and a few pointers on putting himself across as a performer. We think it's really important and could make a big difference to the campaign.'

'Well,' I said, 'I don't know how much help I can be, but anything I can do . . .'

I have always been a great fan of Keating's. I found his prime ministership inspiring and brave and regard it as a tragedy for Australia that he lost government when he did, giving way to an era of unspeakable mediocrity.

So early Sunday morning I flew to Canberra, met Don and we had breakfast at the Gazebo. 'If he's nervous he'll talk about the economy,' Don warned me.

Arriving at the Lodge we were shown into a sitting room and said hello to Annita. Shortly after, Paul appeared in slacks and a lumberjack shirt. I was struck immediately by a palpable maleness, earthiness and lack of the kind of polish I associate with most politicians. We sat down and he launched straight into the economy, dazzling us with a battery of statistics. He didn't look at me directly but shot me many a sidelong, almost suspicious glance.

As he relaxed a little he shifted into more anecdotal mode. He made some slightly disparaging remark about Gough Whitlam's love of panoply and when I interjected, 'I didn't think Gough would go for that sort of thing,' he looked me full in the face.

'Listen, let me tell you,' he said, 'I had this guy from Bankstown doing some plastering for me. He was Portuguese and when he'd finished the job he said to me, "Mr Keating, the Portuguese community think very highly of you and would like to make you a Knight of the Order of Saint Agatha of Portofino." I said, "Well thanks, mate, I'm not really into all that; but I'll be happy to come along and watch the ceremony." So I go along and there's all these blokes lined up to be invested. And Gough's one of them! Standing there in a sash with a great hubcap on his tit. So I go up and say, "Hello, Gough!" He spins around and booms, "Fuck ME, comrade . . . I didn't know *you'd* be here!",' and Keating slapped his thigh and rocked with laughter. The chat and small talk went on for a long time until I managed to broach the subject of why I'd come. It was decided to get down to work after lunch.

Mealtime was a strained affair, presided over by a rather dour Dutch cook. Annita didn't seem impressed by the cuisine and I tried to make small talk with the charming but shy schoolgirl daughters, aware of the doleful eye of my distinguished pupil watching me sideways.

Lunch over, Don and Annita announced they were going for a walk and Paul led me to the lounge room like a man dragging his feet to the scaffold. I felt pretty uneasy myself, uncertain how to put him at ease or how to proceed! So I suggested that he take a recently written speech and let me hear him deliver it. It was an odd sensation, sitting on a sofa at the Lodge with a palpably nervous prime minister standing in front of me, bumbling his way through a speech to the Queen.

The reading was flat and colourless. He was dry-mouthed, shifting from foot to foot. I didn't prolong the agony too much and after a short time offered some observations. 'I think it would be a great help if you stood straight and looked up more,' I suggested. 'When you lower your head all the time it looks a bit morose, a bit hangdog.'

'The trouble is,' he complained, 'that wherever I go the microphone and podium are too low. I have to bend down to reach them.'

'Well, I reckon your minders should go ahead and adjust them for you,' I said, 'or even carry a portable lectern with you that's just your size. I bet George Bush has one . . .

'Another thing is, it doesn't sound like you talking. Your own way of speech is in short sentences, simple and straight to the point. The speeches you read are too convoluted— no wonder you don't feel sincere, even though you believe in the sentiments they're expressing.'

I couldn't think of a lot more in terms of practical advice except to reassure him as strongly as I could that he was a powerful personality, terrific on his feet, speaking off the cuff; and that he must retain that spontaneity and humour in his formal speeches. I made out the strongest case I could for public speaking being an honest and sincere occupation, to be despised only if one were deliberately lying. He must not be distrustful of good old-fashioned showmanship if it was getting his message across.

My little lecture finished, he looked heartily relieved that the ordeal was over and offered to show me around the garden. He was like a dog busting to get out for a walk. So we strolled around the garden for twenty minutes or so, and he gave me a guided tour of the veggie patch.

When we returned to the lounge room Don and Annita were waiting with afternoon tea, curious as to our progress. Don wasn't too impressed when I suggested his writing style was part of the problem, and Paul got out some of his old Parliament Question Time videos to remind us of how good he was when adlibbing. His favourite bit was of himself pulling silly faces at John Howard and sending the Opposition into a flurry. He hugged his knees, chortled with delight and played it over and over, while Annita looked down her nose and muttered, 'Really, Paul! How childish!'

That done he produced his CD collection and invited us to marvel at his latest discovery, Cecilia Bartoli, singing Mozart and Rossini, comparing her handling of particular arias with other sopranos. I've no doubt a lot of this came from Ross Gengos, the proprietor of the best music store in Australia, and Paul's musical mentor; but there was no doubt that Keating was totally transported, sitting on the floor amongst his CDs and flicking from one version to another—'Listen to this bit'—with a childlike absorbedness.

'What sort of music do you like?' he asked me. 'Oh all sorts, but mainly Baroque,' I replied. 'And especially Bach for solo instruments.' I looked at my watch and asked if I could ring a taxi for the airport.

'No, forget the taxi,' he said. 'Hop in the car, I'll drive you.'

I protested but—'No, no worries. Hop in the car.' So in I hopped and Don came for the ride; no escort, no security, just the three of us. As we said goodbye at the terminal he handed me a double CD recording. 'You might like this,' he said a little shyly. It was Jascha Heifetz playing Bach violin sonatas.

As I made my way to the plane, I wondered how many prime ministers would say, 'Hop in, I'll drive you to the airport.' And how many countries were there where it was so easily done?

# The ensemble
# spirit develops

In 1993 I added *Romeo & Juliet* to the company's repertoire, again with spectacular costumes by Sue Field and
music by Nigel Westlake. As well as directing I played the
Chorus and the Prince, small parts so that I could watch
most of the show each night. Because with *Richard* I found
both directing and performing too compromising, the following year I invited a promising young director named
David Fenton to direct Anna and myself as the Macbeths.
Anna had appeared in every production so far, as Gertrude,
then as Nerissa, Queen Margaret and Lady Capulet.

David's production was bold in the extreme, somewhat
futuristic with the witches as aliens dabbling in genetic
engineering; their cauldron scene was a high-tech lab and
their incantations scientific formulae. The banquet scene
featured, as a backdrop, a crucified white horse with its
entrails spilling out. Banquo's Ghost made its appearance
amidst the offal. The production created huge controversy

and copped a lot of flak (most productions of *Macbeth* do). It was wildly popular with young audiences, but set us back financially as its budget blew out considerably. But I was impressed with David's talent and invited him back the following year to direct *Twelfth Night*.

*Macbeth* is a more mature piece of work than *Richard III*, but the leading character is harder to play, despite their many similarities. Macbeth must *grow*, not dwindle as the play progresses. A lot of Macbeths don't manage this. The getting of power is exciting. Having it can be boring. Like Richard, Macbeth lacks any love of goodness or virtue. He doesn't hate evil—just the sight of himself committing it. What Macbeth lacks and Richard has in spades is a sense of humour, which enables Richard to captivate an audience.

The Macbeths are not a couple you'd care to spend the evening with. Their relationship is riddled with guilt, blame and resentment. Anna and I had to work extra hard at being nice to each other off stage and not let the characters' angst spill over into our own relationship.

The Macbeths are not 'in the moment', but live in the future. Referring to his letter she tells him that it: 'Transported me beyond the ignorant present and I feel now the future in the instant.' And how many times does the word 'tomorrow' occur? Right to the end of the play he is still saying, 'Tomorrow and tomorrow and tomorrow . . .', he is still living in the future, but now sees it as futile: 'And that which should accompany old age . . . I must not look to have . . . I have lived long enough.' Macbeth not only lives in the future because it is more real than the present: 'Nothing is but what is not.' He craves to *control* the future through his dynasty. He must destroy what he cannot control.

Why is there such a set-up before Macbeth first appears, telling us what a merciless butcher he is? What kind of monster is the audience expecting?

There is something sexual in the description of Macbeth's savagery: 'bathe in reeking wounds . . .' We gave a lot of thought to the probability that for the Macbeths killing is a substitute for sex. Maybe Jan Kott is right when he suggests, 'The Macbeths have suffered some great erotic defeat.' I studied the role, considering killing as an aphrodisiac. Anna and I both undertook some repugnant research into Brady and Hindley, the child murderers. Macbeth targets children—he is determined to exterminate the children of Banquo and Macduff. There is mention of the Macbeths' children, but it's ambivalent. Have the Macbeths' babies died? Is their relationship undermined by guilt, mutual blame and grief?

The language of *Macbeth* is more complex and subtle than the language of *Richard III*. Shakespeare was mastering a depiction of psychological states. Take, for instance, Macbeth's soliloquy of Act I, Scene VII. It swings violently between a physical urge and an intellectual restraint. Thus in the first line and a half: 'If it were done when 'tis done, then 'twere well/It were done quickly . . .'

The words are monosyllabic, of Anglo-Saxon origin, crude, physical, from the gut.

But then in the middle of the line, the language suddenly changes: '. . . If the assassination/Could trammel up the consequence and catch/With his surcease success . . .' The words are polysyllabic, Latinate, cerebral. The rhythm is measured, considered.

Then once again, halfway through the line, the language reverts to the urgent, monosyllabic language of gut instinct:

' . . . that but this blow/Might be the be-all and the end-all, here—/But here—' (Hammer blows). The fact that the language and rhythm change so radically in the middle of a line signals that this is not a reflective, meditative speech—it has to go like the clappers; it's the picture of a man in a frenzy of indecision.

To complement *Macbeth*, and play in repertoire with it, I chose *Taming of the Shrew*, that most brilliant piece of comedic construction. I wanted to shift the emphasis from the traditional male chauvinist/female victim slanging match to a critique of the society that produces Katharine. *Shrew* is remarkable for its lack of poetry. Its language is basic, prosaic and obsessed with material goods. Petruchio states at the outset he is here to marry for money. Baptista offers to sell his daughter to the highest bidder and conducts an auction for her. Right to the end the talk is of money as the husbands wager on their wives' obedience. The only poetry in the play is Katharine's great speech about wifely duty. Whether it's sincere, comic or ironic, the fact is that it's a great lyrical passage. It is also the hub of the play. The way we interpret it determines why and how we do the play.

I see Katharine as the victim of a male-dominated, materialistic society, one devoid of spirituality and imagination. I set it in contemporary Australia. Stephen Curtis designed costumes reflecting the vibrant colour and affluence of the Gold Coast—a place where nobody seems to do any work except via a mobile phone or fax, while lazing on their yachts or by the pool. Bianca is made for this society, a pretty doll who acquiesces to her father's wishes and men's expectations. Katharine fights it tooth and nail. She wants something better than this.

Enter Petruchio, an opportunist but with a fine eye for
quality, be it in hawk, horse, hound or woman. He decides
to have Kate not because of the dowry, but because here's
something he can help to realise its potential. Chris Stollery,
who played Petruchio, likened him to a Zen master who
imposes a rigorous discipline but has an underlying wisdom
that can put someone on the path to enlightenment and
fulfilment.

However, even Petruchio is stunned by Kate's capacity
for love and loyalty. She far surpasses his expectations,
which I think is why her great speech has to be seen in
terms of joyous self-knowledge and gratitude to someone
who has saved her from a mediocre existence and allowed
her, like a falcon, to fly free. She arrives not at subservience,
but at a negotiated settlement with the mate of her choice.
The fact that her 'capitulation' is scorned and misunderstood by the other women present is significant. It is also
a great comic turnaround to hear the renowned Shrew
espouse gentleness and humility. But Kate and Petruchio's
pact is not for everyone. They are the lucky ones, bold independent spirits who rise above the conventions of the herd.

Shakespeare provides a theatrical wraparound by having
Christopher Sly and his Warwickshire companions observe
the performance. Given the contemporary Australian style
of the production, I had no room for an Elizabethan frame-
work, so I substituted a chook raffle and talent quest as if
the show were taking place at the local Leagues Club.
David King came out of the floor at his Wurlitzer organ,
and Stollery as MC introduced the talent quest leading us
into the highlight of the evening, a performance of *Shrew*.

Our second, third and fourth Sydney seasons were all
at the Theatre Royal, which in 1995 became unavailable

because of long-running musicals. That year we found ourselves at the Footbridge Theatre on the Sydney University
campus. It was neither an exciting venue to play in nor a
popular one with audiences. I directed *Pericles* and played
Malvolio in David Fenton's *Twelfth Night*. The year was
remarkable for giving me the opportunity to work with my
younger daughter, Lucy, who joined the company for both
plays. We were a little apprehensive about working
together, wondering if tensions would emerge or if her presence might arouse some antipathies or resentments in the
ensemble. We needn't have worried; we had a blissful collaboration and I was bowled over by Lucy's maturity and
professionalism, as well as her sheer magic as a performer.
She played a Marina of great integrity and grounded com-
monsense, and a Viola of passionate intelligence. My one
regret was that as Malvolio I shared only one brief scene
with her—I longed to have more time with her on stage.

·I loved working on *Pericles*—such a rich and resonant
myth, so satisfying in its spiritual dimensions. The sea takes
away and then the sea gives back. There is in the play a
wisdom and acceptance of the cyclical pattern of existence
which is profoundly soothing to contemplate.

Our production was as minimal as possible—an exercise in seeing how to create, with a few sticks and pieces
of cloth, various locations, jousts and feasts, storms and
shipwrecks. David King's shimmering music score drew on
Eastern traditions. Edie Kurzer's costumes were a kind of
Arabian Nights fantasy, but simple and unostentatious. The
show focused on poetry rather than spectacle.

In *Twelfth Night* I based Malvolio on Enoch Powell
(a figure of fun in my university days) and various other
British Tory MPs who had hit the headlines in more recent

times. Their public rectitude was at odds with their closet
fantasies. One had accidentally hanged himself while
dressed in women's underwear with a plastic bag over his
head and an orange in his mouth. So I got a deal of satisfaction from Malvolio swaggering around in yellow
stockings, complete with suspender belt and high heels, in
the belief that this would be a turn-on for Olivia. Malvolio's private fantasies are, after all, both outrageous and
salacious: 'Having been three months married to her, sitting in my state . . . Calling my officers about me, in my
branched velvet gown, having come from a day-bed, where
I have left Olivia sleeping . . .'

A number of actors had now been with the company
for several seasons and a genuine ensemble spirit was developing. Actors like Chris Stollery (Hamlet, Solanio, Catesby,
Tybalt, Macduff, Petruchio); Darren Gilshenan (Grumio,
Hotspur, Pistol, Feste, Dogberry); John Adam (Bassanio,
Rosencrantz, Richmond, Laertes, Claudio); Patrick Dickson (Antonio, Polonius, Clarence, Friar Lawrence) and Sean
O'Shea (Tyrell, Lorenzo, Benvolio, Hortensio, Malcom and
Aguecheek) were now helping to define the sort of company we were, the energy, humour and commitment that
defined us.

In 1995, with our major productions now touring twice
a year to Sydney, Melbourne and Canberra, and occasionally Perth, Adelaide and Brisbane, and with Actors at Work
expanding further interstate, we were aware of one neglected
sector of the community. Primary school kids (aged, say,
seven to twelve years) weren't getting much exposure to
live theatre designed especially for them. I remembered my
conversations in the early days of the Old Tote (mid sixties) with the European Jews who were the mainstay of our

audience. They told me how they'd been hooked on theatre as small children, how vital a part children's theatre played in European culture. I saw no reason why Aussie tots should not enjoy the same advantage. So in 1995 we set up a wing of Bell Shakespeare to specialise in quality children's theatre.

We thought that to base it on Shakespeare would be a bit of a tall order, so we focused on Australian stories or books the kids were reading in school. These productions currently play theatre venues with large audiences and are given first-rate production values and casting. The kids are both discerning and critical. We now have five children's plays in the repertoire and add to it every year or two. Des James's production of *Stormboy* with its pelican puppetry is quite magical, as is Chris Canute's *Sadako*, a Japanese child's experience of Hiroshima. This story is not Australian, but is of enormous significance and relevance, especially with its Asian actors playing to a largely Asian/Australian audience. *I Own the Racecourse* and *The Listmaker* are both dramatisations of popular Australian children's books. The 2001 play, *My Giragundji*, is an Aboriginal story about the pains of growing up. It features an all-indigenous cast of actors.

After five years of heading the company I was feeling the need for an injection of new energy, new inspiration. I was beginning to repeat myself as a director and wanted to subject myself as an actor to a new source of energy. I invited Steven Berkoff to direct *Coriolanus* in 1996.

# Berkoff's
## *Coriolanus*

Since I had first seen Berkoff's *East* on stage at the Glebe Valhalla in 1978 I had regarded him as one of the most electrifying performers and theatre-makers working in English. On the strength of that we invited him to direct Kafka's *Metamorphosis* for Nimrod the following year. I had since kept up with his work whenever he came to Australia—his *Tell-Tale Heart, Fall of the House of Usher, Salome* and so on.

He sent me a video of his *Coriolanus* in London (he had also done it in New York and Germany) and I felt it was the right direction for the company to go at this time—highly disciplined, stylised and imaginative in its use of mime, physical imagery and minimal props. I wanted to play Coriolanus because I wanted to work with Berkoff as closely as I could, get right inside his head to see what made him tick. I knew I was probably letting myself in for a hard time, but considered it worth the pain. He couldn't come to Australia for the auditions so I sent him videos and CVs of some sixty actors to help him with the casting. He designed the set and clothes himself and would devise the music with the help of two musicians during rehearsal.

In the meantime, to kick off 1996 with a truly 'popular' piece (financially, again, we were looking down the barrel and the board was desperate for a box office hit), I chose to revise my *Much Ado About Nothing*, which had been so popular at the Nimrod twenty years earlier. Anna and I played Beatrice and Benedick (though feeling we were a bit long in the tooth) and the legendary Keith Bain did his brilliant best to make the cast look as if they could dance. This time I was acutely aware that I was taking on too much, directing and playing a leading role while trying to run the company and prepare for *Coriolanus*. I could do justice to neither the directing nor the acting and swore I would never take on that load again.

Berkoff lived up to his reputation of being a luvvy with the male actors, and a terror to the management and stage crew. He didn't prove too diplomatic with the two musicians or the two women in the company either. On the first day of rehearsal he turned to the two musicians who were standing expectantly by their drum-kit and synthesiser.

'I always create from music,' he crooned. 'I hear a sound and from that I start to create my choreography ... so give me a sound—any sound ...'

'What sort of sound do you want, Steven?'

'It doesn't matter—any old sound will do ...'

The musician tentatively played a chord on the synth.

'Not that fuckin' sound!' Berkoff bawled at him; then turned to me and growled, 'Where did you get this berk?'

And so the music evolved. There were times when I expected the drummer to ram the entire kit down Berkoff's throat, but the musos managed to keep their cool. Volumnia was another matter. Berkoff hectored the poor lady for the first three days, to the point of collapse. Much of his direction (especially since he had done the show before) was to snap out orders: 'You walk very fast round here, you stop there, you carry on round there, you do this with this arm and that with the other, and you talk very loud the whole time . . . now show me! No, no! You walk very fast round here . . .' etc. etc., demonstrating all the while.

By the end of the week Volumnia was a nervous wreck and Berkoff demanded recasting. Luckily I discovered that the wonderful Gillian Jones was available and, moreover, keen on the role; so she turned up first thing Monday morning, script in hand. After the briefest welcome, Berkoff launched into: 'Right! You walk very fast round here . . .' etc.

Looking somewhat baffled, Gillian, with one eye on the script, tried to follow his instructions.

'No, no, no!' he yelled. 'That's wrong! You walk very fast round here . . .'

And so it went on as I watched with sinking heart. This was no way to get a performance out of Gillian (or anyone else I could think of). She stumbled through it a few more times with Berkoff getting increasingly impatient. Finally she stopped in her tracks and with her eyes blazing, hands on hips, she accosted him: 'What! You mean do it just like you?'

Berkoff faced her head on and drawled: 'Daaarling, if you *could* do it like me, I'd be thrilled.'

Gillian was struck dumb but her reaction was priceless. She flung down her script and did two perfect cartwheels across the floor and out the door. As she disappeared

Berkoff yelled after her, 'Temperament is no substitute for talent.' Then he turned to me with an expression of outraged innocence and exclaimed, 'She was rude to me! That was downright rude! I can't understand rudeness in anyone . . . I can only work through joy!'

So I had to sit him down, look him in the eye and quietly explain: 'Steven, it was actually *you* who was rude. Now we can't go on sacking Volumnias. We have an opening night coming up and Gillian is a fantastic actress. We're lucky to have her. She may not give you just what you want here and now—she may give you something better. Now I'm going to find her and bring her back, but you have to work together.'

Berkoff sloped off grumpily to get a coffee while I went in search of Gillian. I found her in the pub across the road, her eyes still blazing, knocking back a gin and tonic. I urged her to come back and have another go, promising her I'd do my best to keep the peace. Reluctantly she came back and rehearsal tentatively resumed with neither Gillian nor Berkoff looking each other in the eye for the rest of the day, but remaining icily polite. By the end of the second day Berkoff turned to me and conceded with a growl, 'The bird's not bad.' My diary notes from this period are scattered with classic Berkoff quotes:

*Steven to Justine, the company manager: 'I'm thinking of moving out to Australia, getting a shack on Pearl Beach and reviving the Australian theatre.' Hmm . . . Steven apologised to Gillian today, Tuesday, and was extremely supportive and patient when she was having difficulty. He sent her off for a rest, then gave me his cheesiest smile and murmured, 'Am I being good?'*

*Sept 21 (end of week 2 rehearsals), Melbourne: Justine
(company manager) and Susie Howie (publicist) went to
Steven's hotel to pick him up for his publicity call. He was
nowhere to be seen. They searched for him for twenty minutes and eventually found him sitting in on the Dalai
Lama's press conference—and taking snaps! 'I thought I'd
just nick in and say hello to the Dalai Lama,' he explained.
'We have a lot of mutual friends and I'm probably the only
person in the room he'd want to talk to. I thought I might
get a photo taken with him—good publicity?'*

*Oct 8: One of the best quotes from today's rehearsal—pure
vintage Berkoff. During the run he suddenly stopped the
show and yelled at the musicians: 'Stop that hideous music!
It's appalling! You're completely destroying the actors' performances! It's all whining and whingeing—dreadful!
Absolutely dreadful!' In the crestfallen silence that followed, Jonathan Hardy, sitting next to me, sighed, rolled
his eyes and whispered: 'There he goes—mincing words
again!'*

*Coriolanus* opened the 1996 Melbourne Festival and
packed the Athenaeum to the rafters for most performances. To my mind the political interpretation was a bit
simplistic (Coriolanus is more complex than a black shirt
bovver boy) and it's true that we were drilled into giving
Berkoffian performances with little or no room for individual interpretation, but I have never been in a production
so thoroughly choreographed with such a perfectionist's
attention to detail. There were scenes of sheer theatrical
magic and imaginative bravura which only Berkoff could
have carried off, and I liked the man a lot as well as

respecting his talent. He is angry, resentful and difficult at times, and finds it hard to relax, but when you see him really firing on the rehearsal floor, creating, driving and inspiring the team, you can forgive anything. Almost anything.

# Auctioning
# Kenneth
# Branagh

In 1993 I had a letter from a young Australian woman who had worked with Kenneth Branagh and his Renaissance Theatre Company in London. She'd told him about the Bell Shakespeare Company and he was intrigued as to how Shakespeare fares in the Antipodes. So I sent him a few brochures and we began to correspond.

When our 1996 fundraising dinner in Sydney was looming and we were looking for interesting items to auction, I wrote to Branagh and asked if we could auction him off— 'Afternoon Tea with Kenneth Branagh'. He replied sure, go ahead and good luck. A very nice lady bid $2000 for the opportunity, so when Kenneth came to Sydney to promote his new movie *Frankenstein*, I put in a call. Afternoon tea was agreed upon at 4 pm one day the following week. The poor man was having a hell of a time with the media because *Frankenstein* had attracted unenviable reviews overseas and here he had to go through the whole media circus with one journalist after another asking, 'So how do you feel about the reviews?'

On the morning of the appointed day I answered a phone call at my office: 'Mr Branagh's secretary here. Can you please tell me who's coming to afternoon tea?'

'Well, the lady who bought it is named Mrs X and she has publishing interests in Hong Kong.'

'I see. Who else?'

'She's bringing her daughter, who's about fourteen.'

'Thank you. Anyone else?'

'Yes, there's a young English actor, a friend of the family.'

'Oh. What's his name and what has he done?'

'Well, his name is Y, but I don't know what he's been in.'

'That's okay . . . we'll see you at the Hyatt at ten to four. Thank you.'

So at ten to four my three highly excited guests and I were ushered into a suite with a silver tea service set out, attended by maids in starched caps and aprons.

Poor Branagh had been in his hotel room all day, doing one interview after another—'So how do you feel about the reviews?' He'll be run ragged, I thought, he'll be a washed-out nervous wreck, poor bugger.

At precisely four o'clock the doors swung open and Kenneth Branagh bounced in looking as fresh as a daisy in an immaculate white suit, his curls all springy and glistening.

First he pumped my hand: 'Fabulous reviews for Lucy in *Twelfth Night*—I'm thrilled the company's going so well.'

Next to our auction winner: 'And how about your publications in Hong Kong! I read *all* your magazines. I'm particularly fond of . . .' and he rattled off a few titles.

'Now!' he said, turning to the teenage daughter with a big wink. 'I bet you're a fan of Keanu Reeves, aren't you?' She nodded shyly.

'Well, you'd love him. Oh, he's a funny fellow! We had a great time filming *Much Ado*. Here's a photo of Keanu and me clowning around on his motorbike; I got him to autograph it. That's for you.'

Then turning to the young actor: 'Ah, maaate! You were fabulous in that remake of *Wuthering Heights*—just fabulous!'

'What!?' the young man spluttered. 'You noticed me? It was just a spit and a cough . . .'

'Maaate!' Branagh admonished him. 'You were a knock-out! You made that movie for me, really brought it to life!'

Then for the next fifty minutes we were treated to the Kenneth Branagh show while he poured tea, told funny stories, did impersonations and displayed the liveliest interest in each member of the assembled company.

At precisely five o'clock he glanced at his watch: 'Oh dear me . . . I have to be off, a few more interviews to do; but before I go, here's a CD for you, a few books for you, a few more photos of Keanu for you—lovely to meet you all, thanks so much for coming . . .'

And he was out the door. We all sat there gobsmacked for a bit. I had never seen anything so totally professional. I thought, He didn't have to do any of that—he didn't owe me a thing . . . But it certainly brought home the old dictum: If you're going to do something, do it well.

Then I remembered I had had one question I'd been longing to put to him—How do you get all those top actors to play bit parts in your movies?

Now I didn't need to ask.

# The Henrys
# and the
# lesser-knowns

There are a number of Shakespeare plays that people complain are 'done to death', yet it's surprising how many people have never seen them or have only the haziest notion of them. 'My kingdom for a horse!' *Henry V,* right? Wrong. It's interesting to sit with an audience watching *Hamlet* or *Twelfth Night* and hear people gasp at twists in the plot you presumed everybody knew.

Still, some plays do seem to get an awful lot of exposure, like *Midsummer Night's Dream.* I think it's one of the most perfect plays ever written and had planned year after year to include it in our repertoire, but every time I looked around it was being done. In one year alone Sydney got the opera and ballet versions, a new Hollywood movie, productions in the park, on the beach, by the pool—and to cap it all, a tour by the Royal Shakespeare Company—all of *A Midsummer Night's Dream*! It seemed a shame that the RSC had only toured to Australia twice in twenty years and both times it was with the *Dream.*

So I took deliberate risks in producing some of the less-performed plays in the canon, partly seeing it as a responsibility for a company such as ours, and partly in the hope that they'd draw large audiences who had seen enough of *Midsummer Night's Dream* and were curious enough to take advantage of a rare opportunity.

It didn't always work out that way. People are frightened enough of Shakespeare as it is, and if it's a play they know nothing about they're doubly scared they won't understand it. Our marketing expertise was growing and we applied it aggressively to sell our 1997 season—one well-known play (supposedly), *The Tempest*, and one lesser known, *The Winter's Tale*, which, alongside *The Tempest* and *Pericles*, is another of Shakespeare's late great plays. Like them, it deals with shipwreck, with loss, rebirth and reconciliation. Leontes is something of a monstrous role—insanely and inexplicably jealous and violent. The play may well be a parable, but the actor playing Leontes has to understand the nature of his illness and portray it convincingly.

To prepare for the role I undertook some research into mental illness. Dr Francis Macnab of the Cairn Millar Institute suggested that Leontes is a paranoid schizophrenic—he suffers irrational, inaccessible rage and quiet subdued submission within seconds; he speaks gibberish and is offended or aghast when not understood.

I also studied the case of Jonathan Deveson from the book *Tell Me I'm Here* by his mother, Anne Deveson. From this I was able to use a lot of significant physical activity: rocking back and forth, hugging myself and keening; sudden, violent mood changes; physical assault and loss of sense of distance, often shouting at someone with my face

very close to theirs; casual brutality then enraged ve-
hemence; talking and giggling to myself; dropping my head
to the left as if unbalanced.

I also found useful information in *Spinning Out*, a TV
documentary in which paranoia is defined as thinking
everything is bugged, that food is poisoned, and that people
are talking about you.

From my conversation with a woman about her schizophrenic brother, I found many traits shared by Leontes:
periods of normality, then symptoms begin to appear—a
nervous tic, watchfulness, sleeplessness, becoming suspicious, wary, keeping one's back to the wall. Most
suspicion is aimed at one's nearest and dearest, with a conviction that they are evil, possessed by evil spirits.

As with medical specialists, I found that psychiatrists
too are intrigued by Shakespeare's observations. Dr Tom
Stanley, a Macquarie Street psychiatrist, said to me: 'Leontes
is certainly paranoid—Shakespeare got it just right, especially the tremor cordis, an attack of acute anxiety to
herald paranoid delusion. He's probably schizophrenic as
well; he has an unshakeable delusion. He sighs; he is brood-
ing, obsessed, always pacing. He's ever vigilant, watching,
listening. Always questioning. Leontes is always cross-
examining people.'

Shakespeare knew a lot about jealousy. It is one of the
major themes of the sonnets and Othello is a good case
study. As with Othello, Leontes' jealousy is easy to arouse,
he looks for signs to verify his fear, it strikes deep and is
hard to dislodge. Rationality and sense of proportion go
out the window. The mind can find no relief from it—it is
all-consuming. There is a demand for proof, an endless
searching for a truth one doesn't want to know.

To me *The Tempest* and *The Winter's Tale* made a good double to reflect the last years of Shakespeare's life and work, with their message of forgiveness and reconciliation and the spiritual serenity they achieve. After the violence, hatred and despair of *King Lear* and the other great tragedies, they make a wonderful coda to the author's personal life-journey.

Playing both Leontes and Prospero gave me the opportunity to make interesting cross-references to Lear and other Shakespearean giants. How often he leads his characters to the brink of madness and then tantalises us with the question as to whether they've toppled over. It's possible to play Hamlet as clinically mad for at least some of the play. You could say the same of Othello, Shylock and certainly Leontes—there is no rational explanation for his behaviour. Lear, of course, is sublimely mad and is at his most scathingly insightful at the peak of his insanity. Prospero, I think, comes close to it. Nursing his resentment, hate and vengefulness for so long has made an island of him. The tempest is all inside him. Only by the good offices of his creative spirit (Ariel) and his virginal sixteen-year-old daughter is he able to accept his darker self (Caliban) and rejoin the great stream of humanity.

It's curious how in all these last plays it is the virginal sixteen-year-old daughter (Miranda, Perdita, Marina) who is her father's spiritual salvation. Cordelia prefigures them. But in the tragedies there is no time for wounds to heal— the plays hurtle along at breakneck speed and people react rashly. In the last plays, Time is the healer and requires sixteen years in each case to effect his cure.

I have been fortunate in having had more than one go at several of the great roles. I have had two cracks at

Hamlet, Macbeth, Lear, Prospero, Petruchio, Shylock and Coriolanus (the first time when I was at university) and three at Richard III. They are all roles which teach you more about life each time you perform them. They are enriching and enlightening. I once heard Kenneth Branagh asked in an interview: 'Do you learn more about Shakespeare the more you perform him?', and Branagh replied, 'Not necessarily, but you learn an awful lot more about yourself.'

1997 marked the end of Virginia Henderson's tenure as chair. Along with Tony Gilbert and my wife Anna, Virginia is the person I most have to thank for sustaining the company and myself through the rocky and difficult passage of Bell Shakespeare's career. Her devotion to the cause, her acumen in recruiting supporters as well as her own personal generosity in opening her purse and her home to the company were matched by the charm, warmth and glamour she brought to her role. Any boardroom of grey suits would light up like a beacon whenever Virginia walked in to woo them.

I have been fortunate in working with boards (both at Nimrod and Bell) composed of exceptional people. Artists sometimes regard 'the suits' with suspicion, but the boards of arts companies, certainly since the eighties, have had a tough role to play. I remember back in the sixties, arts boards were largely cosmetic—respectable names to stick on a letterhead. But as companies have grown, so have budgets and financial responsibilities. Even if directors don't find themselves liable, as they once were, for bad debts if a company falls over, they still have to wear the bad publicity. At Bell particularly, the directors have been people at the top of their various professions and therefore extraordinarily busy. But they have made time to attend monthly board meetings, to form subcommittees, attend rehearsals and performances and put enormous effort into drumming up support, sponsorship and valuable contacts. They have given free advice on marketing, financial and legal matters whenever required, as well as being generous financial supporters in their own right.

Not often acknowledged in public, unless a company goes under, boards like those of Bell are the unsung heroes and heroines of the success of the arts in Australia.

Nevertheless . . . we have had our moments of disagreement. It became a bit of a conviction with some directors that for a show to succeed I had to either be in it or direct it, or both. I had a tough job explaining why this was not a good idea and how important it is to introduce new talent and fresh ideas rather than just keep recycling *me*. In the subsidised theatre I am convinced it's the show which sells, not the individual who directs or performs in it.

*Henry IV, Parts One and Two* have always been among my favourite Shakespeare plays. The combination of fiery rhetoric and earthy humour, and the psychological insights into father–son conflict, sibling rivalry and political machinations are all masterful. And the gallery of wonderful characters—Falstaff, Hotspur, Mistress Quickly, Hal, Justice Shallow, Bandolph—is like a Dickensian novel or Brueghel painting in its variety.

It was not an original idea, but I saw great mileage in presenting the two plays together in one evening, retaining most of Part One, but heavily cutting Part Two. The second play is wonderfully rich in itself, but goes off on a tangent with a new subplot. I was concerned to stick to the story of Hal, Falstaff and King Henry—that marvellous triangle and tug-of-war of affection and loyalty which determines Hal's rite-of-passage and the kind of king he's going to be.

This treatment of the plays has been done several times to my knowledge, notably in Orson Welles' stage version *Chimes at Midnight*, which he later made into a film. And Richard Wherrett had done an exceptionally popular production at Nimrod in 1978 with a medieval feast thrown in at interval. But whereas Richard's version had simulated a medieval environment, I wanted to bring the play into now, a commentary on contemporary Britain, with the king as a corporate tycoon surrounded by ambitious rivals, with no time for his rebellious son. Hal was a dropout in the East End pubs and brothels and the battle sequence was based on soccer riots with rival teams of hooligans chanting their war cries and beating each other up inside a wire compound. I wanted to deglamorise the idea of war and chivalry and to demonstrate that all the high-minded talk by the barons was only a cover for gang warfare amongst a bunch of thugs. To glorify war is the rankest hypocrisy. I believe that is Shakespeare's message too, time and again, in all his history plays.

Justin Kurzell's set consisted of a very steep ramp like a concrete roadway running from the back of the stage straight at the audience. Wire mesh walls enclosed both sides and there were piles of old furniture strewn around as though people had been swept aside to put the road through. The pounding music score by Alan John was heavy rock (four of the cast played electric guitars) but was based on warlike medieval anthems.

John Gaden's Falstaff could be urbane, sly and dirty as well as robust. Joel Edgerton's Hal was disarmingly colloquial—a very convincing modern teenager. Darren Gilshennan's clowning ability as Pistol was doubled with his gutsy and likeable Hotspur, while Richard Piper showed his versatility by playing a forceful and vulnerable king, a hot lead guitar and the race caller at Royal Ascot. This inspired piece of lunacy was of his own devising and kicked off the second half of the evening in a scene where Falstaff, enjoying a day at the races, is arrested by Mistress Quickly and a couple of dopey cops named Fang and Snare.

Looking back over the last twelve years, I'd have to say *Henry IV* is the production that most satisfied me. It was full of rich, enjoyable performances; we managed to invent entertaining mime to suggest props and locations; it was truly contemporary without seeming forced out of its proper context, and the political statement was confronting. One of the most powerful speeches in the play is made by the sick and ageing king not long before his death. He is bemoaning the fact he can't sleep and saying how much he envies the common folk who have no cares. I covered the stage with sleeping bodies dressed in rags and cast-offs. They huddled together for warmth around a dustbin with a fire inside it. They coughed and wheezed and muttered in their sleep—the homeless, the destitute, the detritus of today's Britain. The king wandered amongst them in his expensive suit, topcoat, muffler, warming his hands at the fire and sighing with envy at their good fortune: 'Then, happy low, lie down; uneasy lies the head that wears a crown.' The irony appealed to me, and caught the essence of the production.

What surprised (and pleased) me most was the comment: 'That's the most Australian Shakespeare you've done yet.' I certainly hadn't set out with that in mind. In fact we researched contemporary Britain pretty solidly and had a voice coach to help us get the various dialects accurate— Welsh, Scots, Northumbrian, cockney etc. Because the play is so very localised in terms of place and character names, and because the historical references are so specific, it would have seemed folly to try and 'Australianise' it. But what emerged in performance were attitudes towards class, royalty, mateship, violence, 'honour', sex and humour that were intrinsically Australian in character. It pleased me that we had achieved that unselfconsciously by going for the truth of the text.

All the same, it took me two years to convince my board that *Henry IV* would be a goer. They kept insisting I should play Lear because it would be great box office. Having already played Lear at Nimrod in 1984 I knew what a killer role it was and, much as I wanted to have another crack at it, wasn't willing to do so until I found a director who I thought could do something exceptional with it.

On the first night of *Coriolanus* in Melbourne, Barrie Kosky bounced up to me in the foyer. We'd never met but even before the usual pleasantries were over we found ourselves saying, 'We must do something together.' And almost in the same breath, 'What about *Lear*?' So now I decided to make the call and follow *Henry IV* with Kosky's *Lear*. Everything I had seen of Barrie's had been pretty wild, outrageous and uncompromising. I knew he'd take *Lear* all the way. But I knew that was the only way to go. Anything careful or respectable wouldn't be worth doing.

We rehearsed in a vast, freezing warehouse in the backblocks of Alexandria. Cyclone weather persisted throughout the wintry rehearsal period, so what with the wind howling around the desolate building, the rain crashing on the tin roof, and the corrugated iron doors rattling in a frenzy, we hardly needed the two trumpeters blowing fit to burst, accompanied by six maniacs thumping kettle-drums to convey the impression of a storm!

During rehearsal Kosky was playful, full of beans. He loved sitting at the piano belting out crazy medleys. He was not particularly interested in the precise meaning of the text, more in what images the text threw up, or in his subjective reactions to those images. We had to watch out that he didn't misinterpret the meaning of an entire speech in order to make a visual statement.

'Where do all those images come from?' one intrigued student enquired after a school matinee.

'From the dark recesses of my poisoned mind,' Kosky replied with a straight face. 'It's not somewhere you'd want to go.'

Barrie is pretty much a one-man band. He arrived with his concept worked out, casting done and designs complete. The stage was empty apart from a big gold box on wheels with lots of holes in it. There was a ruched front curtain, tackily glamorous, as in an old cinema. On one side of the stage sat Barrie at a beat-up piano (which he bashed the hell out of), on the other, two ageing trumpeters. All three musicians were in tuxedos, black ties and red fez hats. Otherwise Peter Corrigan's costumes were exotic fairytale fantasies in brightly coloured fun fur which were gradually stripped off. The text was heavily cut and lesser roles disappeared, among them Albany and Cornwall, focusing attention on the sisters.

The elements that proved most controversial were Edgar's coprophilia, Lear's lewd knights (half-man, half-dog, with flamboyant genitalia), the din, wildness and explicit violence. For Edgar's disguise as mad Tom, Matt Whittet stripped down to his jocks from which he scooped a very realistic handful of shit. He proceeded to daub himself and even eat some of it. Gloucester's eyes were sucked out of his head and eaten by Goneril and Regan. The dog-knights I thought were a great idea — they could be as lewd, active and playful as they liked and linked up with Louise Fox's Shirley Temple of a Fool to do a tap-dancing chorus of 'My heart belongs to Daddy . . .'

The noise and madness climaxed in the hovel scene with six actors crammed into the gold box, heads and arms protruding at weird angles from the holes, all shouting, singing and jabbering. One of the most memorable scenes was the one at Dover — not a sea front or cliff face but a transport waiting room with flickering neon lights and blue plastic chairs full of mumbling, crazy, homeless people. It might have been the Channel crossing at Dover, the River Styx, a seedy lunatic asylum, or just one of those bus or train terminals where the dropouts of society gather to sleep. Into this sombre setting Lear rampaged, mad as a meat axe, dressed in Cordelia's pink fur coat and handing out plastic dildos to the bystanders.

We got bags of hate mail, of course. The controversy was great for business and, as always, the young audiences and school matinees were vocal in their approval. For me the greatest relief was not having to play a naturalistic clinical study of madness. The production did all that for me. The gold box full of jabbering voices was the inside of Lear's head. That meant I could concentrate on the more serious business of delivering Lear's blistering satire and commentary on corruption.

A lot of people walked out, especially in Brisbane where some of the actors were abused at the stage door. Sometimes people yelled 'Rubbish' and booed at the curtain call. 'Fuck off,' one of the man-dogs yelled back. Ah, the magic of live theatre . . .

In 1998 we also decided to extend our operations further afield. We were now performing in capital cities and the larger regional centres, but not much live theatre was getting into the outback. So we started a new performing group with that target in mind. Peter Evans directed a heavy metal, grungy *Macbeth* that toured thirty-six outback and country towns, and was enormously popular. In 2000 Des James's Latin American *Much Ado* played the same circuit followed by *The Tempest* in 2001. Audiences in remote areas are grateful for our going there and we are currently enlarging the scope of this activity by boosting the scale of productions and accompanying them with workshop and educational programs for schoolteachers as well as students. So many teachers are desperate for help to bring Shakespeare alive in the classroom.

I had not worked with Richard Wherrett for some ten years and now that he was free of the Sydney Theatre Company and freelancing again, I invited him to direct a new production of *Merchant of Venice* in 1999. This was a polished piece of work, and was followed up by *Henry V*, in which I used many of the cast I had assembled for *Henry IV*, Joel Edgerton in particular. I have always loved *Henry V*, probably because it was my first really thrilling Shakespeare experience, thanks to the Laurence Olivier film. But as ambivalent and anti-war as much of its sentiment is, the play demands a certain respect for heroism, for Englishness, for rhetoric, which are unfashionable right

now. I could find no way to make the play as contemporary as I had made *Henry IV*. The closest I could get was
to set it in World War I, when lads from all over the Empire
willingly laid down their lives for God, king and country.
This gave the play a certain poignancy, especially as I made
Anzac Diggers of Bates, Court and Williams, the three soldiers who debate the morality of the war, and wish the king
'in Thames, up to his neck'.

Again, working with this team of actors was a joyous
experience, and I deliberately provided them with an empty
space in which they could create theatrical images with
mimimal props and technology. It made me hungry to
revive a permanent troupe, an ensemble of actors who
would work and train together over a length of time. This
had gone by the board when I started employing guest
directors, each with different ideas about casting. The
ensemble was revived in 2001.

# A rare and remarkable privilege

I had announced, as part of Bell's initial charter, that we would occasionally present a non-Shakespeare classic and in 1999 I approached Robyn Nevin with the idea of her company, the Queensland Theatre Company, and ourselves co-producing Eugene O'Neill's *Long Day's Journey Into Night*, one of the great twentieth century classics. She and I would play opposite each other as Mary and James Tyrone and I proposed an Australian director, Michael Edwards, who had directed a fine production of Kenna's *A Hard God* in Adelaide. Robyn liked the idea and included it in her subscription season, which meant rehearsing in Brisbane. Unfortunately, because both Robyn and I had other commitments, the play performed only in Brisbane and Melbourne. Some audiences were impatient with the play's verbosity; it's a pity if we have lost the patience to listen, especially when the talk is as fine as O'Neill's.

We tried another modern classic the following year, 2000. This time it was Strindberg's *Dance of Death* translated and directed by Roger Pulvers with Anna Volska as Alice, Bill Zappa as Kurt and myself as Edgar. We opened at the Adelaide Festival where we did very good business, then took the play to Tokyo and Osaka. It was my first step towards getting a large-scale Shakespeare play to Japan, which I hope to do by 2004. Fortunately, *Dance of Death* made a very good impression in Japan and gave us the kind of foothold and contacts we were seeking.

The year 2000 also saw us produce *Midsummer Night's Dream* at last. I saw Elke Neidhardt's production of *Tanhauser* for Opera Australia and thought here was a director with the kinky sense of humour and eye for spectacle who could give us a new twist on the *Dream*. Elke did indeed give us a dark and wintry *Dream* with a brutal chauvinist Oberon and, in Frank Whitten, a lanky, wry and world-weary Puck.

The production did not please those who were expecting a sunny celebration. The *Dream* was selected largely because, as a sure-fire popular piece, it would offset the risk of my other choice for 2000, the rarely seen *Troilus and Cressida*. This is one of those plays much admired by Shakespeare buffs but not familiar to the general public. As far as I can ascertain, it's only had one previous professional production in Australia—by Brisbane's Grin-and-Tonic Company in 1989.

But for Bell to do it was a huge financial risk—a bleak and savage piece of nihilism expressed in language both convoluted and erudite, presuming an audience's intimate familiarity with *The Iliad*. Not an easy number to sell to your board of directors. As always, it was a matter of getting the right number of 'hooks'. The first step was to sell it to a festival and thereby share the financial risk and get some investment upfront. Leo Schofield, director of the Olympic Arts Festival, assured me we could have the Opera House Playhouse during the Sydney 2000 Olympics if we could offer him an unusual item, preferably with some international component. I had long had my eye on Michael Bogdanov, a director whose work I had admired both at the National and the RSC for its boldness and political commitment.

For ten years his productions had aroused controversy and outrage, from the sodomy scene in *Romans in Britain* at the National to his abrasive, award-winning *Taming of the Shrew* for the RSC. We met at a Shakespeare conference in Sydney in 1996 and he agreed to come back and direct a show for me. Other things (a movie, a new baby) intervened. But now I thought I might hook him. Leo Schofield was thrilled with the idea so I rang Bogdanov and asked how he'd like to be in Sydney for the Olympics. He jumped at the idea, and when we debated which play it might be, he proffered *Troilus and Cressida* as one of the Shakespeares he'd always longed to do. Again, Mr Schofield was mightily pleased and so the deal was done.

It was not an inexpensive exercise. Michael wanted a cast of twenty; we had to fly him out to audition and to meet prospective set designers; then fly Michael Scott-Mitchell back to Britain for design meetings. We had to bring Bogdanov's wife, Ulriche Englebrecht, to design costumes, along with their two delightful children. We had to provide them with a house, a car and a nanny. We had to import Michael's favourite fight choreographer, Malcolm Ransom, and an armory of swords especially made in

England. We had to have an extra week's rehearsal and the set requirements included a bank of audiovisual screens, four video cameras (operated by the cast), a stage floor of real mud six inches deep, a spa pool and a jeep. We were to pull all the seats out of the auditorium and replace them with cushions and benches, while the stage was to be extended, losing two rows of audience.

Most of these requirements were met, although we had to scrap the jeep and the real mud. The Opera House balked at scrapping their seating, pointing out that Sydney would be crawling with tourists and overseas journalists for the Olympics, so the Playhouse had to look its best. Still, the show cost us about one and a half million to get on, of which the Olympic Arts Festival contributed $50 000. We were looking down the barrel unless the show sold out, which it did in all three venues, in Melbourne, Canberra and Sydney.

As with Berkoff, Kosky and Jim Sharman, who directed our 1997 *Tempest*, Bogdanov was a director I wanted to subject myself to as an actor—to get inside his head and see how he did it; to get to his inspirational source. I offered myself for the role of Ulysses.

I guess I am lucky in having the opportunity to both act and direct. Most directors don't get the chance to act, to experience what it's like to be directed. There is no way for them to learn except by trial and error, or sitting in on someone else's rehearsal period. I love to be directed by a tough director who will push me further than I would have gone, point out bad habits and mannerisms or make me explore some aspect of myself hitherto kept under wraps. By watching other directors at work at such close range I am able to make my own list of do's and don'ts. First task:

create a congenial, relaxed and stimulating atmosphere to work in. Observe each individual actor and assess what pace he/she works at—some want to make decisions too soon, others put them off until opening night. Never demonstrate—'this is how you should say this line or play that action'—instead, coax the actor along the desired path and let him make his own discovery. That way he will *own* the line or action and it will never become stale. Don't criticise any actor in front of the others unless you intend to do it for a good reason. Never take your frustration or anxiety out on the cast or crew—they'll despise you for it. You are the leader but also part of the team. Give everyone a job to do (those with small roles might take the morning voice or movement warm-up, or teach the group some new skill). Plan meticulously but, no matter how fixed an idea is in your mind, be alert to suggestions or alternatives up to the last minute, and throw out your idea if a better one comes up. No hierarchies. Don't have favourites in the cast. These are just a few of the things I've picked up from watching other directors at work, assessing their strengths and weaknesses.

Bogdanov had begun his career in Shakespeare as Peter Brook's assistant director on the famous *Dream*.

'What's the most important thing you learned from Brook?' I asked him.

'To put on a good show,' Bogdanov replied. 'Despite all the theory, conceptualising and intellectual rigour, Peter loved to sit around for hours working out gags, surprises and theatrical effects.'

From Bogdanov himself I learned (or rather was reminded) of the importance of having a precise time, place and political statement in place to begin with. The audience doesn't need to know all the details, but in your own mind you're working on solid ground, not some hazy, half-baked concept. I also saw how important it was that each scene tell a story, have its own precise location and activity. He has a fine eye for visual effects and will fight tooth and nail to achieve them whatever the expense or safety risk involved. We had a tricky time with the hanging and execution of Hector: Luciano Martucci had to be strung up by the heels and have his throat cut. We spent hours fiddling with ropes and pulleys, blood-bags and tubes (Michael wanted the blood to squirt across the stage). I would have given up much earlier and settled for a simpler solution. But Michael was right to persist and the moment always evoked a gasp of horror from the audience.

I was surprised that he was not more insistent on clarity of meaning with such a difficult text, and never discussed with the actors their motivations or psychological states. In those areas we were left to fend for ourselves. I guess that having directed so much at the National and RSC, Michael was used to letting the star actors do their own thing while he took care of the show around them.

Our tenth anniversary season ended well with finances in good shape, solid sponsorships secure and new recognition from government funding agencies. The Nugent Enquiry into Arts Funding (a comprehensive and significant document) saw us increase our federal funding to some $620 000 annually (or 11 per cent of our turnover, whereas previously it had been 6 per cent), while Bob Carr's state government chipped in with an extra $600 000 over three years to enable us to take our mainstage works to larger regional centres in New South Wales.

The one abiding criticism of the company since the start has had to do with unevenness of casting, and specific cases of weakness in handling the language. Shakespeare makes more demands on the modern actor than any other playwright and cruelly exposes weakness of voice and diction. We had had a number of guest directors since 1996, each director having different casting requirements and frequently casting for reasons of age or appearance rather than verse-speaking prowess.

I took all this on board and resolved not to perform in 2001 but to devote myself to rebuilding an ensemble of actors with a regular training program and particular emphasis on vocal coaching and verse-speaking technique. These are the foundations of any good classical company.

I directed both *Julius Caesar* and *Antony and Cleopatra* using the same fourteen actors in both. Each play had three guest artists. The ensemble changes year to year, but most actors carry through for at least two or three seasons. We are building that company identity and expertise you simply can't achieve with a scratch company and five weeks' rehearsal.

In *Julius Caesar* I have always enjoyed the tension between hard-nosed politics and the fact that so many of the characters (but not all) set store by omens, prophecies and dreams. There is nothing archaic about that; we citizens of the twenty-first century are every bit as superstitious as our forebears and support a multi-billion-dollar empire of clairvoyants, astrologers and gurus.

Because *Julius Caesar* depends on a sense of foreboding and relentless tension, I encouraged my designer, Jennie Tate, to draw inspiration from the paintings of de Chirico. His haunting, deserted city-scapes are full of menace; weird perspectives, unexplained shadows, lowering sickly skies. I wanted the same eerie sense of the supernatural to pervade the storm and battle scenes. Our resident movement designer, Gavin Robins, drew from the actors' extended improvisations and created movement sequences that were expressive and athletic. I found, through working on *Henry IV* and *Henry V*, that a battle scene on stage can be more effectively created through evocative images rather than aiming for realism. (Though I must admit that in Bogdanov's *Troilus and Cressida*, the sight of gigantic Marcus Eyre trying to beat the crap out of Luciano Martucci with a length of chain and a steel pipe had the audience's hearts in their mouths.)

One of the chief delights of *Julius Caesar* was Chris Stollery's manipulative Antony steering the dead Caesar on a hospital trolley through the audience, and murmuring his tear-jerking funeral oration into a hand-mike accompanied by a syrupy music soundtrack. It was a sharp reflection on media manipulation and propaganda (especially on TV) so familiar to us all. When the crowd, swayed by his oratory, applauded him, he signed a few autographs and even kissed a baby!

*Antony and Cleopatra* is a longer, untidier play and a bit of a struggle to hold together—something like conducting *Götterdamerung*, I expect—so many characters, so many scenes and so many *battles*! I decided to set the play in a glamorous casino where the rich and powerful rubbed shoulders with thugs and low-life. Thus the Romans had a mafioso uniformity about them—elegant in black ties and dinner jackets—an exclusive and very male club, shades of *The Godfather*. The Egyptians, on the other hand, represented the female—soft, flowing, sensual and free. The maleness of Rome cannot abide the 'other' as manifested by Cleopatra—the Romans have to contain and eventually destroy her.

The text is full of references to gambling, cards, dice, chance and fortune; and Antony, dallying in Egypt, neglecting his family and his business, is like one of those inveterate gamblers seduced by the phoney glamour of the casino. The lights never change, so you forget what day it is, you lose all sense of time. The drinks keep coming round and the flashing lights urge you to risk all you have on one last throw of the dice.

I'd been waiting some years to give Paula Arundell a crack at a great role and Cleopatra was made for her. She rose to the occasion magnificently, well-matched by the animal passion and apprehension of mortality in Bill Zappa's ageing Antony.

The end of 2001 brought me an unexpected bonus when Robyn Nevin invited me to re-direct *The Christian Brothers* with Peter Carroll for the Sydney Theatre Company. It was a great joy to get together with Peter and the original designer, Larry Eastwood, and revisit this little masterpiece of both writing and acting.

As I sat day after day watching Peter reconstruct his superb characterisation, testing every cadence, meticulously refining every gesture, I can honestly say it's one of the best acting lessons I've ever had.

As I write this, I approach my thirteenth year of heading Bell Shakespeare. I feel myself blessed, not only by good fortune and an excellent board of directors, but a superlative office staff (fourteen in all), remarkable for their dedication and good humour as well as their expertise in administration, marketing, fundraising and so on. In short, what we seem to have created is a very happy extended family, and when I look around there is nowhere I'd rather be and nothing I'd rather be doing with my life.

Anna continues to work by my side, either on stage or, as an Associate Artist of the company, passing on skills and advice to the younger actors. Our domestic contentment is sealed by Hilary and Lucy being happy in their relationships and in their careers; and enabling us to undertake the longed-for role of doting grandparents . . .

I see myself heading Bell Shakespeare for at least another decade, hopefully creating more and more opportunities for young actors and directors, and, little by little, settling into the role of mentor and guide.

I am nearing the end of a tour of Michael Gow's production of *Richard 3* which has played near-capacity business in six major cities. In Melbourne, it marked our third consecutive season at the Victorian Arts Centre. Since we vacated the decaying Athenaeum, we have increased our Melbourne audience by over 30 per cent.

I felt in top form as Richard and delighted in witnessing the growing prowess of the ensemble.

The company is now performing all over Australia, in every state and territory: capital cities, regional centres and the outback. We are approaching an average of three performances a day every day of the year, somewhere on the continent. Our annual attendance figures are over 200 000 and growing steadily.

From our office in Singapore I hope to build a regular Asian circuit for our mainstage productions. I have little interest in touring Europe or the USA. Asia fascinates me and I want to encourage more interchange of artists— actors, directors, designers, and composers. If corporate sponsors and government agencies can't see the mileage in this, well, that's a blind spot we'll just have to fix.

Amongst our many education initiatives (Actors at Work, teachers' workshops, an executive leadership program, publications and an interactive website) the latest is our workshop program for 'kids at risk'. This gives young people in severely disadvantaged circumstances the opportunity to express themselves, work together, and enjoy a feeling of achievement and self-respect. It may help break patterns of harmful behaviour and low expectations. It's an area of our work I am most keen to see flourish Australia-wide over the next few years.

I regard it as a rare and remarkable privilege to have my own theatre company, doing the work I most want to do alongside the people I most want to share it with. To my mind, it doesn't come any better than this.

# Index